STRAIGHT
SHOOTER

heidi belleau

RIPTIDE
PUBLISHING

Riptide Publishing
PO Box 6652
Hillsborough, NJ 08844
www.riptidepublishing.com

Straight Shooter (Rear Entrance Video, #3)
Copyright © 2014 by Heidi Belleau

Cover art: Vivian Ng, viivus.tumblr.com
Editor: Sarah Frantz Lyons
Layout: L.C. Chase, lcchase.com/design.htm

ISBN: 978-1-62649-090-1

First edition
April, 2014

Also available in ebook:
ISBN: 978-1-62649-089-5

STRAIGHT
SHOOTER

heidi belleau

RIPTIDE
PUBLISHING

To everyone who supported me throughout the writing of this series: my editor Sarah Frantz; my beta readers Hannah, Sam, and Julio; the staff at the various local coffee shops I camped out in; and of course my husband and my mother, who took on my neglected parenting duties. This is it, folks! The end!

table of
contents

prologue

Austin hated playing goalie. Actually, when it came to the otherwise well-loved PE 11 floor hockey unit, Austin didn't know if *anybody* in his school really liked being the goalie, but today it was him stuck in the helmet. He stomped around morosely in the net, drowning in too-big pads stinking of all the gym classes that had gone before.

Meanwhile, all his teammates ran free across the floor with sneakers squeaking and sticks clacking and not a single pad or helmet between them. Nothing burdened *them* but the red flags of their pinnies hanging out of their back pockets.

Being the goalie, Austin actually had to wear his pinny over his T-shirt. Fucking rank.

"Come on, come on," he muttered, watching that asshole Timber Durston barrel right through the other team's defence with the ball. How he wished that was him, soaking up the glory, scoring on the other team even though he was pretty positive the teacher wasn't keeping score so much as making sure nobody snuck out the side door of the gym.

But no, Austin was here, on the empty half of the floor, standing around fucking useless, tapping his stick on the ground while Timber Durston showboated and everybody in pinnies gave him pats on the back and everybody in T-shirts glared jealously and then regrouped.

Lame.

The ball dropped. The shouting and clacking and squeaking started up again. The teacher resumed her hawkeyed watch of the side door. Austin continued to stand around like an asshole, sweat dripping down his face inside the hot old helmet. Too much to ask that the side door be propped open to let some air in. Too much to ask that he didn't have to wear this fucking helmet, be the only one in a fucking helmet, as if a little plastic ball was going to do the kind of damage a puck could. Fucking stupid, especially since nobody else had to wear one.

On the other hand, could be pretty great to see Timber Durston go down with a plastic ball–related brain injury . . .

"Austin!" one of the girls on his team shouted, and Austin looked up in time to see the crowd of his classmates now turned toward him, stampeding down the floor with Gene Tremblay at the head of the pack, shoulder to shoulder with Timber Durston, sticks cracking together as the ball skittered between them.

Austin blinked the sweat out of his eyes and hunkered down, spreading the surface of his body out. Left or right? High or low?

Why the fuck wasn't Durston passing? He and Gene were knocking the ball back and forth between them like they were two kids playing fucking hot potato. Even with the helmet, Austin could see at least three openings on their team where Timber could get the ball away from the beeline it was making for the net, maybe even get it back into the other team's defensive zone and out of Austin's hair.

All Timber had to do was pass.

"Pass, damn it!" Austin yelled.

Well, *somebody* listened, but it sure as hell wasn't Durston. As soon as Austin shouted, Gene shot the ball hard to Austin's left and *oh, shit* Alison Greyeyes was right fucking there, nobody covering her, and *tap* went her stupid plastic stick, and Austin fell to his knees and shot his left foot out for all it was worth, but still the little plastic ball rolled happily into the net like this was a game of fucking minigolf and Austin was the windmill.

The stampede slowed. Alison's teammates shouted encouragement while she fixed her ponytail.

Timber Durston, meanwhile, went straight for Austin. He was looking pretty pissed for the guy whose inability to pass had almost single-handedly cost their team the goal. Austin was about to say so when Timber beat him to the punch.

"Whose fucking team are you playing on, Austin?"

Oh, *fuck you*, Timber Durston. Austin ripped the sweltering helmet off his head. "Uh, yours, ya shithead?"

"Funny, because it looks to me like you just fucking gave that goal away to your boyfriend—"

"Austin! Timber!" the teacher snapped, rising from her seat to enter the fray. "One more word and I'm writing you both up."

Austin's face burned hot. Gene wasn't looking at him, and he didn't know if that made it better or worse. Alison had been the one to get the goal, but somehow he couldn't bring himself to point that out aloud. *Pussy.*

Timber snarled and turned, and the teacher went back to her seat. Alison had retrieved the ball and was carrying it out for the next face-off, and Austin thought that was the end of it, was about to put his helmet back on, but then Timber cast a look over his shoulder and said under his breath, "Sweaty faggot."

And what the hell did Austin do about it?

Here's what Austin did about it: he popped a boner.

CHAPTER 1

"**T**ime to come out, Austin."

Austin shot a look at his locked bedroom door, curled his lip in disgust, and returned to his biceps curls. He had nothing to say to any of his roommates right now, not even last-straight-man-standing Noah. And if Noah didn't like it, he could put on his landlord panties and hand Austin his eviction notice, because otherwise Austin wasn't doing shit.

"Seriously, Austin. Open the door." This time, Noah's knock was distinctly landlord-like.

Okay, so Austin wasn't expecting things to get this serious this fast. He gulped, dropped his hand weight with a dangerously heavy-sounding thud, took a second to check that the thing hadn't busted right through the floorboards, and finally clambered to his feet.

He still made sure he had his arms crossed and a suitably surly expression before the door opened. "What?" he barked when he and Noah finally came face-to-face for what felt like the first time since the big gay art show.

"You know what." Noah gave him a dad face. "Can I come in?"

Austin didn't make any move to get out of the way, ignoring the way Noah kept doing these abortive little trying-to-slip-around-you dekes. "Do you have to?"

"Well, I don't want to have this conversation in front of Bobby—"

"*Rob*," Austin corrected.

"—and I'm not sending *him* out for something that's your fault, so it's either in here, or on the lawn. Your pick."

Austin rolled his eyes. "Fine." He stepped aside, and Noah made his way into Austin's room, shutting the door carefully behind him. "Does the door have to be closed?"

"Yes," Noah said. "Now sit."

Austin found himself plopping down onto his bed before he even had a chance to *consider* refusing. Damn those deeply ingrained be-a-team-player habits of his and the way they made him respond to certain tones of voice as obediently as a golden retriever.

Noah sat down too. "So it's been two weeks."

"Since?"

"You know damn well what since, Austin. Since Bobby came out."

"Rob," Austin insisted, but even he had to admit he sounded pretty halfhearted this time.

"Bobby. His name is Bobby now, and this is exactly the kind of shit I need to talk to you about."

"So talk." Austin reached for the foot-long novelty Canucks hockey stick propped on his bedside table and gave it a couple of fidgety swings.

"I'm trying. You keep interrupting me. You think you could maybe cut that out?"

"Sure," Austin said. *Whoosh, whoosh* went the little hockey stick as it sliced the air.

"And could you put that fucking thing down before you accidentally hit me with it?"

Austin tossed it onto the floor. "Fine."

"So it's been two weeks," Noah said again, "since Bobby came out."

Austin didn't say anything, even though he was pretty sure his eye twitched.

He stared resolutely at the floor, refusing to look at Noah as he got on with his lecture: "And look, I'm not blaming you for being a little taken aback by the whole thing. I mean, I'm not sure I really get it myself. The guy wears more makeup than Adam Lambert, and I'm pretty sure I've seen him in high heels, but he says he's not a girl and he's not a drag queen and his boyfriend is gay. So I get that you're confused. I'm confused too. But would it be too much to ask that you take him at face value?"

Yes, actually, it would. Because it's fucking crazy, and why should I have to change when he's the one who sprung all this shit on me? But he didn't say anything.

"He's too shy to talk to you about it, but you really hurt his feelings when you stormed out of his show. And now it's been two weeks and you've pretty much stopped speaking to any of us. So I'm going to ask you straight up, Austin. Do you have a problem with gay people?"

"No!" Austin yelped, then squirmed under the pure daddishness of Noah's gaze. "I mean, no. No, I don't. Of course I don't. I was cool with Christian, wasn't I? Even played along with your whole pretend-him-and-Max-aren't-screwing act, when he first moved in, didn't I? And I'm cool with Max, too. And hell, even that Dylan guy is okay when he's not looking like he's gonna punch me in the face."

"You kind of deserve that. But fine, okay. You're cool with Christian and Max and Dylan. I'll accept that. So why not Bobby?"

"You're going to get mad at me if I say."

"I'm already mad. So spit it out."

Austin balled his hands into fists. Twisted his lips. Squeezed his eyes shut. The bottled-up feeling didn't take long to explode. "Because he's such a fucking *fag*."

Noah recoiled, blinking in shock, then took a deep breath. "Oookay." He cast a quick look over his shoulder, as if the pride police were about to bust down the door and arrest them both. "So, what was that about being fine with gay people, again?"

Great, now Austin felt like an asshole. "Ugh. You know what I mean. There's gay people, and then there's fags. I mean, Christian kind of walks the line a little with the sweater vests, but he's generally pretty cool. He keeps it toned down, you know? Not R—Bobby. He's right in your face with it." Austin flapped his hand on his wrist in demonstration. "Like, shit, I don't want to be seen in public with a guy in fucking lip gloss, okay? Does that really make me a bigot?"

He realized after he said it that he didn't really mean it as a rhetorical question, even though he'd phrased it as one.

Did it make him a bigot?

Noah sighed. "I don't know. I'm not an expert on this shit, I just ..." He scrubbed his face. "Bobby's my friend, and he's our roommate, and I'm sick of seeing him sneak by your room like a kicked puppy. So, look. I didn't want to do this, but here it is. Whatever your issue with him is, you need to fucking sort it out, or you need to find a new place to live."

Even though Austin had been planning for this exact eventuality, it still hurt like an elbow to the gut. "You're kicking me out?" he asked, unable to smother the pathetic insecurity creeping into his voice.

"Looks like it." Noah didn't make eye contact. His voice was cold.

"But I've lived here longest out of anybody here other than you!"

"I know that. You're also the only one here being a complete fucking prick."

Really? Okay, so he'd been rude to Ro—Bobby, sure, but was the way he felt really that beyond the pale? Okay, maybe among *his* roommates. But that didn't mean it didn't make logical sense in, y'know, the real world. Anywhere else, most people would agree that the way Bobby was acting and dressing was weird, even if some of them didn't necessarily approve of Austin's behaviour. Hell, the guys on his team at SFU would probably have acted worse than him. If anything, Austin had been pretty considerate to make himself scarce over the last couple weeks. "So that's it, then," he said, dejected.

Noah didn't even turn from staring at the door. "Yep. Consider this your one month's notice. You've got until the first of June to either fix your attitude and make things right with Bobby, or find a new place."

Austin didn't much feel like looking Noah in the eyes just then, either. "Fine."

"Fine," Noah echoed, and stood. "Good talk."

"Yeah. Sure."

One month.

One month, one month, one month. Austin recited it to himself as he peeled a banana and dropped it into the blender. He wasn't even sure what it meant. One month until he was out of this gay hellhole? One month until he was homeless and friendless? One month to clean up his act and get his head on—*ha!*—straight?

A scoop of protein powder. A big blob of peanut butter. Flax seeds.

Buzz. Pour.

He didn't know. Well, at least he had a month to figure it out.

His first instinct was to cut and run, hit Craigslist and find a new place to live pronto. A month wasn't long to look, and his budget was, uh, about a third of the price of even the worst housing Vancouver had to offer, but he might be able to manage it if he got creative. And relaxed his already low standards.

Except that if he cut and run now, he had a feeling Noah wouldn't be giving him any glowing recommendations.

Stays to himself, doesn't party, pays rent mostly on time—and he's a homophobe, because that's what we're calling it now.

Well, maybe Noah's bad review would be good, in the eyes of some.

If Austin felt like rooming with a bunch of Bible-thumper types. He groaned as he grabbed his gym bag and headed out the front door, protein shake in hand. Wasn't there a middle ground between accepting everything and everyone and being one of those assholes with the GOD HATES FAGS signs? The question gave him something to distract him while he waited for his bus.

The guys on his team, he'd concluded by the time he took his seat. Insulting gay guys was pretty much expected on the ice, after all. Maybe one of them had a room going. If SFU had fraternities like a normal university, this wouldn't even be a problem. Austin would have been well settled in a frat house by now with a couple peon pledges to do his bidding. Instead, he was about to get kicked out of the gayest house in Vancouver if he didn't learn how to magically be cool with a dude in lip gloss and a bra.

Speaking of gay, if he got kicked out of the house would he lose his job at Vancouver's gayest porn store, too?

Not that it paid all that well, and the novelty of working there had *definitely* worn off since they'd gotten rid of the normal straight-dude porn in favour of lesbian autobiographies and dirty gay comics about motorcycle gangs. But that didn't mean he wanted to get fired because of Rob. Bobby. Whatever.

For a while there it had been kind of cool working at a porn store. Free porn. Talking about sex with female customers, some of whom had this habit of getting *real* candid when they told him about their taste in vibrators and crotchless panties. And as far as the guys on his team went, it was probably the only minimum wage job they'd ever be remotely proud of him for having. Sure, they ribbed him as much as a guy flipping burgers or selling electronics, but there was an air of grudging respect there, too, if only for the pure fucking balls it took to work such an out-there and embarrassing job.

He wondered if the same respect would come into play if they knew it was now a *gay* porn store. Not like he was planning on telling them, but it did kinda make him think. Could he really move in with people he couldn't trust to be cool about such a dumb and basic part of his life? He'd seen what that kind of bullshit paranoia had done to Christian, after all. Turned the guy completely fucking squirrelly, that's what.

But if he got fired at the same time he got kicked out, would it even be an issue?

Could they fire him? Maybe they'd expect him to quit.

No, because if Bobby was working at the store and uncomfortable with Austin's "homophobia" in that setting too, then Christian's aunt would be well within her rights to fire Austin just for that. His eviction from the house wouldn't even come into play.

But damn, that was cold. Put a guy out on his ass *and* cut off his income? He'd have to really kill it with the grades this semester so he didn't lose any scholarship money.

Speaking of which, his bus was pulling into the campus loop now. He had an hour and a half in the gym with a few of the other guys, time for a shower, and then it was off to his summer classes, filling all those credit hours he couldn't take during the regular season when he practically lived on the ice. Summers sucked. Hours and hours of drills, no games, *and* academics? And now roommate drama on top of it all. Shit.

When Austin hopped off the bus from downtown, their left wing forward Drew was just getting off his bus from Coquitlam, his SFU Athletics duffel bag over one shoulder. He gave Austin a bleary wave. Hungover, probably. The guy couldn't resist thinking summer equalled drinking time, even though in a way summer was *more* hard work than normal. And did he really think Coach wasn't watching them all, taking note of their off-season behaviour? Not to mention the fact that slacking on summer training meant Drew would let the whole team down when fall rolled around. Austin wasn't spending this much time in the gym and jogging and choking down fucking protein shakes and five-egg breakfasts for fucking fun.

"Hey," Austin said, unable to keep his frustration out of his voice. "Late night?"

"That obvious?" Drew asked. The guy had huge dark circles under his eyes, still fucking *smelled* like booze, not to mention had the vague stain of permanent marker he hadn't quite scrubbed off one temple. Distinctly dick shaped, Austin might add. Not that he was about to mention it. Nope, he'd let Drew walk around with dick face all day, as punishment for his sins against the team.

"Uh, yeah." Austin snorted. "You gonna be able to keep up with me today, or am I gonna have to ask one of the girls on the ellipticals to step in for you?"

"Ha-ha. Looking for a convenient excuse to partner up with someone more your speed, ya fuckin' pussy?"

The familiar insult gave Austin the same sick, involuntarily twinge as it had given him since puberty, but at least now he was pretty well practiced at smothering it. Which didn't help how fucked up it was to have to *be* practiced with something so twisted, but anything was better than the alternative. "More like looking for a convenient excuse to look at some tits on my spotter instead of smelling your balls all day," he replied without missing a beat.

See? Smothered.

Austin was fine, totally fine. He could definitely live with some of his teammates if push came to shove. His suddenly gay lifestyle—Rob's makeup and the leather daddy comic books at Rear Entrance Video and Christian and Max making out on the same couch he sat on to play video games—hadn't quite tainted him yet. He was still in control. He was.

"Don't lie. You fuckin' love the smell of my balls, pussy boy."

Shit. Maybe Austin wasn't quite as well practiced at smothering his reactions as he thought. *Shit, shit, shit.*

CHAPTER 2

You fuckin' love the smell of my balls, pussy boy.

He paused mid-crunch to shudder in reaction to that familiar, heady mix of nausea and horniness that had dogged him for years. Pictured himself on his knees, leaning in—

No, fuck no, he was not doing this here and now.

He grimaced and clenched his abs, forcing his back off the floor. It fucking hurt. His abs spasmed like they'd been electrocuted. At least his uncooperative dick softened a bit.

The workout schedule for that day was gruelling: crunches and side planks and squats and one-legged Russian dead lifts, and it still wasn't tough enough for Austin. Maybe it would have been, if he hadn't had that exchange with Drew, or if he'd at least reacted to it better, but now that the not-so-proverbial hammer had dropped, there could be no mercy.

He'd doubled up on his reps, which ate into his allotted time for rests, but fuck it. He'd upped the weight on the dumbbells. He'd huffed and puffed, muscles screaming with strain, body running with sweat, but he hadn't let himself stop. He wanted to hurt. Wanted to wake up tomorrow morning *still* hurting; the kind of hurt you didn't forget.

Beside him, Drew half assed his way through the same sets, occasionally pausing between wussy shallow squats to give Austin a bug-eyed look.

It's called putting out an effort, he wanted to say, *You should try it.*

Except he really had no right to talk. Oh, sure, busting ass like this *looked* good to the rest of his team—especially Warren Phillips, newly promoted to team captain—but it was all a lie. As hard as he was pushing himself, hockey was the last thing on his mind right now. After all, if he was really thinking about his game, he'd be working out smart instead of working out hard. But he wasn't chasing power or endurance or flexibility, all important qualities on the ice.

He was chasing pain.

Punishment.

Sometimes it felt like he'd spent his whole life punishing himself. Cold showers to start with, as stereotypical as it was to take one when you were turned on but didn't want to be. Banging his head against hard surfaces, although that was more an impulse thing than a planned punishment. Which led to a short-lived affair with cutting himself, always on the inner thighs so he wouldn't have anybody asking questions. The fact that his chosen spot was so close to the source of all his troubles, well, that was just a bonus.

Cutting yourself was fucked up, though, and it didn't work anyway. But he'd eventually figured out a kind of equation, a way to balance shit out. Get turned on by being treated like a pussy and a fag? Do something ultra manly to even the scales. So he worked out. Hard. And if it left him too fucking tired and sore to jack off, all the better.

And it had worked. Worked so well, in fact, that it had been months since the last time he'd had to do this to himself and longer still since he'd had boner timing this bad.

You fuckin' love the smell of my balls, pussy boy.

So much for his winning streak.

"Watch your elbows," Warren said, and knelt down beside him on the mat. Austin fell back onto the floor like a sack of potatoes and wheezed. Shit, he was massively out of breath. How much of it was overexertion and how much was the ball-smell-related horniness he was still (unsuccessfully) fighting off? Warren's eyebrows knitted together. "Are you okay, man?"

God, fuck, the last thing he needed was Warren's people skills. Asshole. "Yeah," Austin puffed. "Just pushed myself too hard, I guess."

"Don't hurt yourself," Warren scolded him gently, in that way he had that never made you feel bad or humiliated, only determined to prove yourself and make him proud. "Although at least *somebody* here is pushing himself..." He cast a mildly aggravated look across the gym to where Drew was standing by the ellipticals, unsuccessfully chatting up some chick in short-shorts who still had her earbuds in.

"He was drinking again last night," Austin blurted, half out of genuine resentment for the guy's lack of commitment and half out of a need to get Warren and his look of genuine concern away from him pronto. "I saw him this morning majorly hungover with a dick on his face."

It worked. Warren shook his head, fully focused on Drew now. "That guy. What am I going to do with him?"

Austin was angrier than he thought, because he sat up and said, "Put him on the fucking bench until he gets his act together. Calabresi would jizz himself if you gave him Drew's spot. And he'd probably play better too."

"Language!" Warren snapped, but then he nodded. "I might have to. His grades are slipping too. I practically had to write his papers for him last semester just so he could keep his scholarship." His eyes widened. "I shouldn't be telling you this. Shoot."

"Make me alternate captain, and then you can," Austin tried. God, he wanted that. To finally get recognition for his three years' dedication to the team. To contribute even more than he was already. Maybe then he wouldn't feel so inadequate all the time and his weird fetish would disappear, too. He'd belong. Be normal. Being alternate captain and winning games and—God, he fucking wished—getting drafted would put so many points on the *manly* side of his inner scales that they'd be permanently tipped in that direction. He'd be cured.

"Maybe," Warren hedged, and stood, striding across the gym in Drew's direction as he shouted out, "Hall! How're your squats going over there?"

Austin gave his head a shake and got back to his grind.

Someday . . .

Until then, doubling up on his crunches would have to suffice.

The last thing Austin wanted on a day like this was to shower with his teammates, so when they all headed to the changerooms, he made up some bullshit excuse about needing to work in some cardio because he'd gone to Vera's for a cheeseburger last night. Then he hit the treadmill, pumped up the incline, and ran until he felt like his legs were going to give out.

By the time he hit the shower, it was clear of his teammates. He soaped his body—trying not to clean his dick too thoroughly—rinsed off, and got the fuck out of there.

He caught up with the team in the cafeteria closest to their next class. Got his plateful of lasagna and an energy drink and joined them. Sat as far as humanly possible from Drew, which meant squeezing in next to Ben Kibby, their goalie, at the opposite end of the table.

"'Sup," Ben said, then turned back to defenceman Tim Cooper, who was in full redneck mode wearing his Confederate Flag ball cap and picking his teeth. "I'm telling you, it costs a couple hundred bucks, but I hear it totally works. You do a web conference with this guy for an hour, and he gets you more pussy than you know what to do with."

"I already get that much pussy. They're called puck bunnies." Tim examined the lump of whatever he'd managed to catch on the end of his toothpick then threw the thing over his shoulder onto the floor. "Don't know what your problem is that you gotta pay some dude to get you some."

Ben frowned. "It's not the same for Asian dudes, man. Girls don't want us. They all think we got small dicks."

"Get a T-shirt that says, 'I'm half-white,'" Calabresi advised.

"Yeah," Austin piped up, trying to get into the swing of things. "With an arrow, you know?" He pointed downward with both hands.

Calabresi and Tim both laughed, but Ben scowled. Man, the guy wouldn't be so down on himself if he knew what Austin was going through sexually.

"At least you're not a fuckin' virgin like Warren over there," one of the other guys added.

"If you think I'm going to be ashamed for saving myself for marriage," Warren said evenly, not looking up from where he was cutting up a chicken breast into bite-sized pieces, "you're sadly mistaken. And anyway, at least I'm not wasting money or time chasing after meaningless sex. Maybe that's why I'm team captain, and you spent most of last season on the bench, eh, Ortega?"

"Buuuuuuurn," Riley Campbell shouted obnoxiously. A table of Asian girls all looked over their shoulders to scowl at him.

"Wow," Ben said, voice dripping with sarcasm. "Good for you, Campbell, you contributed!"

"Yeah, way to get those two brain cells rubbing together!" someone else said.

Austin shovelled a few mouthfuls of lasagna into his mouth, wondering which would be worse: living with this band of horny idiots or in the Gayest House in Vancouver.

"So did everyone get the assignment done for Professor Walton's class?" Warren asked through his teeth, obviously trying to direct the conversation back to a more palatable topic. The table responded with a chorus of *Yeah*s and *Mostly*s . . . except, predictably, for Drew.

"Oh shit!" Drew said, slapping his hand to his forehead. "Was that today? I totally forgot."

Yeah, right.

"Oh come on, Drew," Warren moaned. "Homework is worth thirty percent in this class, and you've already missed two out of three assignments."

"It slipped my mind, okay?" Drew's tone was peevish. He turned to Austin's end of the table. "Hey, Ben, do me a solid and let me copy your answers, bro. I'll play wingman for you at this party Friday if you do. Won't even charge you two hundred bucks."

"Wingman, eh?" Tim guffawed. "You gonna stand around telling all the chicks that he's only half Chinese?" Ortega high-fived him.

Ben glowered. "Forget it, man. I already got in shit last semester when you came into that open book exam with a binder of my photocopied notes."

"Fuck you too, man. You're the world's worst Asian," Drew complained. "What about you, Tim?"

Eyes on his tray and with a mouth full of lasagna, Tim said, "I don't need your help to get pussy."

"Not the wingman thing. Can I copy your homework?"

"You want mine?" Riley asked, as desperate as an SPCA puppy.

Calabresi snorted. "Nobody wants to copy your assignments, man. You probably do them in crayon."

"*Nobody's* giving you their homework to copy," Warren finally announced. "Nobody on this team is cheating. On anything. Period.

And Drew, you need to get your stuff together if you're planning on playing on the team come next season."

"Stuff?" Drew taunted. "You mean *shit*, Warren? The word is shit. C'mon man, this is a hockey team, not your fucking Sunday school. Shit. Say shit."

"We're not talking about my religion right now. We're talking about the fact that you need to start taking things seriously on *and* off the ice. Austin says you got drunk last night."

Drew rounded on Austin while their teammates stared. "Oh did he, now?"

"Come on man, leave me out of this," Austin protested weakly, wishing he could slither under the table and disappear. Just what he needed to add to his roommate drama: team drama. Because even if he was right about Drew, betraying a teammate that way wasn't done. Your teammates were your brothers, and that meant sticking by them no matter what. Drew may have needed to get his fucking act together, but for Austin to narc on him like this? That was the worse crime by far, and it showed: his teammates *glared* at him.

Drew, sensing his advantage, laid his victimhood on thick. "What the fuck else did you tell him, huh, Austin? You tell him I don't say my prayers at night?"

Warren was looking seriously exasperated now. "You know I keep my beliefs off the ice." His voice was calm, but his nostrils were flaring. "Look, we talked about your drinking already, Drew. The drinking, the missing assignments, and then today I had to remind you that you were in the gym to work out. It's the last straw. You need to be a team player."

"*I* need to be a team player? *I* need to be a team player? What about Ben, who won't help me with my schoolwork, huh? What about Austin throwing me under the bus? Don't *they* need to be team players?"

"Team player doesn't mean letting you get away with everything. You need to shape up or ship out."

Drew cast a glower around the table. "Seriously? You're all just gonna let him sit here and chew me out?"

Nobody spoke.

"Tim?" Drew tried. "Calabresi? C'mon, *Ortega*? You at least gotta have my back, Ortega."

Nothing. But Austin didn't take their silence as approval for his behaviour, either. His punishment would come.

"We want to win games, Drew," Warren said solemnly. "Maybe even place. We want to get drafted. We can't do any of that if you're dragging us down with your slacking."

"Oh, I see how it is. You're the new team captain, and you need to make an example of somebody. And Austin's sucking your dick, so it can't be him."

"Oh, fuck off!" Austin shouted, fury fed by the sick twitch his dick did in his pants. "Everybody's sick of your me-me-me fucking attitude, Drew. Sick of it. We're sick of picking up after you. We're sick of losing games because you won't fucking practice hard enough. And yet we've all put our necks out for you by helping you fucking cheat at school so you can keep your scholarship, even though you don't even contribute to the team and you're not worth the fucking effort. And you know why? It's called fucking loyalty, man." One of the other guys snorted at Austin's use of the word, but Austin barreled on with his speech. "It's called sticking to your fucking guns. It's called standing by your teammates even if they're total fucking douche bags or you don't like them or they're fucking weird." He gasped for air. Realized he was standing, chest heaving, and everyone at the table was staring at him. Scratch that: everyone in the entire cafeteria was staring at him.

And he wasn't just talking about the hockey team. Especially not at the end there.

Because sure, SFU's hockey team was a bunch of assholes, some of whom Austin would never associate with if it weren't for a shared love of the game, but none of them—not one—could be called "weird."

But his roommates sure as hell could.

CHAPTER 3

That settled things, anyway. Austin wasn't a quitter, wasn't a traitor, was better than Drew in every way, including on the ice. Which meant that weird or not, he was going to have to learn to live with "Bobby." Because as tempting as it was to move the fuck out and leave all this confusion behind him, that was something Drew would do.

Austin was made of stronger stuff than that. Austin had morals. Austin had *balls*.

It also helped that today's disastrous boner-and-betrayal-filled lunch had solidified the fact that living with any of his teammates—especially considering his . . . problem—would be absolute hell. He thought things were uncomfortable now? Just wait until his new roommates spotted one of his inappropriate hard-ons. Sure, he'd managed to avoid detection up until now, but how long could you live with a group of guys before they figured out that a specific subset of insults gave you a boner every time? Living in the gayest house in Vancouver may have had its pitfalls, but nobody there called him *fag* or *pussy* on a daily basis.

He had a closing shift at Rear Entrance Video tonight, which would be a good test of his new resolve. He'd make nice with whoever was scheduled to work days, and then he'd sit right there in the middle of all that gay LGBT shit and force himself not to be grossed and/or weirded out by it. And hopefully he'd come up with a way to do the same thing around Rob—*ahem, Bobby*—so he could keep his place in the house and prove his loyalty.

If he even could.

Without the ultimatum, he maybe would have been able to get better at handling Bobby by way of desensitizing himself to The Gay, but he wasn't sure if a month—even one spent living with two and a half gay dudes and working in a porn store absolutely saturated in gay—would be enough to bring him to that point. The past two weeks sure hadn't resulted in any progress, but then, Austin hadn't exactly been *trying*.

But maybe if he purposely exposed himself to critical levels of the stuff, even beyond what he was currently dealing with . . .

Which was a possibility, he guessed, except he had a feeling trying for that much exposure would involve marching in a pride parade before going drinking at Celebrities and then heading home to raid Christian's personal collection of dirty movies for his own nightly presleep jerk-off session.

And by the time it got to *that* point, why not suck a bunch of dicks while he was at it?

Argh.

He scrubbed at his face in frustration, more than a little concerned at how detailed the image of himself sucking dick was.

And not, like, lovingly either. Not like girls did in porn, licking their lips and smiling like the dude they were sucking off was their personal god. Not even like girls sometimes did to him, borderline disinterested but still willing so long as he returned the favour. More like a brawny guy cornering him in some grimy bathroom and shoving him to the floor, pinching his nose to force his mouth open and fucking into him like a blow-up doll. And he'd hate it. It'd taste disgusting, and it would choke him and feel wrong all around, but he still wouldn't fight it, wouldn't bite the guy or anything, would just—

Shit. Now he was getting a boner on the fucking bus.

He needed to get this thing under control.

Except he wasn't sure he even *could*. As much as the guys at the house all joked about the gay being contagious like it was the most absurd thing they'd heard of, Austin couldn't help but wonder if having so much of it around wasn't making his problem worse. After all, he'd had his problem pretty well dealt with before Christian and Max had started fucking and Rob had started wearing lipstick and Rear Entrance Video had become Queer Entrance Video.

And now? Now it was back to square one, except instead of being a terrified teenaged kid, he was a terrified grown-ass man with a much more seasoned—okay, more like plain fucking perverted—

imagination. Austin pulled his backpack onto his lap to hide his shame. Couldn't move out because it would be betraying his roommates, and his problem meant he had nowhere else to really go, anyway. Couldn't stay where he was because being around so much gay was clearly affecting his hormones or something.

And his only solution was to expose himself to *even more* gay? God, if he did that, by the end of the month he'd be popping a boner every time someone so much as looked at him funny. Of course, if he was also making nicey-nice with his rainbow roommates, maybe the boner problem wouldn't matter anymore. He'd be one of them.

Oh, who was he kidding? Of *course* it would matter. Austin wasn't like Drew, but he also wasn't like Rob or Christian or Max, who all could say "Screw what other people think; I don't need them anyway. I'll do what I want."

Austin needed to play hockey. And for that, he needed his team.

He needed to be straight.

No, he *was* straight. But he needed to be a *normal* straight guy. His roommates could blab about how there was nothing wrong with them all they wanted, but that wasn't Austin. There *was* something wrong with Austin, and he couldn't lie down and accept it. And if he didn't fix it, and soon, he'd lose everything that mattered to him. He'd lose *himself*. Because he wasn't just on a hockey team, he *was* the team. The team was him.

The more he thought about it all, the more he realized: he was fucked.

He was also at his stop.

And of course it was Rob working the counter.

Of course it fucking was.

Rob, who didn't look any more happy to see Austin than Austin was to see Rob. First, he looked up with a smile, then he startled, then he opened the till and started counting out the bills without a word.

Make nice, Austin reminded himself as he walked in. "Since when do you work days?" he asked. And, like the fuckstick he was, made it sound like an accusation. Not on purpose or anything, but there it was.

Rob snorted. "I have the summer off, *remember*?" he said, and then mumbled something into his lap that may or may not have been, "Or have you taken too many hits to your thick head?"

"Oh," Austin said, forcing himself not to get lippy right back. "Uh, well. That's cool." He swallowed hard and took the seat beside Rob, unintentionally catching a glance of the black lace bra peeping out from the top of Rob's half-unbuttoned white shirt. Imagined someone forcibly putting something lacy like that on him and watching him squirm in embarrassment. His face went hot, and he turned away from Rob, staring at the bills instead. He was beginning to see why Rob couldn't take his eyes of them today. "Look, uh, R—Bobby, about how I've been acting. I'm sorry."

Rob turned on him, his face insufferably smug. Not the face of a guy about to accept an apology, that was for sure. "Oh yeah, is that so? And I'm sure how sorry you are has nothing to do with the fact that Noah told you he was kicking you out at the end of the month."

Jeez, what the fuck had happened to the old pushover Rob from before? The one he could steal food from and never have to pay back? The one he could make small dick jokes about, who'd never punch him in the face for it the way Ben once had in the locker room?

"Well, look who it fucking is. Here kissing ass, I take it?"

Dylan, of course. The fat fuck sauntered in, giving Austin the kind of scowl that didn't turn him on at all.

So *that* was where Rob was getting his new balls from. Hell, the guy had probably coached Rob on exactly what to say.

"Why, you want in on the action, gay boy?" Austin snapped back. Oops.

Dylan's shoulders went up, and shit, Austin had forgotten the guy was fucking *huge*, at least as big as their team enforcer Riley, except with brains to back up the brawn. "You know what I think, toolbag?" Dylan said. "I think you're such a dick to Bobby because it makes you uncomfortable to see him embrace himself."

"Uh, yeah, duh," Austin replied, because with the *gay boy* comment, he'd already fucked this thing up and he might as well go down swinging.

"And you know *why* I think that makes you uncomfortable? I think it makes you uncomfortable because you're jealous. I think you're a little bit of a jock closet case." Oh, *there* went Austin's boner. He crossed his legs, meeting Dylan's fierce stare. He wasn't going to let this guy intimidate him, big or not. "I think sometimes you stare a little too long at your teammates' dicks in the locker room. I think maybe sometimes you jerk off thinking about your coach. And I think seeing Bobby happy makes you jealous, and it also scares you, and I think that's why you treat him like shit. Straight guys—actual straight guys—have no reason to be threatened by people like Bobby. People like Noah are secure in their sexualities, but you're not." Dylan smirked in triumph. "You're repressed, and you're unhappy, so you're lashing out at Bobby because he's brave enough to do what you can't. Admit it."

"F-fuck you," Austin managed to spit. That was all he had. Just . . . "Fuck you, Dylan. What the fuck do you know?"

Rob slammed the cash drawer shut and snatched his man purse from under the counter. "Let it go, Dylan," he pleaded, then stood and walked out from behind the counter, taking Dylan by the arm. "Come on, he's not worth it."

"I know, baby," Dylan said, brushing Rob's long hair from his forehead and pressing a kiss there.

Austin stood there, dumbfounded, with a boner, feeling like a complete fucking asshole. An asshole who was going to be homeless at the end of the month, if things kept on the way they were going. Maybe he should apologize, maybe— "Hey!" he yelled, when they turned their backs on him like he really wasn't worth their time or attention. "Just so you know, I am not a closet case, okay? I am *straight as fuck*!"

No reply other than the jingle of the bell over the door as they exited. Not that they needed to bother; did a statement that pathetic and desperate really require a comeback? Seriously, *straight as fuck*? How straight was fuck, even?

Fuck fuck fuck fuck fuck.

He banged a fist down on the desk. He'd literally *just* decided to make things better, and yet in the time since making that decision he'd somehow made them ten fucking times worse?

Shit, if he'd decided to say *fuck it* and embrace getting kicked out, would he and Rob have miraculously kissed and made up?

Okay, no, that was stupid as fuck, and not just the part about him and Rob kissing each other, even metaphorically.

The issue was, *deciding* to do something and actually making it happen were two separate things. If they weren't, he'd already be in the NHL by now, captain for the Canucks, taking home the Stanley Cup and single-handedly preventing another riot. And he'd be straight—without exceptions.

But he was none of those things. He was just Austin Puett, playing for one of the shittiest college teams in Canada, getting kicked out of his place at the end of the month, and springing wood every time anyone suggested he was anything other than macho.

To get what you wanted, you had to do more than want it and decide to get it. You had to make a plan, and then you had to execute it. Get on a college team. Train hard. Kick ass. Win games. Make captain. Get drafted. Kick more ass. Win more games. Get traded. Kick even more ass. Win even more games. Take home the fucking cup.

Austin knew all about discipline, all about planning and making those plans fucking happen. With hockey, at least. So why not with Rob?

Bobby.

So maybe he hadn't hammered out any kind of plan yet, but whatever that plan ended up being, Austin was pretty sure that calling the guy by the name he'd chosen would likely be a part of it.

"Bobby, Bobby, Bobby," he muttered to himself, practicing the word as he returned to his seat.

"Who's that, yer boyfriend?"

Austin recoiled, torn between surprise and—God fucking damn it—horniness; his wheelie chair flew back and slammed into the wall behind him.

The guy draped over the counter laughed, then blew a big pink bubble of gum. Popped it. Snapped it. Smiled.

Holy shit. A customer. Had Austin missed the bell? Was this guy some kind of gay ninja?

And oh, he was definitely gay. Spiky hair with frosted tips. A V-necked T-shirt tight enough that Austin could see his nipples were pierced.

And gay porn in his hand. That too.

Austin wheeled his chair forward again and snatched the DVD out of the customer's hand. "I'm straight," he said, probably way too late for it to sound like he wasn't lying.

The customer flashed him a crooked smile. "No shit, really? Isn't that weird, working in a gay porn store?"

Weirder than you know.

The DVD was some locally produced BDSM thing called *Master Puck and Mistress Titania's STRAIGHT SUB SETUP 4.*

Austin stared at the case. At the main title in bright red, bolded capital letters.

STRAIGHT.

SUB.

SETUP.

His face burned. The customer cleared his throat, and somehow even that came out gay-sounding.

"Oh!" Austin snapped his gaze up. The guy had asked him a question. Shit. "Uh, well. It wasn't a gay porn store when I first started working here."

The customer smirked, dark eyelashes dipping over his eyes smugly. "So you could say you . . . got set up?"

Oh God. Austin was at the point of giving fourteen-year-old boys the world over a run for their money when it came to involuntary boners. He squirmed and yanked the DVD case open so he could scan the bar code into the system and process the return.

Beep. Three days overdue. He threw it into the TO BE SORTED pile, forcing himself not to give it a second glance. "Will that be all?" he rasped, then tacked on, ". . . bro?"

Yeah, real straight, Austin. Straight as fuck.

"Don't I, like, owe you late fees?" Snap went the guy's gum.

"Oh, uh, right. Um. Yeah. Six bucks." Austin licked his lips, refusing to meet the guy's gaze as he took the ten from his hand and opened the till.

His boner pulsed. *STRAIGHT SUB SETUP*, his mind taunted, those red capital letters floating through his mind. He wondered what a movie with a title like that might be about. He knew enough about BDSM from working here and from his own "research" on the internet to know that the SUB part meant submissive, as in someone who got off on being ordered around and spanked or whatever while wearing a collar and one of those creepy zippered hoods.

Doing whatever some sexy chick in a corset and thigh-high boots told you to do? Yeah, Austin could go for that. But when it turned into her calling you a sissy and paddling your ass like a little kid and making you suck her lovingly realistic strap-on complete with wrinkly balls, Austin started to get weirded out—and turned on, and then weirded out again even worse. So, you know, even if it was a guy and a girl together, he stayed away from the BDSM stuff. Back to the normal porn of blondes in pigtails with fake tits pretending to be babysitters and fucking black pizza delivery guys.

"Um, hello? My change?"

Shit!

"Sorry. Uh, fuck. Four bucks, right?" he fumbled in the cash drawer for some toonies but kept grabbing and dropping the same three over and over again, unable to gather the dexterity to get exactly two. Three. Zero. One. Three. Zero. "Fuck!" he snapped, on the edge of crying like a bitch.

"Are you okay?" the customer asked. Blew a bubble. Popped it. Snapped it. "You seem kind of high-strung, sugar."

"I'm not a tweaker," Austin said. Finally, he managed to pick up two toonies and hand them over. "Four dollars."

The customer put up both hands defensively, rolling his wide eyes. "Nobody said you were, sweetie. But between you and me? I don't think you're quite straight, either."

"What do you know, huh?" Shit. That didn't come out angry so much as . . . pleading? Was that the word for the desperate whine in his tone just then? Also, yay, another fail on the *not being hostile to gay dudes* front.

"On this subject? Quite a bit, babycakes. Not to brag, but I've sucked so much supposedly straight dick in the last few years, that when you say *straight* I hear *convince me.*"

"D-does that really happen? Straight guys? They let you . . . let you . . ." *Suck their dicks? Fuck them? Get fucked by them?* "Let you?" he finished, unable to make his mouth say anything more explicit.

The customer threw back his head with a gloating laugh. "Let me? *Let* me? Oh, honey. They *beg* me."

Beg you.

Austin nearly passed out.

CHAPTER 4

The customer—Zeke, according to the sloppy scrawl on the back of his receipt—wound up giving Austin his number before he finally left. And he'd signed it with *XOXO*.

Austin, of course, balled up the scrap of paper and chucked it into the garbage, then prematurely tied off the bag and took it out to the dumpster in the alley.

There. No evidence.

He returned to the counter and fell into his seat, feeling like he'd run five miles. Which he may have, earlier today. Shit, he was going to fucking *hurt* tomorrow, and it was going to destroy his workouts for the entire week, and it hadn't even helped his problem at all.

Maybe he was going about this all wrong. Maybe the punishments weren't the solution, but a part of the problem.

Maybe Zeke and Dylan were right about him.

Not about him being gay, fuck no. Austin was straight, he *was*. Whatever Dylan thought about him, he sure as hell *never* looked at his teammates' dicks or asses in the showers, and he'd never been tempted to, either. He didn't think they were sexy to look at the way girls were. He liked tits and hips and long hair and, oh yeah, pussy. He was sitting here at the counter with a stack of gay porn DVD cases—returns processed and discs filed away, ready to be returned to the shelves for the next gay dude to rent—and he wasn't even remotely turned on by them. Guys sucking dick, guys with cum dripping down their chins, guys spreading their ass cheeks and showing you their assholes . . . not one image appealed.

But, oh, getting called gay or thinking about being forced to do gay shit, yeah, that got him off. That wasn't gay, it was just twisted. A twisted part of him he'd been fighting for years to bottle up and put a lid on, so no wonder the top of his head was blowing off now.

Okay, the tops of *both* heads.

What was that thing Dylan had said?

"You're repressed, and you're unhappy, so you're lashing out at Bobby because he's brave enough to do what you can't."

If that was true, if Austin really was being such a dick to Bobby because he was *repressed*, then would fixing his repression fix the way he was acting, too? Would he stop being so disgusted and frustrated by Bobby and so *angry*?

He stared down at the stack of DVD cases on the counter. Slowly sorted through them until he found the one he was looking for. The only one that turned him on: *Master Puck and Mistress Titania's STRAIGHT SUB SETUP 4.*

The cover was black and white with bold red lettering. On it, a buff guy in black leather pants and some kind of chest harness thing—Master Puck, Austin figured—was standing facing the camera, his legs spread dominantly, with a naked guy kneeling in front of him, looking up at him in fear and awe. Austin's throat thickened. So did his dick.

Not because of the men—naked or half-naked—but because of the positioning. Because of the expression on the STRAIGHT SUB's face. Afraid and sick to his stomach and helplessly turned on. And Austin, in turn, felt exactly the same. Turned on by the image. Sick with himself for liking it so much. Afraid of what it all meant and where it would take him.

He flipped the case over.

OhthankGod. On the flip side was a picture of a woman in some kind of skintight red vinyl thing that hugged every feminine curve. Her tits practically spilled out of the top of her dress, and in her hands, she held what looked like a riding crop. And she was smirking. At Austin. *Dangerous*, that was what she looked like. Man-eater. He bit his lip, his eyes sliding over to the text.

Mistress Titania is back to her old tricks, and this time well-hung str8 frat boy Danny Domino is her prey!

The setup: After answering an online ad for a straight submissive willing to do absolutely anything *for a sexy and demanding mistress, unwitting Danny arrives at the Mischievous Pictures studio for a classic bait and switch. He thinks he's gonna be licking Mistress Titania's stiletto heels and begging for her pristine pussy, but he's going to get a mouth and ass full of cock instead!*

What Mistress Titania wants, Mistress Titania gets, and after Danny signs a contract promising to obey her every command (and letting us film, of course), she brings out her best friend and partner in crime, brutal Master Puck, who never gets (or hits) harder than when he's with a virgin str8 boy. Now, to please his mistress and fulfil his contract, Danny must perform the ultimate act of submission: swallowing his str8 pride in order to swallow gay cum, all while Mistress Titania watches. But after taking Master Puck's monster pierced cock, will Danny ever give her—or any other woman—a second glance again?

Austin could watch this. He could. There was even a woman and a straight guy in it, so it wasn't even *really* gay porn. It was porn for sick fucks like him. Straight sick fucks.

He could take it home without renting it—no paper trail—and put his headphones on, and watch it. Tonight, in the middle of the night. He could watch it, and if he got a boner, he could jerk off to it. Return it to the store tomorrow before anyone noticed it missing. Steam let off. Repression fixed. And then he'd have no reason to be so angry at Bobby anymore, and he wouldn't say douche bag things without meaning to. Eventually Bobby would have to forgive him, and once Bobby forgave him, the other guys—Noah, specifically—would too. He wouldn't be kicked out of his house. He wouldn't lose his job. Maybe his problem would even stop "popping up" at inopportune moments (like with his team, specifically) if he had an actual outlet.

And it would all be a secret, and Austin would still be straight. He'd have hockey and his team.

Yeah.

This could totally work.

He wheeled his chair back to the filing cabinets where the rental discs were stored, found the one he was looking for (and discs one, two, and three of the same series!), took both DVD and case, wrapped them in his workout T-shirt from this morning, and stuffed them into the bottom of his bag.

Oh, there was one more emotion that he'd seen on Danny Domino's face but been unable to identify before now: anticipation.

The longer his shift went on, the more the anticipation built. It was a shifting thing, moving from arousal to anxiety to disgust and back again. His stomach roiled. It felt a little like the hours before a big game, excitement and fear and grim determination all warring inside him. And just like before a game, he felt the need to stand, jump up and down on the balls of his feet, clap his hands, and do jumping jacks; anything to get that energy out. At least having a plan and a desired outcome took a little of the pressure off him. In one way, he was a mess of emotions, but in another, he felt better—freer—than he had in years.

When a middle-aged gay couple came in partway through the night, he barely blinked, even when he overheard them describing, in detail, what they planned to do later that night after watching the DVD they were currently in the process of selecting. And if he could handle gay Mr. Clean telling gay Jackie Chan that he was gonna pound his cute ass until he couldn't walk straight—as if either of those dudes could do *anything* straight—then maybe, given some time and, um, release, he could handle Bobby too. And Bobby's bras. And Bobby's girly hair. And Bobby's big butch boyfriend.

Damn, this porn was gonna have to blow his socks off to make up for all that.

Well, he thought as he locked the door and turned off the OPEN sign, *I'll know for sure by the end of tonight.* And if this particular volume of the series didn't work, there were three more to serve as backups.

It was sick how much the thought of them excited him.

No. If this video worked, that would be it. He wouldn't watch the others. It was meant to be a treatment. A medicine like his mom's prescription pain pills: use them past the point where you were cured, and they became an addiction.

In fact, he should take the other DVDs in the series off the table completely. If this didn't work tonight, then more of the same wouldn't, either. He couldn't be simultaneously looking for a way to fix himself *and* looking for an excuse to watch as much gay porn as possible.

One porno. One viewing.

Hands trembling with building excitement, he counted out the till.

Three times, because he could never quite get his numbers right.

CHAPTER 5

Doubt hit right after Austin put the DVD in his computer's disc drive.

His headphones were jacked into the computer, but he wasn't wearing them yet. He could hear some kind of tinny music coming out of them, overlaid by a sound that, even at low volume, was definitely moaning.

The disc menu was the same black and white and red kind of thing as the case, but now the black and white images were *moving*, and that made them even more obscene. Two men kissing, one of them grasping the other by the jaw. A gob of spit dropping out of frame onto the fat head of a pierced dick, then a big masculine hand rubbing the wetness around. An asshole that was opening and closing on its own, like it was fucking winking, and holy shit, was Austin's hole clenching along in time?

Jesus. He couldn't do this. He couldn't. He could not sit here and watch gay fucking porn with his asshole twitching like this. It was fucked up. It was totally fucked up, and if he wanted to be straight this was the exact wrong way of going about it, and how the fuck had he even justified this crazy fucking plan to himself?

A man with a mouth full of fabric, face flushed dark, eyes wet. A flash of bright red on the black and white: a close-up of the woman's dress over the curve of her hip. Latex. That's what it was made of.

Austin liked what he saw. His boner didn't get harder—not that it could, by this point—but it didn't go away, either. Looking at the woman wasn't better than looking at the degraded man, just different. Hot, but without the nausea or the asshole clenching.

See? Still straight. You can do this.

He put his earbuds in and pressed play. Instantly squeezed his eyes shut.

He could do this. He could do this. He could do this.

Holy shit, was he hyperventilating? His breath puffed in and out of him like he'd been running for miles. His hands clenched into fists. Should he take his pants off for this? Would it be more effective if he jacked off, or did he only need to watch?

Shit, he was supposed to be watching this thing.

He forced his eyes to the screen. Danny Domino was sitting on an office chair, looking as scared and eager as Austin felt. He had the collar of his pink shirt popped and his white ball cap on sideways. Across from him, a prim librarian type with a severe bun in her black hair and nerdy thick-framed glasses to match was looking over several sheets of paper attached to a clipboard. She had the kind of look where somebody at the porn studio obviously had wanted her to look ugly and un-sexy, like she wasn't part of the production, even though she clearly was. "Well, everything here seems to be in order, Mr. Domino," she said. She had a clipped, lilting accent. Sexy as hell. Indian, if Austin had to guess. "All we need now is your signature, guaranteeing that you identify as heterosexual and granting me your full and complete submission."

Submission. God, the way she said that word, as if it tasted like candy in her mouth. The way she said *complete*, too, snapping on the T aggressively. Austin reached down and rubbed the heel of his palm over the rigid line of his dick through his jeans. This was okay, wasn't it? It was gay porn, but he was jerking off to the woman. That had to be okay. He'd stop once the ass fucking got up and running. He would.

Danny Domino took the clipboard from her. The camera zoomed in on his throat and his bobbing Adam's apple as he gulped.

(Austin gulped, too.)

Then it zoomed in on Danny's hand as he signed.

(Austin didn't have anything to sign, but he'd irrevocably committed to this all the same, the minute he'd stuffed the DVD into his bag. Maybe even before that.)

What happened next wasn't surprising. "Well, well, well," the woman said, and stood. She reached back and loosed her bun. Shook out her long black hair. Now she'd take off her glasses—

But she didn't. She unbuttoned her prudish little grey blazer and let it slip off her shoulders to the floor. Walked around the desk, and the camera crawled up and down her body so that Austin was eye-fucking every inch of her. Because behind the desk and underneath the blazer, she was—of course—the woman in the red latex dress. And she wasn't taking off her glasses. God, she was like every strict stick-in-the-mud-but-still-impossibly-hot teacher he'd had in school. And—holy fuck—just as likely to *punish* him.

He licked his lips and unzipped the fly of his jeans, watching as the woman—this must be mistress Titanium? Tatiana? Titania?—strode around the desk to where Danny Domino was still sitting, pinned by fear to his chair. Austin felt pinned to *his* chair, too.

"You are one stupid son of a bitch, Danny. Can I call you Danny?" She tapped her lip with one finger. She had red nails to match her dress. Sharp. Viciously sharp. "Oh, that's right, I can do whatever I want now. Because you signed my contract, didn't you, Danny? Didn't anybody ever warn you about blank cheques?"

"N-no, ma'am," Danny said sheepishly, and wrapped his hands around the sides of his stiff-backed chair.

Mistress Titania gave him an exaggerated pout. "How very sad for you—and how very fortuitous for me."

Danny's and Austin's eyebrows both furrowed in unison.

"Oh dear. Don't tell me you don't know what the word 'fortuitous' means, now, Danny."

He shook his head.

Titania snatched him by the chin, fingernails nearly piercing his skin. "It means you're *mine* now, bitch."

Bitch, that wasn't a word to call a man, it was one for catty women and dogs in heat, but here she was, calling Danny that, and he could easily overpower her and make her *his* bitch, but he wasn't. He was sitting there taking it, and God, Austin wanted to take it too. From her? "My straight bitch, my toy. Mine to do anything I like with." She tossed a glance over her shoulder, not loosing her hold on Danny, who must be sweating with fear by now.

(Austin was.)

(Or maybe that was the hand wrapped around his dick, already working hard and fast.)

"Puck, dear!" she called. "You can come in now!"

Austin's hand on his dick stilled. He stopped *breathing*.

This was it. This was the point of no return.

Austin didn't *want* to return.

"Wh-who?" Danny squeaked, just as the door behind him opened.

And in strode Puck. *Master* Puck. Easily six feet tall and built like a brick house, with massive shoulders and pecs and powerful thighs and a slightly padded belly. Like a hockey enforcer in peak fighting condition—there was no other way to describe it.

Austin really didn't care one way or another about the shiny black leather fetish wear the guy was sporting: the studded harness crisscrossing his broad chest, the buckled bands around his wrists and up his forearms, and especially not the tight pants with the huge fucking bulge in the front.

No, what Austin cared about was the way Puck grabbed the back of Danny's chair and forcefully spun him so that they were—well, not eye to eye, but eye to abs, yeah. Danny's eyes flicked up. "What the—" he shouted, and tried to push his chair back, get some distance between them, but Mistress Titania was behind him, blocking the way, and Master Puck had already knocked the ball cap from his head and grabbed him by the hair.

He grinned ferally at Titania over the top of Danny's head. "Titania, baby, you have outdone yourself this time. He signed?"

"Signed and sealed," Titania confirmed with a nod. She bent over, so her arms were draped over Danny's shoulders and chest and her tits were pillowed against the back of Danny's head.

Danny whimpered. "What's going on?" he asked.

"Didn't I warn you about blank cheques, boy? This is my good friend Master Puck. He's got a taste for straight boys and I like to help him out. Well, technically he pays me to help him out." She kissed his temple and turned his face up. "You like my dress, don't you? I saw you looking. Puck bought it for me. Why don't you thank him?"

"No way!" Danny shouted in disgust, but he didn't struggle.

(And Austin didn't turn off the DVD, either.)

Puck bent until he and Danny's noses were touching. Had Puck's nose been broken, once? It looked a little off, a little crooked, so rugged compared to Danny's perky perfect Hollywood features. Austin had the sudden urge to see Danny's perfectness messed up, to see him taken down a few pegs until he was the bitch Titania had named him.

"Way," Puck replied, easily.

"Sorry, Puck," Titania said, stroking Danny's face now. "Forgot to mention he's a little bit stupid. Let me spell it out for you, Danny. You signed over your body and submission to me, and with that power, I'm telling you, serve *him*."

"How, how . . ." Danny squeezed his eyes shut, then opened them again, then shook his head.

(Austin didn't close his eyes. Didn't shake his head, didn't even blink.)

"Serve. Him." Titania's stroking hand took another handful of Danny's hair. They both had him, now. He was helpless caught between them. Signed himself away, and now they had him. "You can start by thanking him, like I told you to."

"Thank you," Danny spat.

Titania twisted her hand in his hair until he grunted in pain. "For?"

"Thank you . . . for buying Mistress Titania her dress."

"Sir," Titania finished.

Danny swallowed hard. Glared up at Puck defiantly. "No."

Sweat beaded on the back of Austin's neck. Cold sweat. Time seemed to stop. He stared at the two men, at the camera's close-up on their two faces in profile, at Danny's pathetic fury and Puck's cool smirk, just the two of them in the frame, like Titania didn't matter, wasn't there at all. Maybe for them, she wasn't. She certainly wasn't for Austin, not anymore, not in the face of this clash of wills so heavy with testosterone he could practically smell it.

His dick throbbed in his hand, trapped in the vice grip of his fist.

He let out the breath he was holding, still hanging on the edge.

Puck tossed his head back and *laughed*.

Austin recoiled in shock.

So did Danny, but more because Puck had hauled off and backhanded him across the face.

And it was no staged strike, either. Austin had taken enough hits to recognize Danny's stunned face and slack lip, and the hot red rising on his face, of course. Austin palmed his own cheek, trying to capture that pain, that humiliation of being hit the way pimps hit whores.

"You 'n' me are gonna have fun, straight boy. Now pick up your fuckin' hat."

Danny seemed like he was still dazed by the hit, holding his face and looking around blindly. Puck didn't hit him again, though, not even when the seconds stretched out to minutes, out to their breaking point. He stood waiting, arms crossed and occasionally looking at one of his bracers as if it were a watch. It was almost comical, totally the opposite of the raw power and authority he'd displayed.

It made Austin nervous.

Maybe it made Danny nervous too, because he eventually ducked a look up at Puck then crouched to the floor to retrieve his hat, as ordered.

"How's it feel down there?" *At my feet?*

Austin was expecting more disgust, more resistance, but what he got was Danny looking up, face bright red with shame, and saying, "Better than . . . better than I wanna admit. Sir."

Lip curling, Austin snorted. Pathetic. Fucking pathetic. Austin would have put up more of a fight.

He wouldn't have . . . admitted to it.

Admitted to secretly wanting it. Wanting to be on his knees at Puck's feet like that, looking at him still stunned and afraid, but eyes wide wanting more.

Because you don't want it. You don't want it. You don't. You just want to get this out of your system so you can stay in your house.

The voice in his mind that whispered back to him was Puck's, deep and gravelly and with that unpredictable mean humour: *But boys who don't want it don't* need *to work it out of their systems.*

"That's right," Puck said with a laugh, like he could hear Austin's thoughts, but then Austin remembered there was another conversation happening here: the one on his screen. To Puck, Austin didn't exist. "Get a straight boy on his knees at my feet, and suddenly he finds the fag inside him waiting to claw his way out."

What, like magic or some kind of psychic hypnotizing force field? Or was it instinct, like when people went with their guts, or when you *just knew* something, the way Austin's mother said when he met the right girl he'd *just know*?

Did Danny . . . just know?

Did Austin?

The scene cut. Opened on a dank, open warehouse space and Mistress Titania lounging on an out-of-place, fancy fainting couch filing her nails to dagger points, half an eye on something in the background, the way she might watch a TV show she wasn't particularly interested in.

Except there was no TV in the background, only Danny kneeling naked on the hard cement floor, arms tightly restrained behind him with a complicated arrangement of thick white rope that shot up to some ceiling hook outside of the camera's field of view. He was panting with exertion already, eyes glassy and startled.

And he had a raging hard-on.

So did Austin, coincidentally. One that he was stroking gently with the tips of his forefinger and thumb, like if he touched it any more firmly he'd burn his palms. Or grow hair on them—wasn't that the old wives' tale?

Whatever it was, he was fucking terrified of getting a good grip on himself but simultaneously way too into it now to even consider putting his dick away to remove all temptation.

Hadn't he decided only to jerk off to Titania?

No, he'd decided to not jerk off to the ass fucking. No asses were getting fucked, therefore this was fine.

Right?

Titania blurred into the foreground, then disappeared entirely as the camera zoomed in on Danny. Puck was beside him now. Standing. Free and fully clothed, of course. He put the white cap back on Danny's head. Turned it. Stepped back. Adjusted it half an inch until it was positioned just so. Then he crouched in front of Danny and slapped down hard on his erection, making it spring and Danny yelp.

"Who's this for, straight boy?"

"Nobody!" Danny shouted. "I don't know!"

"I see you didn't say it was for Titania. Not a very good liar when you're under pressure, huh?" As forceful as he'd been before, now he seemed strangely laid-back. Maybe that was how he got, once he knew the other guy couldn't fight or run away. "That's okay. I happen to like it *way* more when my boys are squirming. So let's try that again. Who's this—" He flicked Danny's balls. "—for?"

Danny clamped his mouth shut and shook his head.

"So that's how it's gonna be, huh, tough guy? Vell, ve have vays of making you talk!"

God, Austin couldn't take it anymore. Not even Puck's terrible imitation of a German accent could make that not hot as hell. He wrapped his hand around his dick and pumped. Hard. Pictured himself tied to the chair he was sitting on, and Puck interrogating him, but he wouldn't give up, wouldn't give in, not when Puck clamped his nipples with wooden clothespins, not when Puck wrapped thin rope around his balls until they turned fucking purple. Not even when Puck stuffed fingers into his clenching asshole, or when he replaced those fingers with a thick black plug covered in lube so creamy and thick it looked like margarine.

(Jerking off to Puck doing exactly that to Danny—tied over something resembling a sawhorse with his ass exposed—didn't count as getting off on ass fucking, did it? Fuck, who was he kidding, it probably did.)

Puck kept jacking off the plugged-and-clipped Danny, getting him right to the edge of orgasm before asking again, "Who's this for?"

It felt like he was asking Austin, looking right through the computer screen at Austin with his hot, heavy dick in his hand.

And then Danny still refused to answer, and Puck brought out the ziplock baggie full of ice and pressed it against Danny's dick and balls until he tilted his head back and howled and cried like a little bitch. And then he pulled the bag away and wrapped his hand around Danny's dick—even as Danny begged him not to—and started the process over and over again. Brought to the edge, over and over again. Asked "Who's this for?" over and over again. Austin found himself halting the motion of his hand every time Puck pulled off. Pinching himself—on his ball sac, on the head of his dick, on his nipple—every time Puck brought out the ice.

"Who's this for?" Puck asked him, watching Austin arch in his chair and whimper and abuse his chafed dick, jacking himself to orgasm through the multiple points of pain all over his body. Where he'd pinched himself, but where he'd exercised to the point of injury, too. He felt it all. Felt every inch of his body throbbing with heat and pain and sensation, and then Puck asked, "Who's this for?" and Austin was shouting, "For you, damn it!" as he shot ropy cum across his computer keyboard and right onto his monitor.

He gasped. Panted. Didn't realize Danny had gotten to the same point until he looked up and saw Puck kissing him deep and dominant, a tight hand in Danny's hair keeping him exactly where Puck wanted him. Even something as sweet as a kiss—and in a way, it was still sweet, the way Danny tried to arch up into Puck's grasp, the way he trembled and whined—turned into a power play for Puck.

Austin gasped and trembled too, too sated to feel disgusted with himself . . . yet.

No, the disgust came about two minutes later, when the soundtrack of the porn went to boring dialogue and Austin realized someone was knocking on his door.

CHAPTER 6

Banging on his door, actually.

He yanked his earbuds out, then, disgusted, wiped his sticky hand on the leg of his jeans.

"What?" he yelled at whoever was making all that noise.

Max's voice came back through the door at him. "What the fuck are you doing in there, man? Would you answer your fucking phone already? Or at least put it on silent? I can hear your shitty fucking ringtone from my fucking room."

"Oh boo-hoo-hoo!" Austin yelled back, embarrassment quickly overtaken by irritation. "I wouldn't have to put my headphones in and turn my music up to eleven if you didn't have such loud fucking butt sex!"

But it was true, Austin's phone *was* ringing.

His ringtone wasn't shitty, though. "What's My Age Again?" was a *classic*.

"Who the hell can have butt sex to Blink-182?" Max shouted.

"Calm your tits and shake the sand out of your panties!" He rooted through his bag for his phone, but it was harder to find than the hidden DVD had been—shit, how had Max heard it, but not Austin?

No, he didn't want to answer that. He tapped the screen to wake it up. Swept his thumb across to unlock the thing.

Four missed calls. Eight new texts. Shit, how long had he been jerking off for? God, who the fuck was calling him this late at night?

Warren.

Warren had been calling. But it was past midnight . . . wasn't Warren's bedtime like 8 p.m.?

No need to call the guy back and risk waking his *Leave It to Beaver* parents though, because the line of texts said it all.

12:16 a.m. Drew quit team.

12:20 a.m. . . . . . . .Ok didn't quit per se.

Austin's eyebrows popped up, all thoughts of gay porn and ass fucking and Max's loud sex life and bad taste in music forgotten in favour of hearing the dirt on Drew.

12:22 a.m. I tried to find him after class to talk to him about missing assignments + found him in the bushes on the quad smoking marijuana

12:22 a.m. Had to talk to coach

12:22 a.m. Couldn't even bench him

12:22 a.m. Had to kick him off team

Wow. Not that Austin was at all surprised Drew smoked pot—even Austin indulged occasionally, although not since getting really serious about his hockey career—but to be smoking it right on campus when he knew Warren was already on his ass?

Guy deserved to get kicked off for that. Austin refused to feel guilty for moving things along.

Hell, Drew himself had revealed how behind on his studies he was. The drinking—and Austin ratting him out for it—barely played into it at all.

12:27 a.m. You said Calabresi would b good replacement so I'm giving him Drew's spot

12:29 a.m. Trusting yr judgment on this man, hope u know yr stuff

12:32 a.m. And I'm promoting u to alternate captain

12:36 a.m. Don't make me regret it

All it took was a handful of texts to grant Austin's greatest non-NHL wish: Alternate Captain.

After years of hard practices and early mornings, it had finally happened. Austin had literally dreamed of this day, right down to the showboating victory dance he'd do when he got the news, and how many drinks he'd have afterward in celebration.

So why the hell did he feel like someone had elbowed him in the solar plexus?

This was what he wanted. *All* he wanted, if you left aside the higher-tier goals like getting drafted and winning the Stanley Cup. And hell, he could probably make an argument for how achieving this was the first rung of the ladder to bigger and better things. Taking on a leadership role. Improving his team. Getting noticed. Getting drafted. One thing led to another.

Except there was another, lower, rung that he hadn't anticipated: that he'd earn the A on his jersey after being openly involved in having someone else kicked off the team.

And sure, what had gone down with Drew proved Austin was able to take on the less-savory parts of leadership, and sure, their team was probably stronger already with him gone, but shit—

How the fuck was it going to look to his teammates?

Had Warren promoted Austin because of his skills and drive, or to reward him for narcing?

Or worse, was it a calculated attempt to take some of the heat off Calabresi, who thanks to inheriting Drew's spot would otherwise be the easiest target?

But not with Austin newly promoted as well, and seemingly as a reward for getting Drew kicked off the team. After all, Calabresi may have benefitted from Drew's expulsion, but it wasn't like he'd planned it. Austin, on the other hand . . .

Oh God, was this a *punishment*?

As much of a dead weight as Drew had been, he'd been one of the team. A brother. By ratting on him, Austin had contributed to his downfall. Maybe the pot wouldn't have been as big a deal if it wasn't compounded by the other problems Austin had created. Maybe then, Warren wouldn't have felt the need to take drastic action. Unthinkable, irreversible action. It was like cutting the spleen out of the team. Sure, it was basically a worthless organ, but it was still a part of them, full of the same blood from the same heart.

Austin was a traitor. Jesus.

They'd rake him over the coals for this.

And here he was jerking off to gay porn like some pussy fag? No wonder he was a backstabber, he was bathing in a concentrated tub of wuss-juice. Semen. Fuck.

Right there in front of his eyes was the menu screen for *STRAIGHT SUB SETUP 4* with its shifting black-and-white images, Danny's face and Puck's chest and Titania's latex-wrapped hips and waist. Taunting him. Reminding him.

You came thinking about a guy. Thinking about a guy turning you. Sissy. Traitor. Not a manly bone in your fucking body, except for the one you want up your ass. How can you expect your team's respect or approval like this?

Austin hit eject on his computer in disgust, and the drive spit out the disc like it tasted bad. Austin grabbed it and threw it against the wall; it bounced.

No, no, not good enough. It wasn't the disc's fault he was like this. The disc was an object. Puck and Danny and Titania were just doing what they did: for money or because their parents didn't love them enough or because they were just that perverted.

This, what was happening here in this room to Austin? It was Austin's fault. Austin's perversion. Austin's defect.

He threw on gym clothes that still stank of this morning's sweat and headed out for a run.

As long and as painful as he could make it.

He ran until his chest burned, until his eyes swam, until his muscles screamed with every step, until the impact of his footfalls felt like it was shattering his knees. Didn't have a route planned, no turning point when he'd loop around, not even a sense of direction other than *away*.

He ran until the exercise endorphins faded, until he was working on pure adrenaline—fear hormones. He didn't time himself, didn't pace himself, didn't alternate sprints and slogging, didn't put on his US Marines–inspired music playlist to keep himself pumped. Who needed music when you had self-hatred? Now *there* was a playlist that never ended, that never seemed to lose its motivational power.

He ran until he puked.

Luckily, by the time he got to that point, he was somewhere in Chinatown, so he didn't have to worry about the mess he left. Not that he had anything against Chinese people—*just the gay ones*, he scolded himself bitterly—but Chinatown in Vancouver was a complete fucking slum, one step up from druggie central on the intersection of

Hastings and Main. What was one puddle of vomit in an alley full of used needles and soggy condoms?

Unluckily, when he was done, he was still stranded in a bad part of town in the middle of the night, too exhausted to even contemplate making his way home again. He'd run himself past the point of pain. Just like that, his punishment was complete. There was no pushing himself anymore, not now. The ritual was complete, and according to tradition, he was supposed to collapse into dreamless, overtired sleep, wake up to twinges of pain like battle scars, and move on.

Instead, he was slumped against the metal shutters of one of those Chinese medicine places, chest and muscles burning, wet and tired and *weak*. He shivered as the adrenaline left him. It left him empty and hungry and . . . so . . . tired, in a way that went so, so far beyond the physical.

He was tired of fighting. Tired of struggling.

So why not just stop?

He slammed his fist back against the metal wall behind him with a rattling clang.

Because he didn't want to end up like Bobby, damn it. Because that was what happened when you stopped fighting yourself, stopped struggling to fit in. It wasn't a minor slip, something with a reasonable limit. It never just *stopped*. It turned you into a runaway train and you wound up going completely off the rails: no rules, no boundaries, no guiding anything, not caring about what anyone thought about you, whether they mattered or not. Which may be fine for somebody like Bobby doing some pussy art degree where they all got off on his he/she act and transvestite painting projects, but Austin was a hockey player. People expected better of him. He was on a team.

No, more than that, because as of tonight he was a *leader* in his team, for better or for worse. Which came with more prestige and recognition, but also more responsibility and way more pressure.

Being a part of a team meant conforming. It always had, even playing Peewee. That was all there was to it. Not on everything—they all had their hobbies, their quirks, their ethnic backgrounds, their personalities—they weren't like Hitler Youth or some shit. But to completely let yourself go the way Bobby had?

No way. Even in the magical fairy kingdom where his teammates could accept Austin following Bobby down the gay rabbit hole and not rip him to shreds for it and humiliate him back into line, it still wouldn't make Austin's going there *right*.

Acting out was putting yourself before the team. No different from Drew's drinking and pot smoking and homework dodging.

That was the problem with living with who he was living with and working where he was working and watching the porn that he was watching. It all conspired to convince him that there was another way when there fucking *wasn't*.

It wasn't okay.

He turned, limping. His spiralling mind mechanically plotted a route home, and he set himself to it like a dead man walking, like the maze of city blocks was the march down death row.

It wasn't okay.

None of this was okay.

Austin wasn't okay.

The next morning, Drew didn't meet Austin at the campus bus stop like he usually did.

That shouldn't have come as such a surprise. Why would Drew show up early for a training practice he didn't have any reason to participate in anymore?

Would Austin have to see him later in class, though? (And why was he so anxious about that possibility? Pussy.)

Or had the guy dropped out of school entirely? That would be what Austin would do, if he lost his place on the team. Sure, some of the guys (*cough, Warren*) might get something out of college without hockey, but Austin definitely wasn't one of them. There was nothing for Austin here.

In fact, it wasn't just college that would lose its meaning and purpose, it was the world in general. Austin was nothing without hockey. What else was he gonna do, flip burgers? Become a plumber? He had no idea. None. He didn't understand how other people functioned, how they decided, how they found passion in anything else.

Hopefully that sense of dedication would be enough to get him through today, though. Help him weather the punishment waiting for him.

Eventually.

Because when he got to the campus gym, he quickly realized there was no reason for any of his teammates to know, at least not yet. It wasn't like Warren would have called them *all* up in the middle of the night. Nobody would think to question Drew's absence, either. They probably just assumed he was hungover. Warren would probably make the announcement when they sat down for lunch, like he did with other team business during the off-season.

Which meant that the waves and *Hey*s they were greeting him with—no trace of anger or revenge or distrust, just the usual early morning lack of enthusiasm—were nothing but the calm before the storm.

He squirmed all morning, trying to predict who'd fall on which side, and tried to pretend like his aloofness toward his teammates was because he was super focused on his workout and not because he was busy trying to figure out if any of them would soon be turning on him.

By lunch, he was a nervous wreck. He bought a plate of lasagna knowing there was no way he'd be able to eat it, but some paranoid part of him thought that if he didn't have food when the news dropped, he'd look sorry or scared, and what he needed right now was to look confident and unaffected. He needed to stand behind Warren's decision, but also behind the fact that he'd benefitted from it. If they smelled any weakness on him, they'd be on his ass like dogs on a bitch in heat. He knew that.

It didn't stop him from smiling and waving as sheepishly as a coach at his first press conference after being caught with his dick in a player's mouth when he sat down in the chair Warren had saved for him.

The guys all seemed content to ignore his weirdness and get to their usual conversation topics: the upcoming NHL draft picks, mainly. Not for long, though. Warren, in that dignified way of his, put up his hand.

Of course, the conversation didn't die down until Tim shouted, "Shut the fuck up!" at which point the whole cafeteria seemed to go silent.

Warren cleared his throat awkwardly. "Uh, thank you, Tim. But maybe try not swearing next time."

Tim snorted and sat back, sweeping his tongue between his teeth and lower lip. "Shut 'em up though, didn't it?"

"That isn't the— Never mind. Look, guys, I'm just gonna say it. Drew's gone."

"What, like, hungover?" Ben asked. "Because yeah, I noticed he wasn't at the gym this morning."

Warren shook his head. "No. As in, kicked off the team for drug use. Let this serve as a reminder to all of you that SFU Athletics has a zero-tolerance policy when it comes to substance abuse. So . . . don't."

"Seriously?" Ortega protested. The first to come to Drew's defence, as always. "You gotta come down on him that hard? What, was he doing meth or something?"

"That's beside the point," Warren said carefully.

"Bullshit! It was pot, wasn't it? You kicked him off the team for smoking a fuckin' joint!"

What, had Ortega magically forgotten all the other shit Drew had been pulling? Hell, yesterday when Warren had given Drew that public scolding and Drew had begged for someone to stand up for him, Ortega had been silent.

Yesterday!

And now suddenly he was fighting for Drew's honour?

Not that Austin could point that out. Nope, he needed to stay the fuck out of this and keep his head down. Not draw attention to himself in case that attention turned him into a target.

"Bullshit," Ortega muttered again, leaning back in his chair and crossing his arms moodily.

"Anyway," Warren continued. "Since Drew is gone, I've decided to make Calabresi our star left winger. Think you're up for it, Calabresi?"

"Shit yeah!" Calabresi shouted, jumping to his feet and punching the air before catching Ortega glaring daggers at him and sitting down again. "I mean, not that I'm, uh, happy about Drew getting kicked off the team but, you know, if the spot is open anyway, it might as well be me, right?"

That was a good way of putting it. Why hadn't Austin thought of saying something like that? Well, no reason he couldn't jump onto the bandwagon now. And it would look good for him, too, sticking up for Calabresi. That was a quality of a team leader, right? Keeping the peace. He nodded furiously, if belatedly. "Exactly. Exactly," he said, and wet his lips quickly. "Drew's actions led to this. If people benefit, that doesn't mean they're happy he's gone or that they, uh, planned it."

Warren gave Austin a sideways look. "That's right. And speaking of promotions, I've decided to promote Austin to alternate captain while we're at it—"

"*What*?" Ortega roared.

"Man, that ain't right," Tim added. "Rewarding him for tattlin' on a teammate?"

"I'm not," Warren said evenly. Not that anyone cared what he had to say at this point.

"So, you're saying Drew gets kicked off the team after Austin went crying to you about him drinking, and then Austin gets alternate captain, but it's *not* because of that?"

Why the fuck wasn't Austin standing up for himself? Why wasn't he shaking the table and shouting *Because it wasn't, motherfuckers! It's because I know this team and I know Calabresi's the best person for the spot and Warren trusts my opinion and I've been gunning after this position for two years now and I earned it.*

But he wasn't saying any of that, because he didn't believe it, not really. He'd betrayed his team. Betrayed them by ratting out Drew, but not just that. Betrayed them with his urges and the fact that last night, for the first time, he'd embraced them. Let them take him over.

"Ha-ha!" Riley shouted, slapping his palm against the table and rattling their trays. "I got it! Austin got alternate captain because he really *is* sucking Warren's dick!"

Betrayed his team, and it hadn't even fucking *worked*. Austin flushed and stared mutely at his lap, at his hands fisted in the denim of his jeans. At the huge fucking hard-on trying to rip its way out of his fly at the thought of submissively sucking dick for favours like the faggot he secretly was.

It hadn't even worked.

CHAPTER 7

It hadn't worked, but somehow Austin still couldn't bring himself to feel completely cheated by the fact that he'd watched it.

Maybe because he'd liked it so much.

As much as he hated himself for that, he really had liked it. Kept on thinking about it on the bus ride to the store that afternoon. Every time his eyes landed on his bag and he remembered it was in there, wrapped up in his gym tee. How could such a small, concealable object contain so much meaning and significance? Master Puck's teasing smile, his sexy-mean laugh, the way he'd manhandled his pussy sub until he was crying and totally debased.

But it hadn't worked. Had Austin really expected it to work? Porn didn't cure sexual deviants. It made them worse. He'd been desperate, though. He'd always been desperate.

And yet there he went again, looking down at his bag, thinking about the DVD hidden inside it, remembering the things he'd seen. The things Puck had *done* to him.

Done to Danny Domino, he reminded himself. Austin was watching the porn. He wasn't starring in it.

God, he was losing his grip on reality.

Well, soon he'd be at Rear Entrance Video and *STRAIGHT SUB SETUP 4* would be back on the shelf where it belonged and hopefully having it out of reach would break the horny trance Austin was in. Out of sight, out of mind.

Then all Austin would be left with was his boner problem—and oh, yeah, the fact that he was getting kicked out of his place at the end of the month.

He trudged up the block from the bus stop to the store, feeling like every gay dude he passed could smell it on him—the fact that secretly, he was one of them, that he was breaking down and giving in and soon there'd be nothing left of the person he used to be. How could that thought be so fucking terrifying but exhilarating at the same time?

Because Bobby was happy, Austin realized as he slipped through the door of the store.

Bobby, who'd gone through the same change Austin was fearing now—his old self peeling away to something new underneath—was *happy*.

He hadn't yet looked up from the cash drawer he was counting out, didn't know yet that it was Austin who'd walked in. And in that unguarded moment, he was happy. Smiling and humming as he counted a fistful of crinkled fives.

He was a weird freak of a he/she person wearing a black corset and nail polish, but holy shit, he was happy.

A part of Austin just wanted to be happy, too.

But not like that. That wasn't his future he was looking at, any more than Christian's class of snot-nosed kids was.

Who didn't want to be happy, at the end of the day? Not Austin's fault that all his examples of so-called "happiness" in life seemed to come from weird gay dudes.

Austin needed his own happiness. He needed to chase *that*. Okay, so he needed to figure out what the fuck it was first. Then chase it.

"You should do what makes you happy," Austin blurted out, and Bobby's head snapped up. He gaped at Austin through eyes wide with surprise. Austin flushed and kicked at the floor awkwardly, making his sneaker squeak. "I mean . . . You seem happier, now. That you've changed. We all just want to be happy, and we deserve to be happy, and if that's what makes you happy, then you should go after it and do it."

Bobby's expression softened for a second, went all watery and girly and sweet, like he wanted to kiss somebody, but then he narrowed his eyes and crossed his arms. "And?" he asked.

Austin took a deep breath through his nose. "And I don't have the right to stand in the way of your happiness. Or judge you for what your happiness looks like."

"You mean that?" Bobby asked, expression suspicious.

"Yeah. I do." Austin found it hard to look at him. Couldn't look into those dark, questioning eyes, as timid as a deer's. So he didn't. Instead, he stared at the poster of a dude's hard dick in profile, which hung over Bobby's left shoulder. "Look, I'm not gonna lie to you, man. It's still fucking weird to me, and I don't get it. At all. But I don't really need to get it, do I? There's nothing *to* get. Not for me. All I gotta do is stand back and let you do your thing and be happy for you that you're happy."

Now Bobby's lower lip stuck out and trembled, and before Austin could react, he'd leapt over the counter and was throwing his arms around Austin's body in a crushing hug. "Oh, Austin!" he proclaimed tearfully as he pressed his face against Austin's chest. "I'm so glad you see it that way."

Austin carefully peeled Bobby's arms off his body and pushed him back, but not urgently enough to seem like he was worried about getting cooties. "Okay, man. Don't get all sappy on me. I'm sorry for being a dick, but I'm not planning on painting each other's nails and watching *The Notebook* anytime soon, okay?"

"You wouldn't catch me dead watching *The Notebook* anyway. Now, *Infernal Affairs* is another story." Bobby smiled. "I do appreciate you saying all that, though. From the heart, and not only because you want to keep your room. And if it helps any, I don't really know exactly what my deal is, either. You think *you're* confused by all this?" He gestured down at his outfit—the corset over the white button-up top, the tight men's pants and women's high-heeled boots. "Try *living* it."

Austin laughed nervously. "Thanks, but I'll pass."

Bobby left him on good terms. Not best friends or anything, but they'd spent an entire changeover not avoiding each other's eyes, so that was a win by itself. They'd even joked around a little.

As soon as he was alone for the night, Austin put up the BACK IN FIVE MINUTES sign and locked the door. From there, he scuttled behind the counter to retrieve *STRAIGHT SUB SETUP 4* from its place hidden in his bag. Returned the disc to where it belonged in the cabinet, then put the case back on the shelf.

There.

Done.

But of course he didn't leave it at that, and of course he *wasn't* done.

He stood there like an idiot staring at the case and the ones next to it, like if he did it enough, one of the grim, sexy faces pouting back would tell him what the fuck to do.

It *had* worked, kinda. He thought it hadn't, but it kinda had. Not with his boner problem, no, but with the Bobby one. He'd finally said the right things to Bobby. Said them from the heart, like Bobby said, not out of a desperate desire to not be homeless. It seemed kind of weird in hindsight that watching a dirty video could cure his so-called homophobia, almost hilariously simple, and Austin had this mental image of strapping down the Westboro Baptist Church and forcing them to watch gay porn until the only things they wanted to protest anymore were bad tattoos.

For whatever reason, though, it had worked.

It hadn't fixed his other issue, but then, the exercise punishments that he'd always been able to rely on in the past weren't working anymore, either.

Maybe he was looking at it the wrong way. He thought back on that thing Dylan had said: *something something something repression, something something something jealous.* The point was, he'd thought maybe if he'd let off some steam, things would get better. And as far as his relationship with Bobby went, they had.

But when it came to the turned-on-by-humiliation thing . . . well, that didn't have anything to do with repression or jealousy. It . . . it was what it was. It was an illness. An addiction. Something he'd lived with for a long time. The cycle of denial and punishing himself hadn't worked, even when he'd taken it to extremes that left scars. But giving in to his urges hadn't worked, either. And he wasn't about to sign up for one of those bogus fucking Jesus cure camps, because c'mon, Austin may be a bit stupid and ignorant about things, but he wasn't *that* stupid.

What if he treated it like smoking, though? It was an addiction, right? Sort of? Quitting cold turkey hadn't worked. He didn't think they made gums or patches or sprays of gayness for him to wean himself with, but there was one more option. That kid what's-his-name . . . Derek or something. He'd taken up smoking in grade eight, their first year of junior high. His dad hadn't bargained with him or grounded him or stood by and let him do whatever; he'd gone to the corner store, bought one of those jumbo bulk-sized packs of cigarettes, and then had sat Derek down and made him chain-smoke them right there in front of him. One smoke after another, over and over again, until Derek had started hacking and puking and hadn't touched the fucking things again.

Old school.

Austin wasn't sure there was a way to physically make himself puke with gay porn, but if there was, he was going to fucking find it.

He nodded to himself in determination and headed to the filing cabinets behind the counter. Five movies to start with, he decided. Enough to really overdose himself if he watched them in full back-to-back, but not enough to cause alarm when they went missing all at once. Four of them he picked at random, grabbing the first discs he saw printed with pictures of dick or abs or assholes. For the fifth, he chose *STRAIGHT SUB SETUP 3*.

And tried to pretend that was anxiety and not anticipation making his stomach twist and turn.

With all five discs and their matching cases wrapped up in various items from his workout wear and zipped safely in his bag, he returned to the front door of the store, took down the sign, and unlocked it. Returned to his seat behind the counter and steeled himself for the long, *long* night ahead. Not even a quarter of the way into his shift, and then five plus hours of porn waiting for when he got home? Well, hopefully he wouldn't feel compelled to run for three fucking hours like last night, or else he'd be really tired come tomorrow morning's workout.

Speaking of tired, wow, last night was suddenly catching up to him, a fact that wasn't helped by how quiet and empty the store was, or the soft white-noise hum of the overhead lighting. Austin slumped forward onto the counter and pillowed his head on his arms as his eyes drifted shut. He was so exhausted, he couldn't summon up the will to be revolted or ashamed when visions of Master Puck took shape in the darkness. No Danny Domino here. No pretenses, no sets, no soundtracks. Only Austin, buck-ass naked, bare in more ways than one. And Master Puck, standing over him, looming, speaking, saying—

"Are you guys open?"

Austin startled awake, looked up, caught a glimpse of the guy standing across the counter, and nearly jumped out of his skin.

Master Puck. Master Puck—*the* fucking Master Puck, man of Austin's dreams/nightmares—was standing across from him in jeans and a leather bomber jacket. Smiling.

Act normal. Act normal. Act like he's just another customer and you've never seen him naked and you've never jerked off to the thought of him stuffing his dick down your throat and making you cry.

Austin flicked his tongue over his dry lips. Shook his head hard. "Yeah. Sorry. We are. Had a late night last night"—*jerking off to you and then punishing myself for it*—"and I guess I must have been more tired than I thought. Can I, uh, help you?"

Puck definitely wasn't fooled by Austin's so-called "normal" act, but at least he seemed charmed by it instead of weirded out or—God forbid—predatory. Last thing Austin needed was for Puck to clue into his weaknesses like a wolf picks out the weakest deer and then strikes.

And what the hell was Austin thinking, coming up with something like that? Sure, the guy was a deviant, but that didn't mean he was some kind of sex criminal prowling for vulnerable boys.

Although a very insistent part of Austin really kinda wished he was.

"Actually, you can . . ." Puck trailed off in a way that begged Austin to finish his sentence with a name.

"Austin," he provided, and couldn't help the little thrill he got at doing what Puck wanted.

Puck extended a hand to him across the counter, and Austin was compelled to reach out and shake it. He just had to hope his palm wasn't too sweaty. Puck's shake was powerful but not painful. Confident but not overcompensating. "Liam Williams." He let go of Austin's hand with an exasperated but good-natured smile. "And yes, that means my legal name is William Williams. I'm the co-owner of Mischievous Pictures." He produced a business card, which Austin took. Right there at the top: Owner, Professional Dominant. Liam Williams and Master Puck getting equal billing. "You guys have a couple of our titles, I believe?"

Austin leaned back in his chair and stroked his chin, making a show of trying to remember. "Mischievous Pictures, Mischievous Pictures . . . Gay BDSM, right? I'm not sure . . ."

That act seemed to go over as well as the first, because Liam smiled knowingly, eyes twinkling. "I'd hope you would, seeing as you've got a poster of me on your wall."

"A poster?" Austin squeaked, and turned.

It hit him like a two-hundred-pound enforcer nailing him with a body check.

The poster of the naked man depicted from nipples to hips. The one in profile with the *massive, curving erection.* Austin hadn't allowed himself to look closely enough to notice it before, but the head of the guy's cock had a thick, imposing ring through it, exactly like the one he remembered Danny Domino slavering over.

Austin turned to face Liam again, face so hot you could probably cook an egg on it. "That, uh, that, that—"

"Is me, yeah. Well, it's my dick, technically. You want me to sign it?"

"S-sign? It?" Austin squeaked. "Your dick?"

Liam raised his eyebrows, obviously fighting a smile. "The *poster* of my dick, yeah."

Oh. Well, fuck. "Why would I— How could I—possibly—want that? You think I want that? Do I look like a—like a fan of yours?"

Now Liam did laugh, and it was obvious Austin's offended act had missed the intended mark by a mile, hitting pathetically funny instead of insulting. "Whoa, kid," Liam said, showing Austin his palms. "Cool it with the doth protesting too much, okay? I thought it'd be nice for the store."

Kid? Austin thought hysterically, way too flustered to speak by this point. God, how could something be so very equally insulting and arousing? He was an adult man who could give and take hits on the ice and drink a two-four and fuck women until they screamed. He wasn't a kid. Especially not this guy's kid.

Master Puck's kid.

Down boy, he scolded his dick.

"So that's a no?" Liam prompted, a little more gently than before.

Austin flapped a hand dismissively. "No. I mean no. No, it's not a no. Look, sign the poster if you want. My manager will probably love it." *That's if I don't tear the thing down to hide under my mattress for lonely nights.*

"Cool," Liam said. "You got a marker or something? It'll stand out better than a ballpoint pen."

"Yeah, uh, one sec." Austin bent over and rooted through his gym bag, searching for the black permanent marker he usually had in the side pocket. And of course found the DVD case for *STRAIGHT SUB SETUP 3* first. He pulled his hand back like he'd burnt himself, took a quick look to make sure Liam hadn't seen—he hadn't, or if he had, he was tactful enough to pretend he hadn't—and then finally found the marker. He put it into Liam's hand.

"Thanks," Liam said, and stepped around the counter so that he was standing behind it, right in Austin's space. He didn't usually get this close to other guys unless he was fighting them for the puck. Or they were on an overfull bus, he supposed. Man, Liam smelled way better up close than the guys he usually came into contact with. "So is it the same manager?"

"Huh?"

"Is it the same manager as before? I like the remodel, by the way. Nice to have a queer store. Double nice when they're renting out my stuff. God bless people who still pay for porn, right?" He had an easy, kind-of-lopsided smile. There was a little scar knitted through his lower lip.

"Oh, yeah. Same manager. Some stuff went down with one of our employees and the manager got a gay girlfriend, so she decided she didn't want this to be a normal porn store anymore."

Liam turned on him, eyebrow raised in an undeniably judgmental way. "Normal?" he asked, all but doing the bunny ears around the offending word.

"Sorry. Straight. I guess gay *is* normal to you guys."

The judgmental expression shifted into something predatory and kind of naughty. "'You guys'? Well, that's a fraction better than 'you people' I guess, so I'll give you a couple points for trying. But what makes you think I'm g-a-y?"

Austin nodded toward the poster. "That? And the fact that you just spelled out g-a-y?"

"Aw, bless. Only gay guys do gay porn? You *are* adorable, Austin. A perfect unspoiled flower of straightness in a vast wilderness of cocksucking weeds."

"So . . . what, you're straight? Straight but pretending to be gay?" *Not like the poor saps in your videos, straight but tricked into doing gay stuff and loving it.*

"We in the biz call that 'Gay for Pay,' but no, I'm not straight." Liam's explanation was mostly patient, though judging by his expression the guy was obviously feeling pretty smug about his superior gay porn knowledge. "Except I'm not gay, either." Austin's first reaction must have been a look of blank confusion, because Liam added, "Bisexual. You know, like 'em different from me, like 'em the same as me."

Oh. Right. Duh. Bisexual was a thing. Austin knew that. Of course he did. "Well *I'm* straight." God, did that come out a little too forceful? Judging by Liam's reaction—another lift of his eyebrows—yes.

And yet, when Liam spoke, it was without any trace of sarcasm or disbelief or judgment or any of it. "I believe you, kid."

Austin stared at him, unable to control the weird squeeze in his chest, the urge to smile like a kid watching his dad score a goal in the final few minutes of the last period. "Thank you," he said softly, and though he knew it was sappy, couldn't help but add on, "Really."

And he meant it.

CHAPTER 8

Liam left not long after that, having bullied a promise from Austin that his business card would make its way to Christian's aunt, Beverly. As soon as he'd gone, Austin slumped in his chair, feeling simultaneously like he'd run ten miles but also had a hot shower. Exhausted but refreshed. Worn down but optimistic.

There was no way to get around it: Liam may have been a tiring person to keep up with, especially with his constant little questions picking apart everything Austin said, but fuck, he also made Austin feel *good*.

Maybe the running ten miles analogy was inaccurate, then. More like the feeling he got after a game, because it was a good, uplifting kind of tired. A satisfied tired. Sure, if their meeting had been a hockey game Austin had most certainly lost, but he'd played hard and fair and Liam had proved himself to be a challenging opponent, and there was really no better feeling than that—except for winning against the same.

Except he didn't *want* to win against Liam, did he? He smiled to himself as he shelved returns, the three-dimensional man he'd met combining in his head with the porno god he'd jerked off to last night. He wanted to lose, and badly. Wanted to lose everything to Liam, be taken down to nothing, give in to his terrible urges but take on none of the fault. Because it would be Liam's fault, Liam's responsibility. Liam's responsibility for turning Austin and changing him and breaking him, and then it would be over and Austin would be himself again, and there'd be no guilt at all, except for whatever Liam carried.

And he didn't seem like the kind of guy to feel guilty about much.

Austin wondered what that must be like.

No. Wait. He didn't.

Because he already knew what feeling no guilt or obligations was like. Or rather, he knew what it looked like, what it led to: Bobby.

Shit, how come he could admire Liam for having the same trait that he was so fucking scared of in Bobby?

Maybe Noah and Dylan had a point about Austin after all.

Although God knew what the fuck that point *was*.

Anyway, it didn't matter, because Austin didn't need soul-searching to fix his problem with Bobby; he needed more porn. He'd already gotten through one social encounter unscathed thanks to that first video. Now, like any workout, he needed to ramp up the intensity and increase the reps.

And so, after getting home from his shift that night, Austin stripped down to his boxers, put his headphones on, and popped the first of his five discs into his computer's drive: some muscle-bound thing with guys who looked a little like Austin fucking in a generic living room space and titled *Cody and Darren*—after its two costars, obviously. Zero points for creativity.

And zero points for boners, too. Cody and Darren, both with dyed blond hair and tanned skin and no body hair below their eyebrows, sat around on the couch in jeans and tight T-shirts making small talk with whoever was behind the camera, then after some arbitrary amount of time, they started kissing and rubbing each other. Austin stared, unblinking, as they undressed each other and groaned and kissed with lots of tongue, and his dick didn't so much as twitch. They started sucking each other off next, fists and lips wrapped around their practically identical hairless dicks. Sometimes they said stuff like "You like that, huh?" or "You wanna fuck me?" and then they *were* fucking, or, well one of them was fucking while the other got fucked—Austin wasn't sure whether it was Cody or Darren on the bottom anymore—and still. No. Reaction.

He was about to give up on the whole enterprise when suddenly Cody/Darren pulled his dick out of Darren/Cody's ass and the camera cut to Darren/Cody on his knees at Cody/Darren's feet and Cody/Darren wasn't wearing a condom anymore and he was completely *slathering* Darren/Cody's face with thick ropes of cum.

"You like that, huh?" Cody/Darren said, but this time Austin imagined it as a taunt—*"Little fag, you love cum all over your face, don't you? We should send this video to your girlfriend"*—and it wasn't Cody/Darren doing the taunting anymore, it was Liam. No, it was Master Puck in that tight leather chest harness, with his hand fisted in Austin's floppy hair, coming all over his nose and eyebrows. Not even aiming for Austin's mouth, because he liked the way Austin looked soaked in cum like a two-dollar whore.

Austin twisted in his seat and rubbed at his suddenly thicker dick through the fabric of his underwear. Oh, yeah, *fuck yeah*, that had done it. His head fell back and he groaned, nudging his dick against his palm, not ready yet to take it out and jerk off properly. No, that he wanted to save for later. At least four hours later, judging by the stack of DVD cases sitting on his desk. *STRAIGHT SUB SETUP 3* was at the very bottom of the pile. Saving the best (worst?) for last.

Cody and Darren's bland adventures in dude fucking still weren't over, but Austin hit the eject button regardless. If he sat around for the DVD's entire absurd two hour runtime, he'd be here way longer than the five hours he'd committed to. Just because he wanted to up the intensity on his gay porn workout didn't mean he wanted to like . . . strain something. Especially when that something was most likely to be his dick.

Not that he used it for anything much more than jerking off lately.

Wow, he really needed to get laid, now that he thought about it.

But not until *after* he figured out his gay issues, not unless he wanted to accidentally ask some puck bunny to pull his hair and do him up the ass with a strap-on. He'd never live it down—with girls *or* the guys on his team—if he did. Yeah, better to remain celibate until he had his boner under control.

Speaking of which, time for disc two of his gay porno marathon. He didn't really take note of the title. Just more generic dude names. This one was different, though, because it featured *three* horny hairless guys. These guys weren't all muscular, though. They were skinny bordering on hungry looking, like this was some kind of pornographic infomercial for an Eastern European antihunger charity. And they all looked somewhere around twelve, except for the fact that they were all hung like horses and the DVD case explicitly said ALL ACTORS ARE 18+ on the front. That must be a real boner killer for the pedophiles in the target audience.

Hell, though, maybe they pretended, the same way Austin kept pasting Master Puck over all of these malnourished dudes fucking and sucking each other. Which, he found, was the only way to keep his boner up, because there was nothing inherently hot about a gaping pink butthole with two dicks plunging in and out of it . . . unless Austin imagined himself in the middle, weight on top of him and hands grasping him from below, keeping him still as he squirmed and protested and moaned helplessly. Master Puck would unload his balls into Austin's ass, no condom, like in the scene on Austin's computer screen. Of course, that wouldn't be nearly enough now, would it? Sure, being used as a cum dumpster by a more powerful man gave him a thrill, but he really needed to have his face rubbed in it—his shame, that was. So Master Puck would make him beg for it. Beg for Master Puck to come in his slutty ass instead of on the floor. Oh, no, he didn't deserve that cum, no, but he'd be so grateful, he'd be so, so, *so* grateful to be used that way, if only Master Puck would be so generous. And Master Puck, knowing he was partially responsible for creating the shameless cum slut in front of him, would pump Austin's ass full of semen and then make Austin thank him by cleaning his dick and the spattered toes of his shiny boots . . . with his tongue, of course.

Austin bit his lip to stifle a moan and squeezed his eyes shut. Behind his eyelids, all he could see was cum, cum, cum dripping out of him, shooting onto him, men's cum, and yeah, he was revolted by it, wanted to shudder thinking about the taste and feel of it—but he craved it at the same time, because it represented the ultimate submission. To be used like that. The only way to go lower was to have a man piss on him, but maybe not even that, because sure it was dirtier, but it wasn't nearly as *sexual*. And that's what Austin wanted. To be overpowered and *used*. Sexually. He wasn't about to start scrubbing Master Puck's floors unless he was doing it butt naked on his hands and knees.

He still didn't jerk off. In fact, it became a kind of challenge: to keep himself from getting off or enjoying himself until Master Puck gave him permission. Not that he could—they weren't lovers or fuck buddies or Dom/sub or whatever, only actor and viewer—but maybe Austin could have that last disc stand in for the permission he couldn't get personally. It would have to be enough.

But his resolution turned almost impossible with the next video, which was a simulated prison gang rape with some young guy surrounded by four or five muscled, tattooed thugs. The kid didn't put up much of a fight, but then, Austin didn't really want him to. Didn't want to see him getting his ass beat so much as he wanted to see him give in and submit, fall to his knees and suck one dick while he jerked off two others and a third guy tried to get in there and fuck his ass. And the things *these* men said—damn, they left Cory and Dylan or whoever in the dust:

"Take it, bitch."

"Yeah, bitch, you got a nice mouth."

"Ass like a pussy."

Austin mouthed the words as he pulled his dick out of his boxers and gave it a couple rough tugs. *Ass like a pussy.* Austin wondered if his ass was like that, if a man could get him slick back there and slide his dick in, if Austin would clench around that big invading dick the way girls massaged his dick with their pussies sometimes. Using his ass like a pussy. These men weren't gay, just desperate to get their rocks off, and Austin was weak enough for them to use him as a substitute.

It was humiliation and submission like Austin wanted and deserved.

The men in the video called their victim *bitch* and slapped his face—gentle, teasing slaps, like he wasn't worth the effort of hitting properly—and stuffed nightsticks into his hungry, gaping ass. Now Austin couldn't suppress his moans anymore. Biting his lips only made him hornier with the pain. So he smothered the sounds instead. Slapped a hand over his mouth and wailed into it as he jerked himself off with the other hand. Imagined it was Master Puck smothering him, pounding his ass from behind with that big pierced dick, the one on the poster. Fucking him but keeping his moans silent because bitches should be seen and not heard. Yeah, yeah that was good. That was so good, so—

Shit.

Austin looked down to see his hand webbed with sticky, shiny cum.

Shit, shit, shit. He hadn't meant to do that. Panic flared in him, shame at disappointing Master Puck, until he remembered that the agreement had only been between Austin and Austin, and that Master Puck barely knew he existed, other than as the awkward straight kid working in a gay porn store.

But he still wanted to be punished.

He knew what he had to do. What Master Puck would *command* him to do.

Putting in the fourth disc with his clean hand—back to bland dude fucking, this time with two black guys still in their sneakers— he raised his hand to his face. His *dirty* hand. His shameful hand. His disobedient hand. Dirty. Shameful. Disobedient. He recited the words in his head and forced himself to stare at the nearly naked bodies on his computer screen as he stretched out his tongue to lap at the first drip of cum.

He gagged.

Fucking disgusting. Well, he wasn't a born fag, that was for damn certain. But this wasn't what he was born as, it was what Master Puck was *making him into*: someone who licked up cum and said thank-you, even if it never stopped tasting disgusting.

So Austin licked again, and again, making a face every time. Bitter and salty and the, oh God, the texture was worst of all, not to mention the fact that it was so warm. It stuck to the roof of his mouth like cough syrup, coating the entire inside of his mouth with that awful flavour. He wished he could stop, but he couldn't. He'd committed. He'd lick up every last drop of cum, because that was what Master Puck would want, and he'd watch the rest of this boring porn—every last hump and grunt of it—and *then* he'd get his reward.

Not to mention the rest of his punishment. Because there was no way Master Puck would let Austin watch *his* video without getting himself off. That was fucking rude and disrespectful, on top of the disobedience of coming too early.

But his dick was still floppy and oversensitized as he put in the fifth and final disc: *STRAIGHT SUB SETUP 3*. So what to do?

You know what to do, Master Puck whispered in Austin's head as the video Master Puck swaggered around the screen, menacing his new straight sub. Austin shook his head in token protest, mouthing *no, no* to himself. He couldn't stop himself, though, from reaching down past his flaccid dick, down between his legs, down into the tight hot space there that he'd never touched before. Coarse hair brushed his fingertips, and he almost recoiled, but no, he was doing this. He was man enough to take any punishment, even one like this, one that completely *un*-manned him. And there it was, the tight circle of clenched, wrinkled skin. He touched it with his first finger—not pressing, just stroking, back and forth, back and forth. His heart pounded. Cold sweat drenched his skin.

The angle was all wrong. Too tight. His wrist was bent too far. He leaned back in his chair and flipped his legs over the arms of it, the sole of one foot landing on the flat surface of his desk. Much better. Open. Easier to get his hand in.

Easier for his master to watch, too.

He shuddered with disgust, felt it choking him, wished he could cough it up and spit it out.

Well, he'd have to push through it instead. He closed his eyes and listened to Master Puck's voice, drifting, unable to understand the words. Didn't need to though, not really, because the smooth sound of it, the powerful tone, the teasing rhythm, the hunger rough as sandpaper, those were all language beyond words.

He took a deep breath and held it, chest expanded. Let it out. Found that disgusting hungry place between his legs with one finger and *pushed*.

His body opened up around him, just enough. He puffed out his breath. Realized he was breathing through . . . exertion? Shit, that was exactly what it was. Like pushing himself through the last couple minutes of his workout. He grunted. The feeling of fullness morphed into one of sharp pinpoint pain. He hissed. Gritted his teeth. Opened his eyes and looked at the screen, looked at Master Puck standing with one hand bent formally behind his back as he fucked into his straight sub's mouth. His straight sub, who was on his knees, arms stretched out to either side of him, and tied. Face covered in drool, eyes red with tears.

Punishment. Punishment was pain. Pain was punishment.

Austin jabbed himself harder, forcing through his own resistance, gritted his teeth, and clapped his free hand over his mouth and screamed into his palm.

One finger. Just one.

Couldn't even debase and punish himself properly. Pathetic at being pathetic. Too much of a wuss to be a wuss.

He wiggled his finger a little, testing the walls of muscle that surrounded it so tightly. Bit his lip as his cock twitched against his thigh and thickened.

A miserable moan escaped as he twisted the finger and rubbed everywhere it could reach, massaging himself from the inside. His dick lifted, fell. Lifted again.

Struggling to get it up, Austin? a voice taunted. Master Puck's? His own? One of his teammates'? *What happened to all those super boners of yours? What's wrong with you, can't take a little pain and punishment? Can't submit?*

He shook his head and tasted blood and made some kind of whine/moan that sounded more dog than human. Wrapped his hand around his dick and cried because touching it still fucking hurt.

So what the fuck are you good for?

And came.

CHAPTER 9

It was like a prescription medication. *Take one gay porno nightly before bed. Do not consume alcohol or operate heavy machinery. If you have an erection lasting longer than four hours, seek medical help.*

One gay porno a night, and Austin could trust himself to talk to Bobby without fucking it up irreparably. Could manage to go multiple days in a row without any of his teammates' typical shit talking going straight to his dick. Which was a good thing, since his promotion to alternate captain of his team meant the amount of shit talking had multiplied tenfold.

One gay porno a night. Austin got well acquainted with the various FREE STREAMING PORN websites—and shortly after that, got familiar with FREE VIRUS CHECKER sites. He watched all kinds of porn. If there was two dudes fucking in it, he was there. Even if they pissed on each other (strangely hot), even if they sucked each other's toes (less so). Porn of big burly guys covered in hair, porn of hairless Eastern European teenage guys. Homemade videos of dudes fucking and trying to hide their faces at the same time. It all solidified one thing: Austin did *not* have the hots for men. Abs, pecs, hair, dicks and balls and assholes, it was all about as sexy to him as looking at photos from his stepmother's latest Mexico vacation. (Not at all.)

Night after night, though, no matter what else he watched, it all came back to Master Puck. Watching and rewatching his scenes, picturing him in other people's scenes, just *thinking* about him and concocting his own fantasies where the straight sub who got set up was Austin. The things Puck could do. The things Austin *wanted* him to do. To him. God, fuck. He may not have been attracted to men, but he was sure as hell attracted to Master Puck . . . Or rather, attracted to his power, at least. His power to command and conquer and convert.

Whatever. All that mattered was that Austin didn't feel awkward anymore when he walked in on Christian and Max making out on the couch— He regularly saw far worse, after all. He barely reacted to coming to work and finding Bobby working the counter in a miniskirt. Jerking off all the time was helping him sleep better, too, and he thought that—outside of simply being too tired for it—he didn't feel that compulsion to punish himself as much. Well, not the way he used to, at least. No more exercising until he puked or strained himself. Instead, the punishments were part and parcel with the porn. Pleasure and pain tied together, like they should never have been kept apart. The punishments still hurt, but they felt good, too. They left him worn out and raw after, but in a satisfied way, more like the soreness after a good game—a productive pain that could be soaked away in a hot bath—than like the searing shame and self-hatred of the pain he'd inflict on himself for its own sake. He'd never realized how *alike* overexercising and cutting himself were until now; until he was free of them both and had the perspective that came with that distance. Kinda made him a little sick to think about, honestly.

Two weeks into his "treatment," he came in to work to find Noah working the day shift. Noah looked up at the sound of the bell and smiled when he saw Austin. "Hey, big guy! You working nights?"

Austin nodded mutely. He and Noah hadn't really spoken much since their "talk." Austin had kind of been avoiding him, and he had a feeling Noah had been doing the same in return. The guy hated laying down the landlord law; it had probably been physically painful for him to have to sit Austin down and threaten him like that.

Noah's smile turned slightly awkward as Austin sat down beside him. "So, uh, hey." He rubbed the back of his neck. "Bobby talked to me. Said you've been making an effort."

"Oh yeah?" Austin replied, trying not to give away how eager he was to hear Noah say something *good* about him.

"Yeah. Whatever you've been doing, keep it up."

There went Austin's resolve not to look too eager, because now he was practically squealing. "So I can stay? You're not kicking me out?"

"I didn't say that, not yet. But keep it up." Damn, that was it? All this work, and that was it? Noah patted Austin on the shoulder in a lame conciliatory gesture, and it was all Austin could do not to shrug his hand off like a moody teenager. "Anyway, Beverly is coming in to cover the last hour of my shift. Gotta get back to my other job before dinner service. She should be here in a few minutes to do shift changeover, so I'm gonna split now so I can catch the bus." He stood. Gave Austin *another* awkward dad-ly slap on the back. "Just . . . keep it up, buddy. Okay?"

Austin watched him bustle out the door.

And as Noah left, Master Puck—er, Liam—came striding up to the counter out of nowhere with a shit-eating grin plastered all over his infuriatingly gorgeous face. "How's it going there, *buddy*?" he asked. Austin should have been ashamed and humiliated and furious at having the nickname turned around that way, and by some asshole know-it-all stranger, no less, but shit, this was Master Puck. Master Puck said what he wanted to who he wanted, and you didn't fucking give him lip if you knew what was good for you.

God, there went Austin, unable to separate porn from the real world, again. Liam in his bomber jacket blurring right in front of him with the larger-than-life figure of his Dominant alter ego. The guy Austin had jerked off to. Multiple times. It was fucking crazy, and yet somehow this time the crossing of the streams didn't make him feel nervous and awkward and uncomfortable like before. It made him feel strangely secure. He felt *safe*. Because he'd shared a part of himself with this man, even if he didn't know it, and it had been okay, and Liam hadn't judged him or hurt him or rejected him for it. Austin's secret wasn't Austin's secret anymore. It was almost . . . *their* secret. "Could be better," he replied honestly, and then he laughed. "But God, it sure could be a whole hell of a lot worse."

Liam pursed his lips. "That's . . . pessimistic but upbeat?"

"Masochistic?" Austin suggested, then flushed hot when he realized what he'd said. And to who.

Liam's eyes narrowed, and his smile tilted into a smirk. "You know, straight kid, that sounded an awful lot like you were trying to impress me."

Austin huffed and glared right back. "Get over yourself, *bisexual old man*. You gimp-mask types don't own the word masochist, you know."

A comeback that only made Liam's smirk even more insufferable. "Maybe so, but we definitely own the word gimp mask."

"Yeah, well— Look, you wanna rent something, or what?"

Liam slipped forward, draping himself over the counter with all the natural smugness of a cat. "Nope," he said.

Fucking insufferable prick. Insufferable sexy prick. "Okay, so are you returning something then?"

"Nope."

Beverly bustled up to the counter. "He's here to see me." She dropped a massive purple purse so she could shake Liam's hand in both her own. "Such a pleasure to meet you, Mr. Williams!"

Liam laughed and likewise reached out with his other hand so that they were both holding each other like two overexcited teenage girls. "Likewise, but God, please. Call me Liam."

"Beverly," she replied in kind.

"We call her Auntie Beverly," Austin added, out of some absurd urge to be included in their conversation. Well, to be included in *Liam's* conversation, mostly, although he should really be trying to get on Beverly's good side, too. After all, his home *and* his job were on the line right now, and Beverly definitely had a say in the job side of things.

"You are adorable," Liam said, giving Austin and then Beverly a thoroughly charmed look. "How tall are you, four feet? You're like a porn fairy!"

Wow, he was being so *nice*. Not at all like his Master Puck persona. Austin felt himself smiling in a way he hadn't smiled in a long time. A dopey, genuine smile. Not forced or self-conscious at all.

Auntie Beverly punched Liam in the arm with a tittering laugh. "How dare you! I am five two, I'll have you know, but as for *porn fairy*, guilty as charged. Although I prefer my longer title: Porn and Vibrator Fairy."

Liam's eyes—*green eyes*—twinkled mischievously. "How much is the going rate on burnt-out vibrators left under pillows, these days?"

They went on like that, flirting and pawing at each other like old friends, with Austin feeling more and more like a piece of the furniture—or maybe a blow-up doll was more fitting—as time wore on. He didn't feel bored so much as he felt left out. God, how embarrassing. None of his teammates would have cared; they'd have been glad not to be included in this squealing gay conversation. But here Austin was, practically dying to be noticed or acknowledged.

It was Beverly, not Liam, who finally thought to include Austin, and as terrible as it was, Austin's heart sank that it had to be her. "Liam here owns a local adult production company," she explained. "We carry some of their titles."

"Co-owns," Liam corrected. "And stars in."

"Oh, I know," Austin drawled.

And then immediately froze, realizing what he'd said.

Austin's face went hot, seeing the way Liam and Beverly were looking at him—Beverly with wide-eyed curiosity, Liam with a half a smirk. His shoulders rose. "He came in earlier this week to sign the poster, remember? Guy was *dying* for me to recognize him."

Liam made a mock-stabbed gesture. "Ow! Well. Nobody gets into porn because they *don't* want attention or recognition. A complete and total whore, me, in all senses of the word." He winked crudely. At Austin.

Austin narrowed his eyes.

"Don't let Sandra hear you say that." Beverly's tone was playful but definitely sincere in its note of warning. "Not unless you have at least an hour to listen to her read you the radfem riot act."

Liam flashed her a puzzled look. "What? Sandra your partner, you mean? That Sandra? She's antiporn? And she co-owns a porn shop?"

"Antiporn?" Austin asked. Not that he was close with Sandra or anything, but she hadn't seemed religious or whatever when they'd interacted. How could she be?

"They think coercion is inherent to the industry." Liam rolled his eyes. "Like because we screw on camera, we're too stupid to make our own decisions."

Beverly wrinkled her nose. "Well, that's not fair. Sandra and I may not see eye to eye on the issue, but I *do* know that isn't her point. She doesn't think people working in the industry are stupid, she just thinks that a lot of people wouldn't be doing porn if they had other—better—options. She doesn't necessarily mean *you*. Or your company. I assume you don't take advantage of people in dire straits."

"I definitely don't. My business partner and I are both pretty vigilant about making sure people know what they're getting into and why. I don't want to be the guy who takes advantage of somebody else." His serious expression melted into a leer that he aimed directly at Austin. "Not unless they *want* to be taken advantage of, that is."

Busted.

"I should, uh, put these cases back on the shelves. No wait, I need to take a crap, I mean." *Somewhere I can hide behind a closed door and Liam can't follow me.* "Yeah, that." He squirmed in his seat.

"Aw, sorry, straight kid, don't get all awkward. I didn't mean anything by it." Liam's smile had way too many teeth for his apology to be sincere, but he still took his X-ray Dom gaze off Austin and swung his attention back to Beverly again. "So, okay, say I accept that her heart's in the right place on the antiporn thing. That still doesn't explain why she co-owns a porn store."

"We agree to disagree," Beverly replied with a shrug. "She . . . mostly admits that maybe it's not fair to paint everyone with the same exploited-victim brush, and I take the time to look into the ethics of the companies I buy from. And anyway, she handles the sex toy and dirty book end of things."

"Ohhh, I get it. So you're the porn fairy, and *she's* the vibrator fairy."

Austin snorted. "Have you met this chick? I can think of lots of words to describe her—" Beverly shot him a withering side eye, and he hastily added, "—all of them nice. But 'fairy' is definitely not one of them."

"Nice save," Liam said with a laugh. "Sorta."

"Maybe add 'chick' to that list of words you don't use, Austin." But Beverly still smiled. Maybe he hadn't fucked up too badly, or maybe she was patient enough to give him an A for effort when he got a D for execution. "Anyway, Liam. *Speaking* of ethical companies, Sandra and I looked into Mischievous Pictures last night, and we both agreed we'd be happy to host you for some promotion. We'd love if you could be a part of our grand reopening celebrations the Saturday after next, in fact. Come in, look sexy, flirt, sign autographs, that sort of thing. We can't pay you an appearance fee, but you can promote to your heart's content, if that's fair?"

"Sorry, you're gonna have to match Paris Hilton's going rate for appearances—I kid! That sounds great, Beverly. Auntie Bev." He gave her hand another enthusiastic shake. "What about you, buddy, you gonna be around for the celebration?"

If you're gonna be there?

As Master Puck?

As Liam?

Fuck yeah.

Hell no.

Austin squirmed more. "I don't work that weekend. Practice."

He could have sworn, for a second there, that Liam's face fell, but then he was grinning again, all gay and in your face. "Practice, eh? And what kind of practice are we talking?"

Austin hardly saw how it mattered. Not like gay dudes had any interest in sports that didn't feature half-naked men or feathery spandex costumes. And the second one only if you counted shit like figure skating as a sport in the first place.

Well, maybe Liam was just trying to be a good sport and cross the divide. And hadn't Austin resolved to be nicer to gays and do his part by crossing *his* side of the divide? He wouldn't shut the guy out. "Hockey."

"With *that* perfect face? You're lying."

What the fuck? Austin recoiled. Was Liam hitting on him?

No, that wasn't it. Couldn't be. Liam had hit on him a couple times already today and yeah, it had made him uncomfortable, but it hadn't made him *angry*. Not like this.

So what? Was Liam trying to cut him down by suggesting he was too pretty to play hockey? Because if so, fucker was about to find out you didn't have to have a busted face to be able to take—or give—a good hit.

And then Liam's hand drifted up to cup his crooked nose and scarred lip.

Liam's crooked nose.

Liam's scarred lip.

He'd touched them. Drawn attention to them. Did that mean—

"I'm not! Just lucky on the injuries so far," Austin spluttered before he could finish that thought.

If Liam played hockey, then Austin didn't want to know. Didn't want to know the guy this way, didn't want to know him as a person and not a porno god. But more than that, didn't want to think about him stomping all over everything Austin thought he knew about the lines between gay and straight. The lines girly-boy Bobby and mild-mannered Christian confirmed every day, even if their critical lack of manliness made Austin hate them a little.

But Liam didn't seem to have any respect for lines at all. Straight became gay once you signed his contract. Porn star and real person shared the same business card. Conversation drifted seamlessly from fairies to full-contact sports. Lines, what were those? Liam embodied the grey space between black and white, didn't he? Bisexual, he called himself. Not straight or gay, but something in between, something shifting and dangerous and a little bit of both.

Bobby's fey fashion sense that moved him so easily between girl and guy might have annoyed and confused Austin, but Liam's inability to follow the rules and respect the lines between gay and straight scared the living shit out of him.

Because if *those* lines didn't hold, then what about the lines he'd drawn around *himself*?

The first of June came and went without an eviction notice, and Austin should have been happy not to be homeless, but this latest development with Liam had pretty much destroyed any hope of that.

The fact was, he'd lived his whole life following a certain set of rules. Rules dictated by what he thought were the clear lines between good and bad, man and woman, straight and gay, and now thanks to Liam, they were meaningless. The boundaries hadn't merely shifted; they'd crumbled.

Like playing on a rink without lines.

No, it was worse.

It was like playing on a rink without lines *and* with teammates who'd never heard of zones, let alone icing and offside rules. Chaos. Offensive players in the goal crease, goalies at centre ice, everybody skating around helter-skelter and shooting the puck as far as they could make it go in whatever direction they liked. Hell, since they'd got to that point, why not just do away with the teams entirely? And the rules?

No penalty box, and people pissing in the Stanley Cup. It was like the hockey version of *Mad Max*.

And now it was Austin's life.

As much as he wanted to blame Liam and Bobby and Rear Entrance Video for this, though, there was no denying that the first step across those sacred lines had been *Austin's*. He was the one who'd first brought home that copy of *STRAIGHT SUB SETUP 4*. He was the one who'd put it in his computer and watched it. Let it get under his skin. And then he was the one who'd brought home more porn the next night, and the night after that. He'd jerked off to it. He'd willingly looked at guys fucking and sucking each other. He'd started worshipping at the altar of porn god Master Puck. He'd fingered his own *ass*.

He'd made his bed—his filthy cum-stained bed—and now he had to lie in it.

And "lying in it" meant standing in the group showers after a long, miserable morning of field drills with his bitter teammates, but instead of thinking about how to win them over, all he was thinking about was a porno he'd watched a couple days ago where the water boy had been ordered by his coach to service his whole football team in the showers and "improve team morale."

Well, Austin's team was definitely lacking in morale, that was for sure. To his left, Ben Kibby purposely had his back turned on Austin, making a big show of not including him in his conversation with Tim. Not that Austin cared—he didn't want to hear any more of Ben's blabbering about that pickup artist shit he was so into. Guy was practically a walking infomercial at this point, and he didn't even have a girlfriend or fuck buddy or one-night stand to prove it worked.

It wasn't only Ben giving him the cold shoulder, though, or else Austin might not have minded so much. It was all of them, every single member of his fucking team; the same team he'd been so damn loyal to for the past three years.

Apparently, now that he'd gotten Drew booted and himself promoted, that loyalty counted for nothing. Never mind the fact that he'd been a contender for the alternate captain spot long before the whole thing with Drew—ever since their last alternate captain had graduated out of the program last year. Never mind the fact that Drew had really deserved to be kicked off the team. What he'd thought was his teammates giving him a hard time had turned into a full-blown mutiny.

On the field this morning, they'd harassed him every time he'd slowed down on his pyramid sprints or stopped for a drink of water or slipped up on the wet grass:

You can do better than that!

Aren't you supposed to be good at this if you're alternate captain?

Drew may have been a slacker, but at least he could keep up!

Pick it up, pussy!

And now it was the cold shoulder in the showers, and he couldn't help but think that maybe it was time to find his own table at lunch, too. Somehow, Austin had gone from a valuable member of the team to its whipping boy, like he was some loser freshman again, still to be put through the paces of hazing.

He should have been upset about this, worried, trying to elbow in on the conversation with a joke or a jibe, maybe even cut down Calabresi and see if a bit of his own scapegoating could get him in the team's good graces again, if only by shifting their focus a little.

Should have.

Instead, here he was soaping himself up and thinking that maybe Coach (played in his imagination by Master Puck) could storm into the shower and make Austin get on *his* knees in the name of team morale. Suck Calabresi's dick, and Riley's, and Tim's, and Warren's, and then the dicks of the alternates, too, their entire B-team, and then at the end of it, Drew would swagger in and exact his revenge on Austin's ass. Just the thought of it had Austin biting back a groan.

Ben had his back turned, but Austin could still see Riley's dick out of the corner of his eye. As big as the rest of him, big and fat hanging against his muscular thigh, and Austin knew if he got hard it'd be even bigger, way more than Austin could hope to get into his mouth without choking. But Master Puck—Coach, damn it—would grab Austin by the back of the head and shove him forward until he had a noseful of Riley's blond bush and a chinful of balls.

Aaaaand now he had a boner.

Reflexes honed by experience kicking in, Austin made to hide himself, which was when he realized:

He wasn't wearing pads and a uniform. He wasn't sitting at a table. There was nothing to duck behind. He didn't even have any pants on.

He was standing in a shower completely naked and his dick was rock hard and any one of them could see.

See and tear him to pieces.

Because so far, calling him *fag* was a baseless insult, a word they used on everybody and anybody, regardless of suspicion. If they saw him now, like this, they'd *mean* it.

And then what would they do to him?

Nothing fucking sexy, that was for sure.

Ben still had his back turned. Austin, still with suds all over him, yanked the taps off and grabbed his towel. Threw it around his waist, where it made a humiliating tent. He ran for a toilet stall.

No jeers followed him, no shouts of disgust. Nobody chased after him in order to pound his head against the nearest pointy metal locker or hard wall of tiles. He'd gotten away with it, somehow. Gone unnoticed, thanks only to the fact that his teammates were all pissed at him.

But he wouldn't be so lucky again.

CHAPTER 10

There was only one option left, and Austin knew it.

Denial and punishment hadn't worked. Giving in to his urges and gorging on porn hadn't worked.

But there was still one thing. One person, specifically, who made all this make sense. Who made Austin feel secure even as he was falling off the edge of the world and into a pit of gaping assholes. One man who seemed to see through Austin's solid jock exterior to whatever the fuck was boiling and seething under the surface; who knew it enough to pick at it and exploit it. One man who could combine pain and pleasure together in a way that left Austin feeling like the fucked-up scales inside him of strong and weak—and gay and straight, and masculine and feminine—were finally, *finally* balanced.

So Austin wanted to be fucked? Humiliated? Treated like some disgusting cock slut?

Liam could give him that. Give him it and *then* some. And then, when it was painful and humiliating and Liam had torn his ass open with that big pierced dick, when Liam had taken Austin's fucked-up fantasies and made them real, made them really real, well, there was no fucking way Austin could be seduced by the fantasy ideal again. How could he jerk off to gay porn when his ass hurt too much to sit in front of the computer?

Okay, so it wasn't a flawless plan. A desperate one, more like. But still: Austin had played enough games, been up against the boards enough times, to know that sometimes desperate plans paid off, and even if they didn't, just the possibility of them working was better than giving up early.

But this desperate plan *was* going to work. Because after this, what else was there? Pray away the gay? Electroshock therapy? Go back to punishing himself, only this time upping the intensity even more? He'd wind up having to cut off his own balls if he kept in that direction.

And that was how Austin found himself thinking of an excuse to go to the grand reopening event at Rear Entrance Video—*I'll help out pro bono, okay? I wanna prove I've turned over a new leaf. I wanna be a part of the family again*—and making a show of hanging up a rainbow of streamers while he anxiously watched the door, waiting for Liam. At least standing on a chair gave him a good vantage point over the store.

"Who put the meathead on decorations?" Max griped, standing below Austin with his hands on his hips. "I thought it was common knowledge that he was only good for keg stands and heavy lifting."

Ha-ha.

Well, at least Max was teasing him instead of berating him. That was a step in the right direction.

"They're just streamers," Austin said.

Bobby, setting out trays of local organic catering, scoffed dramatically. "Jeez, Max, stereotyping much? There's no reason a straight boy like Austin can't get in touch with his inner interior decorator."

"They're just streamers," Austin repeated, a little more insistently.

He was already feeling insecure enough about the whole sexuality/masculinity thing, especially after deciding to let Liam fuck his ass. Even though he *shouldn't* be insecure, because wanting it up the ass in order to teach himself a lesson and knock the rose-coloured (or should that be pink?) glasses off his face wasn't as gay as wanting it up the ass for its own sake . . . right?

Max rolled his eyes. "I'm not stereotyping, Nugget, I'm telling you straight up, those streamers look like shit."

"Why don't you come up here and do them, then?" Austin snapped, then grinned, baring teeth. "Oh wait, you can't. Even standing on a chair you couldn't reach, couldja?"

Christian let out a quickly stifled snort of laughter at that one.

It made Austin feel light, like he finally belonged again. He'd never really been in on all of his roommates' high-minded jokes, but before the whole thing with Bobby, he'd at least been able to laugh with them. (Even when he got the feeling that sometimes they were laughing *at* him.)

Maybe this whole crazy plan *would* work, after all.

And after it did work?

Shit, he wasn't going to think about that. No point in trying to get ahead of himself when he was still ten steps behind.

Fuck it. Fuck it all. Why *not* be fucking happy for a little while? He forced a grin onto his face and went back to twisting the purple streamers into gay little curls, taping them up in their happy little rainbows with the rest of the colours.

Max, meanwhile, wandered off to the table of snacks, sneaking samosas and cupcakes behind Bobby's back. Until he snatched one too many and Bobby rounded on him, slapping the back of his hand like he'd been taking lessons from the nuns at Austin's old school.

"Hey, straight kid, nice streamers!"

Austin rolled his eyes and gave an exaggerated shrug, one of the rolls of streamers unravelling out of his palm and onto the floor. "Thank you," he gushed sarcastically. "*Finally* somebody appreciates me." And then he turned. Startled so hard that another streamer shot out of his hand.

Liam. Duh. Of course it was Liam. Who else called him *straight kid* that way, half a term of endearment and half an insult?

Oh and, y'know, the fact that he was the guest of honour at this shindig and the only reason Austin was here in the first place.

Liam stooped to pick up the fallen rolls of streamers and moved to return them to Austin's hand. Shit, up close and upright the guy was a fucking eyeful: full on Master Puck today with those wide leather bracers around his powerful forearms and that leather harness around his chest. Not to mention the soft, well-worn denim jeans, riding low on his hips. Or those spit-shined boots.

Fuck. There went Austin's boner. "Thanks," he mumbled, taking the streamers.

"You do know you've got the colours in the wrong order, though, right?"

"Huh?" Austin stared dumbfounded at the ceiling, trying to focus on the hanging rows of streamers but somehow only seeing Liam's bulge in those tight jeans. Was he really going to take that dick in his mouth? His ass?

Yes.

God yes.

"Rainbows. They go in a specific order. Don't tell me you never learned ROY-G-BIV in straight boy school."

"Who the hell is Roy G. Biv? Is he one of your straight subs you set up?"

Liam's eyebrows shot up. "You watch my stuff?"

Yes. "No!" Austin coughed. Liam's eyebrows rose *more*. "This dude comes in and rents it. So I see it then. Don't take it personally, though, dude. I don't watch any of this shit."

"Hey!" Beverly protested from across the store.

"Sorry!" Austin called back sheepishly.

Shit, he hadn't really considered the logistics of this whole thing. How was he going to proposition Liam when his roommates/coworkers were listening in on every word he said? Shit, shit, shit. He quickly turned back to his streamers, taping up a red strand and pointedly *not* looking at Liam.

"God damn it, what are you doing now, straight kid?" Liam exclaimed. "Oh my God. No. *Stopstopstop* before you pull something." And before Austin could react, he leapt onto Austin's chair with him, crushing their bodies together. He snatched the streamers from Austin's hands, skin brushing skin, and twisted them around. "See?" he said, and was that just Austin's imagination, or did he sound a little bit breathy? "Red first. Then orange." He taped them both to the ceiling. "ROY-G-BIV. What comes next, straight kid?"

"Uhh," Austin said, momentarily caught with too little blood in his head to think about coloured streamers.

"C'mon, kid. What colour starts with Y?"

"Y- . . . Y- . . ." Austin stuttered, twisting, trying to find some position where Liam's huge chest wasn't pressed against his own. The chair wobbled.

"Good job, good job, yes, that's the Y sound."

"I watched *Sesame Street*," Austin bragged, as if it were an obscure European documentary series.

Liam snorted so hard he nearly fell off the chair.

Which meant that to stop himself, he looped his arm around Austin's waist.

"Full of surprises, aren't you, buddy?" he said with a laugh, and gave Austin a squeeze before pulling abruptly, awkwardly away. "Yellow. Yellow next. And then?"

"G! Green!" Austin shouted like an excited schoolkid.

Wow. Embarrassing.

And kinda sexy?

"Okay, okay," he said, focusing on the task at hand and not the fact that though he was a pretty big guy, Liam still dwarfed him. "I get it, now. B's blue, obviously. What's I-V?"

Liam handed him the purple streamer. "Indigo, violet. That's gay for purple."

"Oh. Right." Austin hung the purple.

"Well, you seem to have a handle on things here," Liam said with a cough. He jumped down from the chair and patted Austin's butt awkwardly, like he'd do with a teammate, but at least a thousand times more gay and ten thousand times more brain-frying for Austin.

At least Austin's boner didn't show in these jeans. Small mercies.

And why was Bobby watching Austin so verrry carefully from the table where he was setting out glossy photos of Liam-as-Master-Puck and their selection of Mischievous Pictures DVDs?

God, this was going to be a long, hard day.

Austin had clearly underestimated Master Puck's popularity. When they opened the doors to the store at 11 a.m., there was already a few guys waiting on the sidewalk, looking way too cheerful for a bunch of dudes standing out in the rain waiting to meet a fucking porn actor.

And at the front of the line was Zeke, the guy who'd been so proud of his straight hookups, the guy who'd first introduced Austin to the concept of straight guys ever doing anything gay. Thanks for that, Zeke.

"Oh my God!" Zeke squealed, and rushed through the door with his arms extended like he was greeting a lover at the airport. "It's really you!"

Liam, from his seat behind the table, flashed Zeke a stiff, stern smile. In character now? Austin gulped and ducked his head, determinedly trying to refocus his attentions on greeting their, uh, exuberant guests. These were the dedicated fans, he had to guess, so maybe the people who trickled in later this afternoon wouldn't be quite so . . .

No, you know what, no. It would be a dick move to be standing here salivating over the thought of having Master Puck's dick shoved up against the inside of his cheek, while simultaneously criticizing Zeke and the other grand reopening early birds for acting too limp wristed about their gayness. Drawing lines between what was acceptable and what was "too faggy" had been what had gotten him in trouble in the first place.

And he really didn't have a foot to stand on when it came to those judgment calls anymore.

Master Puck signed autographs and posed and glowered for his loving public, arms crossed, while Austin simultaneously seethed with jealousy and preened with pride that he knew the *real* Liam. Watched him so intently that he didn't notice when a small shoulder bumped his own.

Bobby, of course. "So what's up with you and him?" he asked with a cheeky little smile, his eyelids low.

"Who?" Austin asked, but his loud gulp totally undermined any attempt to play it cool.

"You know who. Liam. You two were getting pretty close on that chair."

Austin prickled. "Nothing. Well, nothing's between us. Maybe he imagines there is. Maybe he wants there to be. You seen his videos? His whole thing is fucking straight dudes. No wonder he's into me." No, that sounded dangerously douchey. "Not that I'm offended or scared of it, okay? Just, no thank you, thanks but no thanks, I'm flattered, whatever."

"Uh-huh." Bobby shrugged, nudging Austin as he did. Surprisingly, Austin didn't mind them standing this close. That was an improvement. Maybe he could stay living where he was after all. "Well, it's cute. Kinda weird when he treats you like a little brother, but cute."

"Weird? What's weird?"

Bobby shrugged again. "It's a strange dynamic, that's all. For him to obviously be sexually attracted to you but then do that whole *kid* thing he keeps pulling."

He's into me? Austin flushed.

"Maybe he's trying to remind himself you're not for fucking." Bobby tapped his lip thoughtfully. "Or maybe he's into that whole pseudo incest daddy-play thing, who knows."

How the hell could Bobby be so relaxed about this? Talk about it so nonchalantly?

Because you played it cool, and now he's following your lead, dipshit.
"Wait, wait, wait," Austin blurted. "What the hell is 'daddy play'?"

Bobby snorted. "Oh, honey," he said, shook his head, and walked away.

Nearly one in the afternoon, and Austin was beginning to think that he'd seriously undercooked his master plan. Sure, propositioning the porn star sounded easy enough in theory, but not so much in a store packed wall-to-wall with people, including, oh, all but one of Austin's coworkers/roommates. Including Bobby, who was *totally* onto him.

The only way this could be worse was if his whole team were here, too.

Luckily, though, they weren't. Because they'd have definitely torn him a new one when he finally figured out how to put his plan into motion.

Because shortly after one, Master Puck stood and announced, "All right, my adoring public, thanks for coming, I love you all, but I need a break for some lunch and some me time. Giving my shaking hand a rest."

And Austin almost—okay, no, there was no "almost" about it—*shouted*: "I'll come with you!"

Liam blinked, and Austin turned to Beverly sheepishly. "If that's okay? I'll buy him lunch on behalf of the store and, uh, make sure he doesn't run off or anything."

Bobby gave Austin a suspicious look but didn't speak. Damn, for a guy Austin had been treating like shit for weeks on end, Bobby sure wasn't holding it against him now.

Beverly looked to Liam, who shrugged. "Well, I wasn't planning on running away to anywhere, but sure, kid, I could use the company."

"Get some money from the cash drawer, then," Beverly said. "Don't take him anywhere too pricy."

"Aren't you supposed to say stuff like that behind my back or outside of earshot or something?" Liam asked as Austin trotted to the counter and opened the till, snatching up a twenty.

Beverly smacked him on the shoulder. "You're lucky I'm not sending the boy to get you a burger and fries off the dollar menu somewhere."

"Yikes!" Liam's eyebrows shot up. "Point taken. Okay, kiddo, lead the way. I hope you like sushi."

Ugh, fuck no. But for Liam? To get a chance at being alone with Liam?—*today*, before he lost his fucking nerve? Austin would eat every raw fish the Japanese could throw at him.

They headed for the door, and it was only when they made it to the sidewalk that Austin realized Liam hadn't put a coat on, hadn't done a single damn thing to cover up his flashy Dom wear. And, oh God, people were *looking* at them. Well, they were looking at Liam, because he was the bare-chested one in all the leather. But Austin was with him, walking beside him, and like it or not, that made them something of an item. Together.

Every person who passed them on the sidewalk, every person who spotted Liam in his eye-catching getup, also saw Austin at his side. Saw Austin and made some assumption, came up with some explanation, as to why they were together. Austin wondered what those explanations were. Did they think he and Liam were just unlikely friends? Coworkers? People who had met on Craigslist to buy and sell a used mattress or bookshelf?

Or did they think Austin was Liam's slutty jock sub and that underneath his hoodie and jeans, he had pierced nipples and a big plug up his ass?

The thought simultaneously made Austin so sick to his stomach he wanted to puke right there on the sidewalk and so turned on his whole body thrummed with it.

He wondered if Liam knew.

God, he kind of *wanted* Liam to know.

Well, soon he would. Because Austin was going to ask. Ask him to fuck him, dominate him, whatever.

Hell, they were alone; he could do it right now. All he had to do was open his mouth—

Open his mouth and admit he wanted it up the ass.

Sign him up for the weekly newsletter and pull out your dicks, boys, because Austin Puett was G-A-Y gay. Oh God, he couldn't do this, he couldn't go through with this, he needed time, he needed—

Shit! They were already at the sushi place. How had they gotten here so fast? Before he could convince himself not to, Austin grabbed Liam by the wrist and gave him an urgent tug, preventing him from going through the front door. "So, uh, it doesn't make a guy gay if he does stuff with another guy, right?" he asked. "I mean, you know, your one series, like, those guys aren't gay, they just, they just do some stuff. With guys. But they're still straight?"

Liam didn't laugh at him, merely gave him a careful look. "You're asking me if Gay for Pay is a thing?" He put a hand on Austin's shoulder, and that was all it took for Austin to breathe deep and relax a little. It was okay. Nobody was going to find out. There were no newsletters. Nobody was going to make him suck their dick just because he'd jerked off to a little bit of gay porn. "I wasn't lying before, little buddy. Of course it is. You gotta do what you gotta do to earn a pay cheque. Doesn't change who you are or what you feel. It's a job."

Austin flushed. Licked his lips. "Yeah. Of course. Yeah. But what if... what if they weren't..."

What if I wanted you to fuck me for free?

What if it's not just a job?

Oh God.

"I mean, I'm straight. Obviously."

"Right," Liam said.

"Well, I'm straight, and I was thinking, you know, maybe I could be in one of your videos. Gay for Pay. Yeah."

Yeah. That made perfect sense. If Austin did this thing for money, then it didn't change who he was at all. It would be no different than any of the other dumb shit he'd done for the dollar, like that time he'd drank straight from a bottle of tabasco for twenty bucks and burnt the shit out of his mouth.

He'd still be him.

Nobody would question his straightness; they'd think he was in it for the cash.

He'd get a wad of money, still be the same straight Austin, *and* he'd get the painful reality of a dick up his ass to deter him from any future fantasizing. It was win-win-win.

Liam was staring at him, dumbfounded. "Waitwaitwait. Did you ask to tag along so you could ask for a job?" He pushed open the door to the sushi place, a hand on Austin's back guiding him through.

"*Irrashaimase!*" called the chefs and waitresses.

Aaaand now they were having this conversation in the middle of a restaurant full of people. He was propositioning a man for sex with the smell of soy sauce in his nose.

"Um, yes?" Austin tried.

"Hooooly shit." Liam laughed. "I did not see that coming, straight kid. I did not see that coming at all. Holy shit. Holy. What makes you think you can *do* porn, anyway?"

Now Austin felt completely humiliated. He squirmed, hands balled into fists, wishing he could say something clever and convincing, but simultaneously macho and not too eager. "Well, I mean, I watch a lot of it. I have a pretty nice body. I work out. I like people looking at me. How hard can it be?"

Liam shook his head. "How hard can it be, he says. Oh, Lord help me." He moved up to the counter. "Chirashizushi to go, please. How about you, kiddo?"

Straight kid. Buddy. Little buddy. Now *kiddo.*

Austin burned. "Nothing for me, thanks."

Liam clucked and rolled his eyes. "He'll have a California roll." He turned to Austin, explaining helpfully, "That one's cooked."

"Right, um." Austin reached into his pocket for the money Beverly had given him. "How much?"

"Forget it," Liam said, and reached into his pocket for his wallet. "I can afford my own lunch."

They waited at the counter awhile, and Austin thought maybe that was the end of the conversation, but after Liam had paid and the guy behind the counter had handed over a plastic bag with two styrofoam containers, Liam gave him that calm, assessing look again. "You must be tight on cash," he said.

"N-not really," Austin replied. The explanation—the lie—came a lot easier than he expected it would, considering he'd come up with the let-me-be-in-your-porn angle on the fly. "I had a scare where I thought I was getting kicked out of my place and losing my job in the same month, and it made me think I should put some money in the bank, you know? For a rainy day type thing. So I thought, I could do a movie for you, and that money could be my rainy day money."

Liam sighed deeply. Grabbed Austin by the shoulders and steered him toward a small corner table still littered with dirty dishes. Sat him in a chair and then took the one opposite. He cleared his throat. Gave Austin a level stare. "Look, Austin. It's gotta be a no, buddy. I'm not looking for any talent right now, and even if I was, I only take guys with experience."

"What do you mean, experience? What about for Straight Sub Setup, those guys aren't gay porn stars, they're straight guys like—"

"Yeah, I'm gonna have to stop you there. That series is all an act, Austin. It's not real. If we did that shit for real, with the bait and switch and the contracts and all of it, it'd be rape. The guys we hire know exactly what they're getting into and what's expected of them."

What? Austin recoiled like he'd been slapped. Damn, was Liam going to tell him Santa and the Easter Bunny and Jesus weren't real while he was at it?

"And as for the 'straight subs,' some are straight, some are bi, and some of them are gay but can pull off *the appearance* of straightness. Or stereotypical straightness, at least. Point is, it's not real. It's staged and scripted and edited into a pretty package. All porn is. If you don't even know that, there's no way I can hire you in good conscience."

A waitress wandered up to clear the dishes from their table, shooting them an irate look as she did so, presumably for seating themselves despite the sign. And the people still standing around the podium *waiting* to be seated.

Liam cast a guilty look at her walking away and sighed. "Look, I understand money troubles. If you're really worried, I can talk to my partner, ask her if she's got some behind the scenes stuff you could do, even if it's, I dunno, stuffing envelopes. Or sweeping floors, or whatever."

"I don't want to sweep floors!" Austin snapped, slamming his fist on the table. "And quit fucking treating me like a kid! First it's *kiddo*, then it's *buddy*, now you're telling me I'm not big enough and bad enough to be able to decide for myself whether I want to do porn. What happened to being all mad Sandra thinks you're too stupid to make your own decisions, huh? Aren't you doing the exact same thing?"

"Lower your voice," Liam said, reaching out to touch Austin's forearm.

Austin snatched it back before Liam could make contact. "Don't you pull that daddy play shit on me. You know what, you can take your kiddos and your floor sweeping and your California rolls and... and..." Oh no, he was going to say it. Nope, correction, yell it. "Shove it up your ass!"

And with that, he stormed out, leaving Liam sitting at their table for two, alone and looking shell-shocked.

CHAPTER 11

He had a copy of *STRAIGHT SUB SETUP 2* pirated on his computer. He booted it up the minute he got home from the sushi place, compelled to hate-watch it. He'd seen this one three times already; he knew at least a third of the dialogue by heart. This was the one where the sub followed the letter of the contract, but passive-aggressively, half-assing all of Master Puck's commands until all of a sudden Puck cut him loose and threw his clothes at him and told him to get the fuck out if he was too much of a pussy to honour a deal properly. Of course, by that time he'd already had a taste of what Master Puck had to offer, and apparently the guy was like a drug—or a potato chip—because the sub needed more despite himself. Couldn't bring himself to walk away.

Austin watched the guy beg on his knees for a second chance, blubbering and moaning, while Puck coldly stood over him, unswayed. Austin wasn't going to jerk off to this. He wasn't. He resolutely ignored his throbbing hard-on, focusing instead on trying to pick out any signs of not-straightness from the sub as he pawed at Master Puck's thighs, then fell prostrate and began to lick the toes of his boots.

"Please," the sub begged, and Austin squinted at the screen, trying to discern any lisp in his voice, any femininity in his posture, any gay tattoos, anything. Anything to prove that what Liam had said was true and not some bullshit meant to send Austin packing. But there was nothing, nothing at all, and the longer Austin watched, the more convinced he was that Liam was giving him the run around. Playing father-knows-best like the hypocritical piece of shit he was. What did this sub have that Austin didn't? Austin was damn sure he could beg better than that, could crawl better than that, could take pain better, could suffer pleasure better. Austin could take a hit and keep fighting.

Austin knew what it took to prove himself, and more than that, what it cost. He wouldn't be caught dead crying and begging, hell no. Liam had underestimated him, treating him like a stupid kid who couldn't handle the consequences of his decisions. And no wonder, if this sub was an example of the kind of guy who usually got tangled up with him, asking for something—no, begging for it—and then crying like a bitch when he got it.

It was almost infuriating, really, to see how bad this guy sucked and know he could do better, but also know that Liam refused to give him a chance. The same way his team refused to give him a chance at being alternate captain. A chance to prove his worthiness, that was all he fucking wanted. How could he prove himself if Liam didn't even give him a chance?

And then Master Puck said a line Austin *didn't* remember by heart, maybe because by this point in the scene, he was usually coming all over himself like a fifteen-year-old.

Well, this time Austin was in a position to hear it when Master Puck said, "That's it. Cry like a little pussy for me. Just like that. Cry, and prove how much you want me."

Not *prove you can handle it*, because the way he'd spoken made it sound like Master Puck actually enjoyed the fact that the sub couldn't handle it.

No. It was *prove how much you want me.*

Liam *had* given Austin a chance to prove something, after all. Only, it wasn't about proving himself, or proving he could handle what Liam dished out, oh no. It was about proving that he really wanted what Liam had to give him in the first place.

And looking at it that way . . .

Liam had said *no* in the sushi restaurant, refused Austin's proposal, shown Austin the same resistance he was showing his boot-licking sub by making the sad fucker crawl and beg. He'd wanted Austin to push back, to beg, to crawl, to prove he wasn't proud, to prove that yeah, he wanted this, wanted it more than his dignity, wanted it bad enough to cry and degrade himself.

And in reply, Austin had given up and walked away.

Prove you want this.

Oh, Austin wanted it, all right. He'd wanted it for a long time, had been gunning for it all of last year.

The alternate captain position, he meant. And the fact that he'd gotten it as a result of some sketchy team politics didn't change the fact that he'd wanted it and earned it.

Too bad acting all apologetic and guilty after Warren had made the announcement really didn't put that across.

Well, that ended today. Because he did want it. Wanted it enough to fight for it. To take whatever abuse his team planned on putting him through for it.

"I have something to say," he announced in the changeroom before their first off-season on-ice practice.

Nobody looked up, of course. They kept lacing their skates, adjusting their pads, bullshitting back and forth with one another, pointedly ignoring him all the while. Like he was a ghost.

So he tried again. "I have something to say."

Nothing.

He stood. Instantly remembered the uneasy feeling of standing on his skate blades on rubber flooring. Squared his shoulders anyway. "Listen up, douchenozzles!"

That got Ben's attention, at least. He looked up from strapping on his massive shin pads with a grin. "Isn't that the part that goes up the girl's snatch? Yeah, the nozzle, right? Nice!"

Austin wrinkled his nose in distaste. "Only you could twist that into a turn-on, Kibby."

Tim laughed. "No shit! Somebody get this poor motherfucker laid already before he starts popping boners at tampon commercials."

"All right, all right," Warren cut in. "I think, for once, that I speak for everybody here when I say nobody wants to hear that stuff. So, Austin, didn't you want to say something?"

Now he had the team's attention. They all stared at him expectantly. "Yes," he said. "I did. I do. I wanted to say that I get what you guys are trying to do, shoving me out, and I want each and every one of you, right now, to give me a good reason why I shouldn't be alternate captain. And if you can't, I want you to cut the bullshit and let me play." He looked around the room, staring down every single fucker there, daring them to interrupt or argue. "One catch. It's gotta be a reason that doesn't have anything to do with Drew getting kicked out."

"What!" Ortega shouted, as usual, the first guy to jump to Drew's defence. "Bullshit, man!"

Austin's heart flipped, but he didn't back down. He jabbed at the air with one finger. "No, I'll *tell* you what's bullshit, Ortega. It's bullshit that you guys are all acting like Drew was some innocent victim here, like he hadn't brought shit on himself by slacking on his training and his school shit and skipping practices and showing up to games hungover. It's bullshit that now that he's gone, you're all pretending you didn't spend all of last season *wishing* he was gone." Nobody said a word. They stared at him, mouths hanging open, skates half-laced, absolutely fucking stunned. "And you know what? You should be fucking sucking my dick right now, because at the end of the day I was the only one who didn't keep it a secret. Because I was the only fucking one on the team who had the *balls* to cut the dead weight. You wanna use Drew as an example of why I shouldn't be alternate captain? Well, tough shit, because guess what? The fact that I was the only one to stand up to him is the exact reason why I *should* be alternate captain. Because I do what's best for the team. I put the team before my friendships; I put the team before my own fucking self. You guys have been treating me like shit for weeks, and you know what, I put up with it. I put up with it, because if that was the price of getting this team into shape to fucking win? I'd happily pay it." He took a deep breath. "So now, who's gonna be the man to tell me why I don't deserve to have the A on my jersey?"

It didn't take long for the answer to reveal itself: nobody. Not one of them, not even Ortega, had any good reasons why Austin didn't deserve to be alternate captain.

"That's what I thought," Austin said, feeling deservedly smug. "Now let's get out there and make sure Ben still has better game in net than he does with chicks."

Prove you want it.

Austin stared at the rental system screen, his anxious leg jiggling making the whole counter vibrate.

Liam William's customer file was open in front of him. His rental history, but more importantly, his phone number. Right there, and the store phone was at Austin's fingertips. All he had to do was pick it up.

Of course, it wasn't that simple. Couldn't be, not with Austin's conscience gnawing at him. He was the type of guy who knew how to relentlessly pursue what he wanted, but he *wasn't* the type of guy to get there any way but honestly.

Thing was, he couldn't decide if it was . . . wrong to use the store's database to proposition a customer. Probably, but what was the alternative? Wait for the guy to come in and hope he was working at the time?

Waiting around on a coincidence really didn't seem like the actions of a guy proving he wanted it.

Going for it, chasing it, that was the way to go.

Which meant Austin needed to call the number on the screen.

Too bad there was such a big leap between deciding to do something and actually accomplishing it.

But then, he'd crossed that divide with his team, hadn't he? He'd gone from apologetic pussy asshole sitting ignored on the sidelines to the tough bastard barking orders.

You wanted it, and you took *it.*

That was what Liam wanted from him, too. That Austin.

He picked up the phone and jabbed in Liam's number.

Nearly puked as it rang.

"Liam Williams here."

Austin's heart jumped, his eyes flicking to the computer screen. "Oh, hi, Liam, this is, uh, Austin."

"Austin?" Liam asked.

"Yeah, you know, from—"

"Rear Entrance Video, yeah, I know. I know who you are. But what I *don't* know is why you're calling me, seeing as I've still got this California roll sitting in my fridge that my roommate won't eat."

"Right, uh, well." *Apologize. Apologize for storming off. Do it. Man up and do it.* "I was just calling because you have—" He squinted at the computer monitor. "—*Bi Boys in Bondage* out."

Liam's normally easy voice was testy. "Yeah, so? It's not overdue, is it?"

"No! No, no, of course not. But I was calling to remind you it's due back this Friday." *A night I happen to be working and could have waited for instead of calling you like this, holy fuck I have fucked this up.*

"Yep, I know that. It's a seven-day rental and I rented it last Friday. So tell me, Austin, is this the usual Rear Entrance Video policy, to ring up people about rentals that aren't due yet? Now, I'm no expert, but it seems like a waste of staff resources to me."

Even over the phone, the guy had the power to make Austin squirm like a preteen kid getting the *masturbation is sin* lecture in Sunday school. "Yes. No. Fuck. Can I start over?"

Liam laughed, and the sound of it was warm and husky with no trace of his earlier annoyance. "Sure, kid. There's nothing good on the telly right now anyway."

"Um," Austin said, and crossed his legs, because for some reason his dick was chubbing up in response to the abject misery of humiliation running through him. "Look. I'm sorry about the other day. About storming out on you."

"And about trying to say me doing the right thing and looking out for your straight ass was 'daddy play'?" Liam sounded offended, for a second there, but when he spoke again his tone was more incredulous than anything. "Which, uh, I know you work in a porn store 'n' all, but do you even know what that *is*?"

Austin twisted his mouth. "Um, it's where you play at being my dad."

"Sexually," Liam said.

"What?"

"It's where I play at being your dad *sexually*. I discipline you like you're my kid. You call me daddy when I'm fucking your ass. That kind of thing."

"Oh." Austin's face went almost as hot as his dick suddenly was. "That's, uh—"

"Yeah. See, that's my point about you, straight kid. You don't know what you're doing. What you're getting into. With porn . . . *and* with me."

"You saying I can't handle you?" Austin snapped.

"That's exactly what I'm saying. The things I want to—I mean, *would* do to you, as in theoretically, as in they're never going to happen . . . those things? You have no idea what you're getting into, is what I'm saying. You couldn't handle it."

A pause, during which Austin panted and groped at himself, rubbing uselessly with the heel of his palm against the huge boner trying to explode out of his jeans. He heard Liam breathing too. Heavily.

"Shit," Liam grunted. "That sounded like a challenge. I didn't mean it that way."

Well, Austin wasn't going to *take* it that way. He'd learned his lesson on that already. "You're right. You're right about me."

"You— Yes." Austin could practically *hear* Liam recoiling in stunned surprise. "Yes, I am right. That's right."

"I don't know what I'm getting into. Maybe I couldn't handle it. Maybe I'm not tough enough or kinky enough to really be a match for you, I don't know. All I know is, I want it. Even if it turns out I can't handle it. Even if I have no idea what I'm getting into, not really. I want it. I want you to . . . to give it to me. No matter how it turns out. I want you to take me there."

For a second, all Austin could hear—all that existed for Austin, period—was the sound of Liam's measured breathing. And just when Austin couldn't stand it anymore, Liam finally spoke. "So what, exactly, is it that you want from me, Austin?"

I want you to dominate me. I want you to rip my ass open so I never even think about letting a man fuck me again. I want you to fix me. I want you to destroy me.

"I want you to hire me for your company. I want to do a Straight Sub Setup DVD."

No pause. No hesitation. Not this time. "No," Liam said, and hung up.

Prove how much you want it.

Like hell Austin was going to take no for an answer. Like hell he was going to let himself get hung up on like some pimply-faced teenager going through his first breakup. Oh no. Liam might be screening his calls, but that only made Austin more determined.

The way Liam had been breathing on that phone call. The thing's he'd said—*The things I want to do to you*—all proved he wanted Austin, too. But Austin clearly hadn't gone far enough to show he was willing to suffer for what he wanted, willing to give it all up, willing to trust, willing to hurt and be scared and confused, all for a greater purpose. So after Liam hung up on him, Austin accessed his customer file on the Rear Entrance Video system one more time. Got out a piece of paper and scribbled down the information he found there.

And the next day after class and practice, he took a shower and, piece of paper in hand, headed to Liam's home address.

A condo a couple blocks away from Davie Street, it turned out. Eighth floor. An older building with shady willows in the front and a retro-cool name printed in bold letters on an aging sign. Unit 816. Austin buzzed up to it.

A woman answered the buzzer. "Hello?" she purred, her Indian accent screaming prim and proper and *holy shit* familiar.

Austin gawked at the buzz box. "Mistress Titania?"

"Who is this?" she replied sharply, and now her prim voice sounded like it came from the kind of nun who could take three layers of skin off your palms. "No. Don't answer that. I don't care. This is completely inappropriate. Absolutely beyond the pale. I cannot believe the gall of you."

Austin tried to speak up, tried to say he was a friend of Liam's and not some deranged fan here to go through her garbage or make a doll out of her (beautiful) hair, but she wouldn't let him get a word in edgewise. With every passing sentence her voice got higher and more urgent and more fucking terrifying.

"I don't know how you got this address, and I don't want to know. But I want you to turn around right now and walk away, and never come back here again. If you do that now, I'll assume this is an honest mistake by a socially stunted young man and refrain from calling the police on you and having you arrested as a sexual predator. In the meantime, I'm calling building security the moment I hang up here, so I suggest you get moving if you want a head start."

Click.

Austin ran. So much for ambushing the guy at home. He definitely wouldn't be able to show his face at Liam's condo again, not if there was the remotest chance that he'd wind up with Mistress Titania on the other end of the buzzer again.

It was only when he reached Davie Street again that he realized it: the roommate Liam had mentioned yesterday. The one who wasn't eating Austin's untouched sushi. Was Mistress Titania.

Mistress Titania and Liam were not only costars in porn, they were *roommates*.

CHAPTER 12

Austin wasn't giving up. He couldn't. Too much was riding on this, and he'd gone too far now to go back.

Sadly, calling Liam (from store phone or cellular) or showing up at his house were no longer options. And he had to assume any email he sent would be deleted unread. He'd exhausted all the information available to him through Liam's customer information, and it seemed like all that was left for him was to hope Liam would show up to return his DVD during Austin's Friday shift.

Which still left the problem that sitting around passively for the next two days and waiting for the guy to come in did absolutely *nothing* to prove how much Austin wanted him. It. Fuck.

Not that he could make any more grand gestures so long as both Beverly and Sandra were in the store, like they were right now, holed up in the so-called "office," either talking business or scissoring or maybe both.

Beverly!

It hit him. The customer file wasn't the only contact information Austin had on Liam. There was also his business card, the one Austin had given to Beverly so they could arrange his appearance at the store. Beverly probably still had the card on file in the office somewhere. All Austin had to do was . . . ask for it? *Excuse me, Miss Beverly, I was wondering if I could borrow Liam Williams's business card from you so I can continue stalking him now that his apartment is no-go and he's screening my calls?*

Yeah, that would sure as hell go over well.

He needed a convincing excuse, or he needed to wait for the pair of them to leave and then sneak into the office after they'd gone. That was, if they didn't lock the office door.

Shit. He needed a convincing excuse.

Folding his hands behind his head, he leaned back in the chair, spinning it in little semicircles on its wheels as he pondered. And then caught sight of the signed poster on the wall behind the counter, the one with Liam's huge, curved dick. He hopped to his feet and found himself at the office door before the excuse had fully formed in his mind. He held himself back from knocking at the last minute, and good thing too, because he could hear Sandra's heated voice through the door, and no way was he getting in front of her when she was on the warpath, hell no.

"—never going to get me to say I'm happy carrying it," Sandra was saying, and whatever Beverly replied with was too soft to make out through the door. "Just because they sign the contract and the director cuts them a cheque doesn't magically make the industry exploitation free. Giving consent doesn't magically make it all ethical. Don't get me wrong, I'm glad the company can prove they've consented, but who knows what's going on in their lives? Would they consent if they didn't have crippling medical debt? Would they consent if they hadn't lost their house in the real estate crash? Would they consent if they didn't have a history of being victims of sexual abuse and now they have low self-esteem and are searching for approval and validation in all the long places?"

A pause while Beverly talked, her voice nothing but a musical murmur to Austin's ears. Sandra, for all her stubbornness, never interrupted. Didn't cut Beverly off. And when she spoke again, she didn't raise her voice.

"People do sex work for all sorts of reasons. I get it. I believe it. But that doesn't mean some reasons aren't healthier than others. What if she consented, but for all the wrong reasons, and once she's in a better place she feels differently about it? Porn is forever. You can't take it back. I can't be a part of that, and I don't like that you're a part of it either."

Austin's heart fell into his stomach. *Wrong reasons. Porn is forever.* Holy shit, he was making a colossal mistake.

The door opened from the inside, and suddenly Beverly's voice came to him loud and clear. "Well, like it or not, you're going to have to learn to live with it if you want this to work between us, because this is a part of my life and you knew it was a part of my life from the start, and yes, I'm willing to compromise, but only if you meet me partway."

Austin should really back away from the door, but if they noticed him running off or skulking away, they'd know he'd been eavesdropping. Better to just stand here. Also, he was kind of . . . compelled to stay and listen. Like a soap opera.

"That's the last word on it, then?" Sandra asked, her voice vibrating with some emotion.

"That's the last word," Beverly replied, in a tone that said she meant it. "Final answer. Take it or leave it."

A pause. "Take it. I'll take it, Beverly." Sandra sounded like she was on the verge of tears now. "I'll take it, I'll take it, I'll take it. For the rest of my life."

"S-Sandy!" Beverly exclaimed. "Is that—"

"Yes. It's a pink sapphire. Certified ethical, of course."

"I didn't mean the *stone*, Sandy. I meant is that—" She lowered her voice to a stage whisper. "—an engagement ring?"

Sandra must have nodded, because one second Beverly was quiet, and the next, she was *screaming*, like a teenage girl at a concert for insert-boy-band-here.

That was also the exact moment she backed through the office door and right into Austin, and before he could stop himself, it popped out: "Can I get Liam's business card from you? I need his production studio address to pick up some postcards he said he'd sign for us."

Beverly was still overcome with emotion, staring at the big rock on her hand with wet eyes. She flapped a hand dismissively—and distractedly—in Austin's direction. "Of course, of course, go ahead, there. It's on the bulletin board."

Dumbfounded, almost in a trance, Austin wandered into the office and reached for the card while everything that had just happened, *everything*, everything Sandra and Beverly had said between them, every word, spun through his head in a dizzying blur.

He tugged the card right out from under the thumbtack. Liam's business address was in his hands. In his hands, and yet Austin had no idea what he was going to do with it.

"You can go do that now, actually," Beverly said. "Sandra and I can watch the store for a couple hours. Actually, we can stay here for the rest of the night, let you duck out early, and you can bring those postcards by whenever."

Austin's stomach twisted and flipped. He looked to Sandra, and she smiled.

Was doing porn in order to have gay sex without it making *you* gay one of Sandra's "wrong reasons" to do porn? Austin wasn't sure. It wasn't like the woman had listed the reasons for doing porn that she considered "right," if there even were any in her eyes. If she wasn't so fucking terrifying, maybe he could have asked her, but as it was, he couldn't imagine any scenario where he could sit her down and spill his guts without her stringing him up by them. God, he wished there was someone he could talk to about this. He was sick of trying to figure out this shit on his own. He was pretty sure that by now he was on a one-way train to stomach ulcers and happy pills. He was a hockey player, damn it. He wasn't fucking built to do this much *thinking*. Split-second decisions, that was what Austin was good at.

Maybe that was why Austin was already on the bus, on his way to Liam's studio, without a single fucking clue what he was going to do once he got there. Whether he wanted to go through with this fucking thing; this thing he'd been so damn sure about two hours ago. Well, split-second decisions had gotten him this far—what was one more once he and Liam were face-to-face?

Shoot glove side.

Shoot stick side.

Fuck me.

Fix me.

Fuck me to fix me.

Fuck.

He was here. He didn't remember getting off the bus or pulling the business card out of his pocket, but he must have at some point because he was standing at Liam's address with the card in his hand. In front of him, a heavy steel door was stenciled with the words MISCHIEVOUS PICTURES.

Place looked like a dive. Shit, where was he, anyway? He peered down at the business card. Hastings, of course. Right in the heart of skid row, because where else would Liam choose to conduct his seedy fucking business?

Look who's talking. You're the one begging to be a part of it.

Begging and scraping, and now he was here at Liam's door like a lost fucking puppy. Might as well knock.

Or rather, not knock, because this seemed to be some sort of big, looming old industrial building, like an old factory, and there was no way you just knocked on a door like that. There was, however, a buzzer. He pressed it before he could second-guess himself.

Looks like nobody's home, better drop this whole thing and get the fuck out of here! some cowardly (sane?) part of him chimed when the door didn't immediately open. But he stayed exactly where he was, like his feet were stuck to the pavement. Actually, since this was Hastings, they very well might have been. With gum or tar or maybe good old semen. Whatever it was, he stayed rooted on the spot even as it became obvious nobody was answering the bell.

He should have turned and walked away. In a movie, if he turned away the door would open at that exact moment. But Austin didn't move, didn't twitch a single muscle, just stood staring at the door in absolute utter disbelief that he could ever get this far only to find nobody home. No, no, no. You didn't make a decision like this and have nothing come of it. You didn't—

"Oh, it's you."

The door was open. Liam was standing there.

Correction, *Master Puck* was standing there. Eyeliner. Chest harness. Braces. Austin stared, dumbfounded.

"Can you make this quick, kid? We're supposed to be filming today . . . if my bottom ever fucking shows up." Liam poked the front half of his body out the door of his studio, peering impatiently down the sidewalk. No bottom, only some dude a block down going through a trash can for bottles.

And Austin.

Austin was here.

This is your chance. Offer to take the other guy's place.

Austin opened his mouth. "I . . ." He stared up into Liam's fierce eyes. "I'm not here to beg you for a part. I . . . I can't do porn with you, Liam."

Liam snorted. "No shit you can't."

Another split-second decision, three seconds left on the clock and here Austin was, taking one last wild, desperate shot. "But I really need to talk."

He thought Liam was going to snort again, but the guy nodded instead, features softening. "Of course, buddy. C'mon." He opened the door the rest of the way and went inside, leaving Austin to trail behind.

All this time, Austin had thought he had nobody to talk to, nobody he could trust not to tear him to shreds or destroy his life, nobody to *believe* him. But Liam had been there the whole time.

Too bad he had no idea what to say.

Not that he could have said it if he did, because the minute they walked into the massive, open space, Austin was swarmed by people.

A woman with an apron of makeup brushes got to him first, but before she could really get her hands on him, somebody else had taken her place.

Mistress Titania. Holy shit. Her hair and makeup done up all vampy, but she was wearing leggings and a bright orange tank top, looking more like she was running down to Whole Foods for organic soy milk than about to star in a BDSM porno. And yet she was somehow *more* beautiful in the flesh than she ever was on camera, so absurdly petite with the kind of hair Austin had to remind himself very firmly he couldn't touch. And she was glowering at him.

"Is this him?" she asked Liam, talking to him like Austin wasn't there. "Is this the so-called professional who apparently doesn't know how to work a watch or a phone?"

"Easy, now," Liam said.

"Don't you *easy, now* me," she snarled back at him. "You condescending shit. This is a business. Time is money." She rounded on Austin. "A lesson you'd do well to learn."

"Baby," Liam said. "Baby. Baby." She finally looked to him again, if only because she was raring up to lay into him. Austin had been with enough women to know that look. Liam didn't give her time to let loose, though. He closed a hand around Austin's shoulder, giving it a gentle squeeze. "This is *Austin*. From the porn store."

It was like flipping a switch. Her face contorted into an exaggerated pout and she slinked forward, chin in one hand. "Oh, *pet*," she said, in horrible syrupy baby talk.

Austin shot Liam a look, wondering what the fuck he'd told her, but Liam was too focused on Mistress Titania to notice.

"Look, babe. This obviously isn't happening today. We're missing talent, we're behind schedule, it's a complete fucking mess. Why don't you and the crew go grab an hour for lunch and I'll try and salvage things here."

Titania rolled her eyes. "Yes, *salvage things*. You do that." She clapped her hands. "You heard the man!" she announced to the rest of their crew. "Lunch is on Liam."

Liam opened his mouth to protest but obviously thought better of saying anything. As his crew filed out, he grumbled to himself, "Guess I'm not paying off this month's credit card bill after all." But then he shook his head and smiled. The front door to the studio slammed shut, and Liam locked it behind them. "All right, kid. I have a feeling my scheduled sub isn't coming, but if he does, he's gonna find what appears to be an empty studio that was sick of waiting for his cute ass, so I bought us an hour and a half at least. For all Lalita talks about *time is money*, the woman sure does know how to stretch out a lunch. So what's up?"

Austin didn't reply, because he was finally cluing in to his surroundings. The place was huge: a big open plan floor space with a high ceiling and old exposed ductwork. It was also old as balls, with exposed brick and huge grimy windows with their little square panes all painted black. And all around him, *stuff*. Chairs and couches and those big lighting umbrellas and tool chests and tables covered in coffee mugs and sex toys. He saw the little table and chairs set they always used for the STRAIGHT SUB SETUP videos. Funny how in the scenes it looked like a small, closed-off room, and not just a table and chairs framed in by two plywood "walls." And then there was all the other stuff lurking against the bricks, stuff that looked like it came out of a medieval dungeon. Metal dog cages and sawhorses and a massive X made of wood.

"It's like a kink factory," he said, still trying to take it all in, and Liam laughed.

"Damn, I wish you were around when we were coming up with a name for the company. Kink Factory is real punchy." He put a hand on Austin's lower back and guided him to a well-worn couch draped with a hideous crocheted blanket. "But yep, this is home. Costs me a fortune in rent, but when you do the kind of stuff I do, it really pays to have a gritty industrial space to play with. Renting out nice houses for an afternoon doesn't cut it in this part of the business."

"I guess not," Austin said, staring at some kind of looming wood-and-rope construction made up of two massive posts filled with metal anchoring rings and strung with bright white rope.

"You like it?" Liam asked, following the direction of Austin's gaze.

"I have no fucking idea." He laughed, the sound maybe bordering on hysterical. "God, I have no fucking idea about anything."

Liam put his big, steady hands on Austin's shoulders again, gently pushing him onto the couch then sitting down himself.

The comfy, warm couch. Austin settled back and took a deep, shaky breath. Tried to imagine he was in a cozy little apartment instead of a warehouse full of whips and dildos.

"Talk to me," Liam said. The natural authoritativeness of his voice soothed Austin somehow, made his heart stop thrashing and that flip-flopping in his stomach settle to a more gentle kind of rocking motion.

Talk to Liam. Liam who had always listened and never judged before. Always accepted Austin at his word.

"I don't know what to say," he admitted.

Liam threw an arm onto the back of the couch, around Austin's shoulders. He clicked his tongue in thought. "Well, maybe you can start with why the hell you wanted to do porn with me so bad."

Austin's face burned. "As if you don't know."

"Humour me," Liam replied.

"I didn't want to do porn. Porn is forever. You can't take it back." Now that he was the one saying them, Sandra's words made so much sense. He didn't understand how he'd ever thought any differently. Oh God, if he'd gone through with it and any of his teammates had *seen*! He put his face in his hands, the very *thought* of that possibility making him nauseous and trembly. "Shit, I have no idea what I was thinking. If anybody saw, it would destroy my life."

"Uh-huh."

"You knew that this whole time, didn't you?"

Liam sighed. "I've seen it go well and I've seen it go wrong, Austin. And you've got *gonna go wrong* written all over you. I'm glad you came to your senses."

"Me too," Austin said, thinking maybe he owed Sandra some kind of thank you, even if it was just him never visualizing her sex life ever again. "But I still—" He swallowed hard.

"You still . . . ?"

"I don't want to do porn with you, but I still want—" He bit his lip, laughed, and coughed into his palms. Didn't lift his head, didn't dare show his face. "I still want you to . . ." *Dominate me.* "Do things to me. Like you did to those guys in your videos."

"Oh." Liam drew away to the other side of the couch. Those six inches or so of hideous orange and brown granny squares felt like fifty hundred miles.

"That makes me gay, doesn't it? The fact that I want that. From you and not from Mistress—from Lalita."

"Oh God." Liam blew out a harsh breath. "This is some heavy shit, kid. Can you answer a question for me, though?"

"Sure. I guess. I don't know."

"Who's the first celebrity you remember jacking off to?"

Oh God. The answer popped up almost instantly. "Lindsay Lohan. *Mean Girls.* Santa costume. Oh."

"Oh," Liam echoed, and Austin could fucking hear the smirk in his voice, as if he was proud of poor little Austin for finally catching on. "Sooo . . . not gay then."

The revelation should have been more comforting. "S-so what, then, I'm like you? Bisexual?" The thought was terrifying, cutting through him and giving him shuddering goose bumps as surely as the high grinding sound of a skate sharpener.

"Not for me to say, buddy."

Austin tore at his hair in frustration, biting out, "But I want you to *fuck* me." He recoiled in surprise the minute the words left his mouth. Shit. He'd really gone for it. Really said it. And meant it, too. No doubt about that. Austin wanted Liam. Wanted to be dominated and fucked, and it wasn't because of some bullshit reason like that whole carton of cigarettes thing or the stupid theory that if it hurt enough he wouldn't want it again. Excuses. Bullshit excuses. He wanted it because he wanted it.

Wanted Liam.

"I believe you."

Austin looked up, blinking away a sudden wetness in his eyes, rubbing at the heat in his cheeks with the heel of his palm. Liam had said those words before. The day Austin had first insisted he was straight. He'd meant them then, and he meant them now too. He was still sitting on the opposite end of the couch, one arm slung over the back, one leg crossed over the other, and he was still wearing his full Master Puck gear, but his face was all Liam, easygoing and nonjudgmental but with a hint of mean humour. He stared at Austin, serious, expectant, and he didn't move a single muscle. He was . . . waiting?

For Austin. He was waiting for Austin. Austin's choice. Austin's move.

Take the shot, or retreat.

CHAPTER 13

Austin hadn't come this far and stripped himself this bare for nothing. He hadn't come here only to chicken out at the last minute.

So he lurched forward and pressed the flat of his palm on one side of Liam's broad chest.

At first, Liam didn't react. Underneath Austin's palm, his chest expanded and his heart beat, but his face stayed the same, and he didn't make any moves for Austin.

Austin moved his hand, dragging it down the smooth hardness of Liam's chest, not really caressing so much as trying to acclimate himself to the feel.

He was no *Mean Girls*–era Lindsay Lohan, that was for damn sure.

But still, Austin had to admit, he wanted him.

Liam's voice brought him crashing back into the real world. "You need a safeword."

"What?"

"You need a safeword. If you want me to dominate you. I mean, you've watched my videos, I presume you know what kind of shit I'm into. So I need you to give me a safeword so I know when it's getting too heavy for you. Because otherwise, I don't plan on holding back."

That threat went straight to Austin's dick, even as the notion of the safeword annoyed the shit out of him. "But isn't that what you do, go hard and heavy on straight guys until they learn to like it?"

Liam leaned forward, rapping hard on Austin's forehead with his thick knuckles. "Hello! Not real. Porn is not real. All those guys had safewords. You need one too."

Austin's confidence fled him. The last of the lies he told himself, gone. Liam wasn't forcing anyone. Liam wasn't taking any kind of blame off Austin's shoulders for what they'd do. What Austin would *agree* to do. A full participant, with no one else to pin this on. "What if I don't want a safeword?" he asked, forcing himself to give Liam a challenging stare.

Liam crossed his arms and shook his head, shrugging Austin's hand off as he did. "Then you leave right now. Look, Austin, the safeword isn't about . . ." He grunted in frustration. "It's not about putting a bunch of lame restrictions on you and wrapping you in bubble wrap and taking all the edge out of what I do, if that's what you're thinking. It's about giving us both *more* freedom. Freedom for me to really let loose on you, because I know you'll stop me if I ever push too hard. And it's freedom for you, too, to fight and struggle and beg and cuss me out and push back, knowing I'm not gonna back off when what you really need is for me to fucking *force* you." His jaw was tight, now. His eyes, dark. And his hand was on Austin's thigh. Squeezing nearly—but not quite—to the point of hurting. "And you need to fight me, don't you, Austin? You need me to overpower you."

Austin's whole body seemed to loosen, somehow, like he was being hypnotized. "Yes," he said, and his voice sounded strange to him.

"Then pick a safeword. Something completely unsexy. Something random, that you're not likely to yell when I start beating your punk ass, so *no* is right out. You'll be saying that a lot."

Austin reached down impulsively and cupped his dick through his jeans. "Luongo," he said, the first unsexy word to come to mind.

Liam's mouth twitched in a smirk. "Thatta boy. Now, how about you get on your knees so I can have a proper look at you, then?"

What, just like that? How desperate to suck some dick did Liam think he *was*?

Considering how desperate you've been acting *lately? Pretty damn desperate, probably.*

Okay, point, but he still found the assumption insulting on principle. "Make me," he spat.

Liam's lips drew back, exposing teeth in some sociopathic imitation of a grin. "I was hoping you'd say that." Suddenly, one of his hands was fisted in Austin's shaggy hair and twisting until Austin's scalp screamed. Austin fell sideways into the pressure, cheek slapping smooth black leather as the side of his face fell against Puck's upper thigh. When the pain subsided and he opened his eyes, his nose was right against Puck's substantial bulge. "You wanna play who's the alpha, huh, tough guy? That's fine by me. Gives me an excuse to come down hard right off the bat. Time wasted is time lost, 'n' all." His grip on Austin's head was hard and heavy, while his tone was light and conversational. "So hey, how's the view down there?"

His scalp wasn't getting yanked off his skull anymore, at least, but Austin still grunted in disapproval when Puck used that grip to rub Austin's face back and forth across the leather. It tugged on his skin, burning his skin, but worse was how close his face was to Puck's crotch, so close it filled Austin's entire field of vision, so close Austin could smell the musk and sex.

That smell wasn't supposed to make Austin so horny. Neither was getting treated like a dog who'd pissed the carpet.

"Answer me," Puck demanded. "That's rule one. I ask you a question, you answer me. You answer me immediately and you answer me respectfully and you answer me truthfully."

"Truthfully?" Austin said, his voice muffled by Puck's crotch and his own squished cheek and lips. "It fucking stinks."

Puck laughed, the sound of it not remotely offended. "That's what a man smells like when he's ready to fuck, kid. And I promise that by the end of the night you're gonna learn to love the smell of my balls. Crave the smell of my balls. Wake up in the morning looking to get a breath of that smell before you even take a piss." He pushed harder, squishing Austin's face right into his bulge. A wave of revulsion hit Austin head-on; too bad it was accompanied by a pulse to his cock. "What about you? Wearing spray can deodorant like all the other little popped-collar kiddies at whatever passes for bars among the douche bag frat boy set?"

What's wrong with spray deodorant?

"Austin. Answer me." He never raised his voice. Just tugged Austin's head back so he could look into his eyes. Theoretically, anyway, because as soon as he'd done it, Austin squeezed them shut to block them out.

"Fine! Yes, damn it! Are you happy now? Yes, I'm wearing fucking spray can deodorant!" Austin's face burned with shame. Even though as of two seconds ago he hadn't seen anything wrong with his choice of scent, being forced to admit to it like he *should* be ashamed somehow flipped a switch inside him and then he *was*. So ashamed. So ashamed, and all he could do was take that shame and present it to Puck in upraised palms and hope Puck still accepted him.

Puck dropped his head, and after Austin had given in and let it rest on Puck's thigh, Puck's hand returned to his hair. This time, though, his touch was gentle: he petted and raked his fingers over Austin's scalp. "That's okay, buddy. You know why? Because we can fix it." He sounded optimistic, and he tapped Austin right on the nose to punctuate his words, like he was comforting a child. "Because Master Puck can piss that stench right off you, can't he?"

No. Austin's heart thrashed. His muscles tensed. He pushed back against Puck's grip on him. *No. I didn't sign up for that. Luongo. No. Luongo.*

But he couldn't say it aloud. Didn't make any noise beyond a slightly high-pitched, miserable moan. He didn't want to get pissed on, he *didn't*, but he also didn't want to refuse Puck. Anything.

Puck continued to pet him thoughtfully. Didn't let up on the pressure that was keeping Austin pinned to his lap. "Hmm. Maybe later, though."

Austin went absolutely boneless with relief.

"There, there. See? See how much easier it is for you if you accept your place? You talk a big game, kid, but like all macho straight boys, you've got a submissive little fag deep down inside you begging to be let out."

This time, when Austin moaned, there was nothing miserable about it. *Fag.* He loved and hated that word. Hated being insulted, hated being thought of as less of a man. Hated his uncontrollable reaction, that sharp arousal he felt every time he heard it used against him.

Loved that for the first time in his life, he didn't have to hide how much it affected him. The way it made him hot and hard and needy, even as he despised himself. Despised being like this.

Loved that Puck didn't send him away or reject him for it. Didn't beat him up or kick him off the team. Puck wanted him like this. *Preferred* him like this. Groaned his approval when Austin compulsively rubbed against the firmness of the couch, wishing it was

Puck's strong thigh he was humping instead. The hand Puck wasn't using to pin Austin's head slipped down his back to cup the swell of his ass and rub firmly against the centre seam of his jeans, mimicking the motion of rubbing across Austin's tight but hungry hole. And Austin pushed through the disgust, lifting up his slutty ass, pressing it against Puck's big hand, begging for more.

"That's it, buddy. That's good. That's better."

Yes, yes. The praise made Austin's head swim. He felt fucking drunk, that feeling right on the edge of vomiting but still good: six cans of beer chased by a shot of tequila, and he knew he couldn't walk straight, and he knew he was a sloppy fucking mess, but he felt so good, too, so free, so good. He didn't need to worry about what happened after.

"Are you ready to follow directions now?"

Austin squeezed his eyes shut and nodded.

"So what do you need to do for me?"

He didn't want to say it. Didn't want to speak at all. It was bad enough to be reduced to this needy moaning thing, would Puck really force him to speak his shame aloud?

"Austin," Puck said. Not buddy, not kid. His name. Drawing him back into himself like tugging on a line. The threat was clear. *I can make you fly, but I can yank you back to earth again just as fast.*

"I need . . ." It hurt to speak. Felt like he was fighting every fibre of his being. Fighting himself in a way he'd never fought before, not for anything. But he could do it. Win this fight. Puck believed in him, didn't he? He wouldn't ask for something he knew Austin couldn't give. All Austin had to do was grasp on to that faith and let it pull him through. "I need to get on my knees so you can get a look at me."

"Very good. What else do you need to do?"

I don't know. You didn't tell me. You didn't give me directions. You need to tell me. Panic swelled. Austin wasn't a thinker. He'd never been a thinker. He was a follower, and that was okay, that was what loyalty and teamwork were made of.

"Austin," Puck said again, and now his hands were cupping Austin's shoulders. "I need you to focus. In order for me to get a good look at you, what do you need to do?"

I need to be naked. I need to show you everything. I need to give you everything. "Take off my clothes?" he asked, because somehow speaking it aloud made him feel so much less sure, so much less secure in his answer.

"So get to it," Puck replied, folding his arms over his chest and leaning back, and it was obvious he was trying to look stern and disaffected, but he was smiling a little, too. Wanting to look tough, but secretly pleased. Austin had seen that expression hundreds of times before, on the faces of coaches mostly. Usually when he was being a showboating shithead.

Not much of that Austin left now, not here with Puck. Puck, who made him feel so small and desperate. (*And safe, and wanted, and understood.*)

Eyes locked on Puck's, drawing strength from him, he started to undress.

Stripping off his shirt was easy; Austin was proud of his body, and he knew damn well that he was hot, and he wasn't quite homophobic enough to mind who noticed. It wasn't like he'd never flexed his muscles or gone shirtless or worked out hoping that Christian or Bobby or Max might notice, although mostly the first two because he liked the way they got flustered. Max, on the other hand, had a decent chance of trying to make something of it, and that was where Austin usually drew the line. Not with Puck, apparently. Puck, who was looking at him with unmasked hunger, not the least bit awkward or flustered.

So yeah, the shirt was easy. Pants, on the other hand . . . Well, it took a bit to remind himself that this was the one man he didn't have to hide his erection from. It was okay, with Puck. It was okay to like what he liked. Okay for his body to respond this way. And Puck was still smiling that half-hidden smile, pretending like he wasn't pleased. With Austin's body. With his submission. With the way his dick popped right out of his newly opened fly and sprung over the elastic waist of his boxers.

"Well, well, well," Puck said as Austin scrambled out of his sneakers and jeans, the worst—hardest?—part over. "Not too shabby, kiddo. You work out."

Austin blushed, and where once he'd be proud of that fact, now *he* was the one flustered.

"Knees," Puck reminded.

Austin dropped to them so hard it fucking hurt.

"Nice." Puck pushed off the couch and up to his feet, moving in a graceful, predatory way: like a cat, or one of the Sedin twins.

Austin put his hands behind his back. Spread his knees a little. It seemed like the right thing to do.

Puck put a hand on top of his head. "Very nice, kid. You're pretty, you know that?"

On his knees and naked, sporting a huge gay boner, but that little sentence—*you're pretty, you know that?*—set Austin off. It was too humiliating to stand. "Fuck you, I am not!" he shouted, but he also didn't get off his knees.

Puck laughed at him, at his anger and denial—*laughed!*—and that only made Austin's dick harder. "Don't like being called pretty, huh, buddy? That's quite the predicament for a kid as pretty as you."

"I'm not fucking pretty." *Hot, sure. Sexy, okay. Maybe even handsome, if you like little old lady words. But pretty? No way. Pretty's for girls.*

Girls and fags.

"Sorry, but you are." Puck petted his head. Circled him, like he was prey. Traced his hands all over Austin's skin, lighting fires in his capillaries, and narrating as he went: "Pretty, soft lips; pretty, pink nips; pretty, cut dick with pretty, tight little balls. Pretty blush that goes from your cheeks to your chest when I call you pretty. Bet your hole is pretty and pink too, isn't it?"

"It fucking isn't."

"Prove it." His hand tightened on Austin's shoulder. Squeezed. *Pushed*, slightly.

"N-no!" Austin reared back against the hand bearing down on him, but it was a lost cause. Puck had at least thirty pounds on him, *and* he had a few feet of leverage. And also? Partway down, Austin suddenly started lowering himself of his own accord.

Because he didn't want Puck to crack his face on the floor, he told himself, but that didn't explain why, as his face went down, his ass went *up*, high and proud without a struggle.

"*Damn*, kid." Puck sounded impressed, a tone that filled Austin with a weird, unwanted pleasure. And then Puck's hand came down on Austin's upraised ass with a quick *thwack!* and Austin's whole body jerked in surprise. It wasn't a hard slap, but heat still rose to the surface of his skin—of his ass and his face. "You like that?" Puck asked, and his hand slipped between Austin's spread legs, down to cup his heavy balls.

"No." Austin squirmed as Puck rolled his balls in the cage of his thick fingers.

"No?" Puck's hand abandoned his balls. Slapped his ass again. This time Austin moaned. "That doesn't sound like a no to me, buddy. How's your hole right now? Twitching a little? Getting hungry for something?"

"It's not— It is *not* twitching."

"Hmm." Puck slipped a hand down the crack of Austin's ass, his middle finger gently rubbing the slight indent of his hole. And sure enough, it twitched at the touch. "Feel that? That's how I know you're secretly a fag, buddy. Say what you like, but your hungry little cunt doesn't lie."

"My *what*?"

"Oh, you heard me. Your hole. Your cunt. Your boypussy. This hungry little spot right here." The rubbing finger *pressed*, and Austin cried out, as much in surprise as in pain. "Nice and tight, isn't it? We'll have to get it all wet if we're gonna have a hope of getting anything in there."

"You're not gonna put anything in there."

"Yes I am." Puck spat, and then his fingers were back, three of them wet with saliva rubbing all over Austin's hole.

Which, yes, was twitching at every touch.

"And you know what else?" Puck crouched down behind him, still rubbing, and his other hand came to cover Austin's shoulder, body draped over Austin's, his mouth at Austin's ear. "You're gonna love it," he whispered.

"No, no," Austin moaned, but despite his words, his hole half opened, like it was trying to capture Puck's teasing fingers.

Another spank landed on his ass, making him yelp. The spanks were starting to hurt, now, the burning changing from humiliation to plain old pain. Austin twisted. Felt like he was trying to climb out of his own skin, away from the hurt all over his ass and upper thighs.

"You can say *no* all you like, boy, but that doesn't make it any more true. I know what you want. I know what you need."

What I need. What I need.

What did he need, anyway? To have this ache—this perverse *hunger*—satisfied? Or did he need to be taught a lesson, one that would ultimately cure him of it? Wasn't that why he was here? To have the gay fucked out of him? Beaten out of him?

"More," he gasped, even though it was a lie, even though Puck was already pushing hard against the limits of his tolerance. He needed more. Needed to stop being such a pussy, acting like having his ass spanked was the worst pain in the world. He needed— "Harder."

"Two of my favourite words," Puck praised. "All right, buddy. You asked for it. Get up on the couch for me, ass up over the arm, and I'll give that slutty little boypussy of yours what it needs."

"Stop calling it that," Austin bit out, face hot with shame, and scrambled to get himself arranged over the couch the way Puck had ordered.

"No," Puck said, and strode away.

As soon as he'd gone, it felt like suddenly there was air in the room again. Cold air, to be specific. Austin heaved a shaky breath, burrowing his face in his arms. His body was trembling. His ass hurt. He didn't want to do this anymore. He wanted to—

He wanted to—

He wasn't sure, actually. He was torn between curling up and crying himself to sleep, or doing push-ups until his gut and calves cramped and he puked.

But he didn't need to punish himself, not anymore. Because that's what Puck was for. Puck would punish him. Puck would fix him, where cutting himself and overexercising never had.

He had to tough it out. Let Puck have his way with him.

He shivered when he heard Puck's returning footsteps. Fought back the urge to get up and grab his pants and fucking run. But no. He had to go through with this. He had to man up and take it.

"I brought you a present," Puck taunted, and Austin shuddered with fear. What if it was a huge black plug, like the one he'd used on

Danny Domino? What if it was Puck's fist in a latex glove? He'd seen Puck do that, too. But it wasn't either of those things. Puck petted his ass, cupped it in his hand, jiggled it a little, then let it go.

And then he slapped it, *hard*, and not with his hand, either. Austin jerked upright. Turned. Puck had a black leather paddle in one hand and was stroking it thoughtfully.

"What the fuck, dude?" Austin shouted.

Puck raised an eyebrow at him. "Language, Austin. Now get back into position before I *tie* you down."

Hands shivering with adrenaline, Austin swallowed a comeback and bent over the couch arm again.

Go through with it. He'd promised himself he'd go through with it. And if making him never want this again was the goal, well, beating him with a paddle was a damn good way to accomplish it. The ends justified the means.

"You need to breathe, buddy. Big deep breaths. Just like exercising, you can't forget. Let's hear a breath." Puck breathed in theatrically, then breathed out. Austin followed suit. "That's it. In, out."

They did three more, and on the third, the paddle came down again, this time on Austin's upper thigh, right at the crease of his ass. "Fuck!" he shouted, his voice raw. He clawed at the hideous afghan thrown over the sofa and squeezed his eyes shut. Those weren't tears in his eyes, damn it. And he wasn't going to let them fall.

Another hit, and it took all his power to stay down. To breathe, the way Puck was coaching him. In. Out. The air shuddered in his lungs. It fucking *hurt*. He choked back a sob.

The next one, he screamed. Screamed this horrible, gritty scream, and now he *knew* there were tears on his face. He shifted his weight from one knee to the other, trying to push through the pain, trying to work it out of his body, but it wasn't going anywhere.

He needed to take it. He needed to take it. He needed to man up and take Puck's punishment, or he was never gonna fucking get better. His body vibrated. The strikes came closer together, now, the pain of them overlapping now, multiplying where the hot lines of them met. Austin couldn't deal anymore. "Stop," he bawled.

He hated this. Hated it. And not in the way he'd hated Puck playing with his asshole, where he'd hated it but, in a sick kind of way, loved it too. This was pure hate.

And fuck, he didn't want to do it anymore. Fuck manning up. Fuck being cured. Pain hadn't cured him before, so why would it cure him now? Because Puck was the one inflicting it instead of his own hand? He was going backward. Any more of this, and he'd be getting out the knife to cut himself again.

Breathe in. Breathe out. Cut. *Thwack.*

The skin on Austin's ass felt like it was about to split open.

"Fucking stop it!" he screamed, high pitched, hysterical. "Stop it, damn it! Just stop!"

No mercy. Puck hit him again. And again.

The tears fell. Austin gave up trying not to cry. Gave up on trying to *hide* that he was crying. No pride left for that. None at all. "Please!" he sobbed, and his voice broke. "Jesus, please, this wasn't what I wanted!"

What I wanted.

What had he wanted?

If not this, then what?

If not pain, if not punishment, then what?

The truth was, he'd liked it when Puck had played with his asshole, when Puck had called him pretty and a fag. He'd liked all of it. Loved it. Wanted it.

But not this.

What did that mean, to want your asshole played with by a man, to have a man taunt you and call you pretty, but to not want it to hurt?

It means you really are a fag. It means you didn't come here for punishment, did you?

"Fine! You're right! I'm a fucking fag! I came here because I'm a fucking fag." He collapsed forward bonelessly. Rubbed his tears and snot across the arm of the couch. "Luongo," he cried at last, remembering. "Fucking Luongo, already."

CHAPTER 14

"**O**kay, buddy. Okay. Okay. You're okay. You're with me."

Somehow, he'd wound up in Liam's lap, Liam's strong arms wrapped around his body. Liam was rocking him. Like a fucking baby. A hundred and eighty pound, totally shredded baby.

"Shhh, shhh, it's all right. It's over now." Liam's hand stroked his hair.

His soaking wet hair. Jesus, had he been sweating that badly?

God, what the fuck had happened just now?

Why the fuck was he naked and sitting in a man's lap?

Because you're a fucking fag, remember? You're a fucking fag who likes having his asshole—no, his boypussy—played with.

"Dude! Fuck! I'm not gay, man!" Austin broke free of Liam's grip and leapt off his lap. Stood there, buck-ass naked, panting and sore and fucking furious.

"I know that," Liam said, and levelled Austin a perfectly calm look. Somehow, his whole composure thing only made Austin angrier.

"Fuck you and your *I know that*! You didn't know it when you were fingering my ass ten minutes ago."

Liam raised his eyebrows. "Austin, calm down. Deep breaths, remember? I didn't do anything you didn't let me do, okay? The *second* you safeworded, I stopped. Didn't I."

Austin's heart pounded. He didn't want to take deep breaths. He should get dressed. He should get the fuck out of here and never come back.

And yet, he stood rooted to the spot, staring Liam down. "Wh-why?" he asked. "You had me. You could have had your way with me. You could have done anything to me, anything you wanted."

"Why? Because that's the way it works, Austin. I'm not in this to hurt you or God forbid rape you. I want you to, well, maybe not enjoy yourself, exactly, but to get what you need out of it. I want to be what you need."

Austin fell into a crouch, caging his head in his hands. "How could I possibly need . . . that?"

"Lots of people do." Liam shrugged.

Austin snorted, then sniffled. His nose had started running again. When he spoke, his voice quaked. "Yeah. Gay ones."

"Oh, give me a break!" Liam rolled his eyes. "Gay ones. Bi ones. Straight ones. Everything in between."

"Yeah, if you give them money!" he protested. "I did all this shit for free. What does that make me?"

A fag. It makes you a fag.

Liam, once again completely oblivious to how much Austin was hurting, laughed and shook his head. "Get dressed and come sit down, would you? You've gone off the rails, here. Do you want a drink?"

"What, like a shot of whiskey?" Great. Now he was hysterical again.

"I was thinking more like water. You must be pretty thirsty after all that screaming and crying you did."

Austin didn't think Liam meant it to be humiliating, more a statement of fact, but Austin's face burned all the same. What was worse, though, his cock chubbed up too. "Yeah, well, you fucking hurt me," he said, as much a reminder to himself (and his dick) as it was to Liam.

"That's—" Liam sighed and scratched the back of his head. "Well, yeah. That's a part of what I do, Austin. Look. Get dressed and I'll grab you a bottle of water, and we'll talk."

"What if I don't fucking want to talk, huh? What if I don't wanna get dressed just because you tell me to? What if I'm sick of you trying to be my fucking dad all the time?"

"Oh, for fuck's sake. See, now, this? This is why I didn't want to go down this road with you, Austin. You're all high-strung and so caught up with worrying about being gay, you can't let yourself need what you need and like what you like. You think you're the first straight guy in existence who gets off on the extra-special humiliation of submitting to a man? Because sorry, you're not. I play with straight guys all the time. Why'd you think I never took my dick out? Believe me, it's not because I didn't want those pretty lips of yours wrapped around it. I'd love to see you choking on my dick, Austin, if only to *shut you up*." He blew out a breath. Ran both hands over his scalp.

Austin felt like he'd been slapped. "I don't understand," he said.

"Yeah, well, no shit. You're pretty, but you're dumb as a bag of rocks, aren't you?" Liam winced. "Sorry. That was uncalled for."

"No. No. It's fine. It's fine. I get it. I'm an idiot and I don't know what I'm getting into and you were right the whole time; I can't handle you. Can't even take a little bit of pain. You won't even trust me with your dick."

"It's not— How— For fuck's— How did you come to that conclusion? It's not that I don't trust you with my dick, it's that I don't generally get my dick out with straight guys, because they want the submission, but they don't necessarily want to have gay sex. You can do that, you know. Be dominated without having sex. I'm here to push your boundaries and get you off, not do shit you don't want me to do to you."

"Oh yeah, things I don't want you to do to me? What, like beating my ass until I'm crying like a girl?"

"To be fair, I personally thought you cried like a grown man." For a second there, Liam smiled, but then his smile fell. "So you're not into pain. I didn't realize. I'm sorry. Dominating people isn't an exact science. You have to play it by ear, mostly. You reacted well to the spanking, so I went for it." His shoulders slumped. "But I was wrong."

"Yeah. You were." As hard as he was trying to stay angry at Liam, though, the guy's stupid apologetic face wasn't letting him keep up the momentum.

Which was a dope move on Austin's part, because it didn't take long for Liam's apologetic switch to flip back to attack mode again. Target: Austin. "But regardless of the mistakes I made, it doesn't change the fact that you have *got* to get over this terror of being gay. You're not gay, all right? Things aren't as black and white as you think they are. It's not like there's a tiny island of straightness in the middle of an ocean of gay, and if you so much as dip your toe—or get splashed by a wave or whatever—then, that's it, you're gay forever. It's not like that. People experiment. They do things that aren't necessarily in line with their sexuality. God, kid, you've turned this gay/straight thing into a fucking noose, and it's strangling you!"

Austin swallowed, and yeah, it sure did feel like he was being strangled right then.

"So I gave you a boner. So you like having your ass poked. It's something you *do*, Austin. It's not who you *are*."

Austin nodded wordlessly, and his ass stung, and he knew his so-called grown man tears were back again. He swiped at them uselessly.

Liam didn't comment on the tears. Just smiled gently. "So here's the deal, buddy. If you want to get dressed and leave right now, that's okay. Leave. Leave and know that regardless of what we did together, you're still you, and you're still straight. You're still straight so long as when you look into yourself—*honestly* look into yourself—that's what you want to call what you see." He patted the couch beside him, eyebrows raised. "So you can leave, or—and this is my vote, personally—you can stay, and we can talk about what happened to you with the pain, talk about why it didn't work, and maybe we can try this thing again. And you know what? If we do try again, you're *still* gonna be straight." He stared at Austin through wide open eyes, as if daring him to argue that last point.

And God, Austin really, really didn't want to.

Could it really be that easy, though?

Austin didn't think so, but man did Liam ever have a way of looking so certain about shit, like he knew all the secrets of the universe, and it made it real hard for Austin not to go along with whatever he said.

Not to mention, it was a real attractive thing, what Liam was offering. Be straight; be straight hockey player Austin with the respect of his team and a puck bunny on each arm, *and* get all his secret needs taken care of? Shit. Whoever had come up with that phrase *Having your cake and eating it too* had obviously never gotten a deal this good.

Well, Austin was hardly gonna be the guy to have his cake and throw it in the trash, now, was he?

He'd have to be a fucking idiot. Or Warren, maybe. Warren seemed like the kind of guy to let an opportunity like this pass him by.

Christians, man, how did they *function* with all those rules?

Well, Austin was no Warren, and he liked cake, so he squared his shoulders and walked right up to Liam. Crossed his arms. "This doesn't make me gay," he said, staring the guy down. "I m-may like it when you *call* me a f-f-*fag*"—he whispered it, not sure whether his shame came from using such a cruel world around Liam, or from admitting to his desire for something so dirty—"but I'm not one, right? You said it, the things I like and the things I do don't make me gay. And seeing as I have a hockey career to think of, I'd rather we kept everything between you and me. Everything we do. Everything I like. I want it to be a secret, all right?" The words sounded a lot braver than he felt, because what if Liam said *No*? What if Liam wanted to go public? What if Liam thought this made them boyfriends, or that it meant Austin was now cool with doing porn with him? Could Austin really walk away from Liam now? Now, after he'd come so close to finally getting what he needed?

Liam sighed and rolled his eyes. "I'm going to regret this, but okay, fine. We'll keep all this in the closet."

"There is no closet, because *I'm not gay*."

"I already told you I believe you, kid. Do you believe me that I believe you?"

That was a lot of believes, so Austin had to stop a minute and do the math. "I believe you," he said, at last, and it was true: he'd never gotten the feeling that Liam was only playing along, or that Liam was secretly laughing at him for insisting he was straight. When Liam said he believed Austin was straight, it was because he did. There was no hidden meaning there, not with Liam, because Liam said what was on his mind, and wasn't that what had drawn Austin to him in the first place?

"Okay," Liam said with a nod. "So all this *I'm not gay* talk you keep spouting . . . who are you trying to convince, if not me?"

Fuck.

Austin flopped onto the couch. "Point," he mumbled.

"Yeah, that's what I thought. So let's just establish: yes, you're straight; yes, you've got a couple kinks that kinda test the limits of straightness; yes, you'd rather not make a public thing of it. Okay, fine. I won't tell anyone what goes between us. And in return, Austin, you're going to tell *me* your story. I want to know why you sought me out, and

I want to know what you think you might want from me, and then I want to talk to you about what happened when you safeworded." He turned to Austin, laying a hand on his shoulder. "Okay?"

For the first time since they'd been talking, Austin realized he was naked. Butt naked, sitting on this couch next to Liam, who was . . . well, not fully dressed, but definitely not naked, either. Funny, but that had felt so natural before now: him naked and Liam dressed. Still did, actually. Maybe it was the *question* that made him feel so raw and not the physical state of being nude.

Or maybe he was full of shit and totally not smart enough to be analyzing things that way. He was naked. That was why he felt naked. And Liam was still looking at him, expecting an answer. Liam, not Puck, but still, he should really start talking if he ever wanted to see Puck again.

"I . . ." he began, but at the same time didn't begin at all, because that was all there was. He didn't know where to start or what to say or any of it, and Liam was sitting there staring at him expectantly and *God, what now*. His face burned.

Liam watched him squirm for a minute or so, and then he smiled, a weird kind of soft, wistful smile, like the kind of expression you'd film in soft focus. "It's okay, buddy. You're having a hard time telling me, huh? What if you got on your knees and tried?"

On his—

Austin's brain shorted out.

On his *knees*?

And then the relief flooded him with warmth, like a cup of Timmies after a skate on an outdoor rink.

He jerked his head in a nod and slipped to his knees. In an instant, all the awkwardness went away. Puck guided his head to his lap and petted his hair. Petted him and petted him, until all the tension had drained from his body, until he was in a calm, not-quite-sleepy place: not as heady as the other places Puck had taken him today, but a softer, lazier version, and Austin liked it fine. His shoulders slumped. He breathed in the smell of the leather.

"Much better," Puck said at last. "You feel better?"

It was amazing how much better. And the best part was, down here on his knees? Austin didn't even feel like he had to analyze exactly why that was. "Yeah," he said.

"Good boy. I'm glad." Puck toyed with Austin's hair, brushing it off his cheek and twirling locks of it between his fingers. "All right. First question. Why me?"

The words were out of Austin's mouth before he could put them together in his mind. "Because I trust you."

Puck's voice was soft, soothing, neither disappointed in Austin's answer or excited by it. "With your secret?"

Yes, Austin did, but that wasn't what he'd meant when he'd said it. "I trust you not to hurt me. Or send me away."

"Mm-hmm. Is that something you're afraid of with other people?"

Um, duh, of course it fucking is! he'd have replied, if this was Liam and he was still sitting on the couch, but this was Puck, and Austin was on his knees. "Yeah," he admitted. He tightened his hands into fists. "How could I not be? I— This thing, this thing that's wrong with me, it's—"

"'Wrong with you'? What's wrong with you?"

"The way I get turned on. Like when you call me fag, it drives me crazy. Not just that. Pussy, girly-boy, cocksucker, all of it. Ever since I was in Bantam hockey, guys would trash-talk each other, you know, and whenever it went that way I would . . ." He swallowed hard, almost couldn't say it, and then Puck gently tugged on his hair, and it fell out of his mouth: "Get hard, okay? I would get a boner. I still do. It's horrible, and I know that one day it's gonna happen and someone's gonna see and then they're gonna *know*—"

"Shhh," Puck said, and his hand slipped from Austin's hair down to his neck, giving it a gentle pinching rub. It was only then that Austin realized how high and panicked his voice had gotten, how hard his breathing. But Puck didn't make a big deal out of it, just touched him, kept touching him, and said, "That's heavy, kiddo."

"Tell me about it," Austin replied, miserably. "I feel like I'm living on the edge of the apocalypse or something. One wrong move and my life is—" He sniffled in frustration. "Fuck. Over. It's over." He snapped his fingers. "Like that."

"I remember that feeling," Puck said.

"You do?"

"Austin, you have a *kink* that makes you feel like you don't belong with other guys. Imagine what it would be like to *be* bisexual or gay?"

"I guess," Austin said. "So that's all this is? That's all that's wrong with me? A kink?"

"Nothing's wrong with you, kiddo. I can't say that enough. Nothing's wrong with you. Look at me."

A few seconds of struggle, and then Austin did. Straightened up on his knees and stared into Puck's eyes.

Puck took his cheeks between his hands, cradling his face. "Nothing. Is. Wrong. With. You."

It was only when Puck's thumbs swept across his cheeks that Austin realized his eyes had leaked a little.

"Nothing is wrong with you. But yes, that's all it is. A kink. A kink that's getting in the way of your life a little, but a kink just the same. Lots of guys are into that. Straight, gay, bisexual. Guys who like to be emasculated, guys who like to be insulted or laughed at, guys who like to be forced to wear women's clothes, guys who like to be dehumanized and act like dogs, guys who like to be used as toilets. Everything in between."

Austin laughed, the sound of it a little ragged with tears. "When you put it that way, I don't sound all that bad."

"You're *not* bad, buddy. Nobody is, as long as everybody's an adult and everybody's consenting. You're not bad. You're fine just the way you are. And I'm going to give you everything you need." He cocked a smile. "Right after you tell me what that is."

"I don't know," Austin said. "I don't know what I need. I need ..." And now he dipped his head again, and Puck let him. Let him rest it on Puck's thigh again. Reclaim the safety of the position, of being on his knees and hiding his face. "I need you to help me," he said.

"I can do that," Puck replied. "We can explore together. So let's start by talking about what we did earlier. One word answers, okay? Yes or no. You like me calling you names."

Austin snorted. "That should be ob—"

Puck yanked his hair. "Yes or no answers, Austin."

"Y-yes."

"Good. Now. You like me giving you orders."

That one was easy. "Yes."

"You like me playing with your little hole, maybe penetrating you."

Austin's eyelids fluttered, and he grunted with effort. "Yes."

"Mmm, nice. That makes me happy to hear."

The pain and discomfort of the questioning subsided a little.

"Okay. You like me emasculating you. That is, you like me treating you like a fag or a girl."

"Yes!" Austin's teeth were gritted, but his dick jerked with interest.

"Points for enthusiasm. Now's the tough part. You like me spanking you."

"I . . ."

"Think carefully, Austin. Spanking. My hand on your ass, maybe you turned over my knee."

God, fuck. "Yes."

"That's what I thought. Last question. Remember, think carefully, because even though it sounds similar, it's not the same as the one I just asked. Okay?"

"Okay," Austin replied, because Puck always wanted answers to direct questions.

"You like *pain*," Puck said.

Pain: Puck's hand striking him one too many times, a little bit too hard. The paddle. Running until he vomited. Punching walls. Bashing his head against things.

Cutting himself.

His hand drifted to his inner thigh, tracing the rows of scars hidden there. Puck's voice: *There is nothing wrong with you.*

"Austin," Puck said, reminding him. "Do you like pain?"

"No."

CHAPTER 15

I don't like pain.

Austin tensed up, waiting for an expression of disappointment or disapproval or rejection . . . that never came.

"That's kinda what I thought," Puck said simply, instead.

"Y-you did?"

Puck sounded bemused, his voice husky. "I had a hunch."

"So why . . ." God, was he allowed to question his Dom's decisions and motivations? Was that allowed?

"Why did I do it? Because I was feeling out your boundaries. That's what I do, kiddo. Push you, see how much you can take and how far you can go. And in my defence, you did ask for *More, harder* right before I switched to the paddle."

"Oh." Well, that made sense. And Puck didn't seem angry that Austin was questioning him, either. That was good. That was . . . that was good. He took a deep, fortifying breath.

"Speaking of which, care to tell me why you asked for that?"

Austin startled. "I . . ." His eyes drifted down to his spread thighs, down to the pale rows of scars. "I don't know."

"Don't lie to me, Austin."

"Shit." Austin moaned.

"Did you think you had to prove yourself to me? Prove you could take it?"

Austin balled his hands into fists. "No! I know I can take it. I'm a hockey player. I can take a hit. I can handle pain."

"Mm-hmm." The unspoken question: *So then why?*

Why did he ask for more? Why did he ask for harder? "I thought it was what I wanted from you, I guess."

"What you *wanted*? Why would you want something you don't like?"

Oh, this was like before, where Puck had teased out the tiny differences between two words. Spanking versus pain. Want versus . . . "What I needed," Austin amended.

Because he didn't *want* to be hurt. It didn't feel good to hurt. He wasn't a masochist. Wants? He wanted a lot of things. He wanted to be dominated, to be satisfied, to give into all these perverse feelings and have Puck take away this burden of repression. Want was pleasure, was giving in to temptation.

But need was a different thing. Need wasn't so generous. Wasn't about pleasure, only survival.

"Why do you need pain, Austin?"

Not *did you*, as in *why did you need pain earlier today?* but *do you*, as in something ongoing. And it was ongoing, wasn't it? Austin's need for pain had always been there, right from the beginning. All the things he did to hurt himself, chasing pain, because pain was— "Punishment," Austin said aloud. "I need pain because I need to be punished."

Austin hadn't realized it before—was too caught up in the porno—but he was here, so some unconscious part of him must have known it anyway: punishment was something Doms did. They punished you. They gave you rules, and then they punished you when you broke them. They punished you for your character flaws, for past transgressions. They punished you for things that had nothing to do with them. It was a kind of absolution—like going to confession, almost—because punishment balanced the scales again, maybe even helped you do better. It wasn't about silly rules like ending every sentence in *Sir* or making sure not to miss a single drop of your master's cum when he told you to swallow. It was so much bigger, so much more, it was practically on the level of karma, except instead of waiting for the universe to reward you or punish you as you deserved, you could seek it out. You could *ask* for it, and have it freely given.

Realizing that lifted such a great weight off Austin's shoulders. Pain was pain and punishment was punishment, but unlike with the overexercising, or the cutting, or any of it, at least now he wasn't in this alone.

That mattered. Austin was nothing on his own. But in a team, even a team of two, he was a giant.

And that was why it was easy to answer Puck's next question, the most painful one of all: "Why do you need to be punished?"

"Because I'm like this," he said, and though he felt strong and brave, it still hurt, still hurt so bad that his eyes watered and his voice wavered. "Because I pretend like I'm a man, but deep down inside, I'm a fag like you said, and I want to be treated like one. Humiliated a-and . . . *used* like one."

He waited for his Hail Marys. Waited for Puck to turn him over for another paddling.

But instead, Liam took him by the chin and delicately turned his face up, like they were in a romantic old movie and about to kiss. His eyes were shimmering, and his voice was raw when he spoke. "And those scars on your legs, Austin? Are they punishment for that?"

Austin didn't want to answer; he'd gone from ecstatic to ashamed in that one look, but apparently his silence was all the answer Liam needed, because he slid off the couch and to his knees on the floor with Austin and gathered Austin into a chest-crushing hug. Liam's face pressed against Austin's bare shoulder, and those tears that had been brimming in Liam's eyes overflowed onto Austin's skin.

"Oh buddy," Liam mumbled into him. "Oh buddy, oh kiddo, oh no. Oh no. I could never. I could never punish you, not for *that*. I could never. Nobody—"

As strong as Liam was, Austin was still able to break out of his grip. Maybe it was all the training.

Maybe it was how *furious* he was.

"Stop fucking *cuddling* me! I'm not gay!" he roared, because he couldn't possibly begin to vocalize the real reason he was so angry.

He'd told Liam his deepest, darkest secrets. He'd trusted Liam to fucking help him, to be the one to absolve him, and if not fix him, to at *least* make the unresolved guilt gnaw at him less. Liam was supposed to punish him the way he needed to be punished. Balance things out. They were a team! They were supposed to work together, help each other. Liam was supposed to let Austin depend on him, lean on him, and in turn, Austin would be loyal, so loyal and so obedient and so good.

And instead, Liam was spitting in his face, abandoning him, refusing to satisfy the one thing Austin really needed. The pain. The absolution.

"I don't understand," he cried, and God, his throat hurt, his heart was pounding, his head was spinning, the whole world seemed to have fucking flipped while he wasn't looking. Puck had promised to give Austin everything he needed, and here was Liam snatching it all away again. "How can you say you can't—you won't—?"

It wasn't worth talking. Not to Liam, who'd taken Austin's confession and thrown it back at him like it was garbage. Austin turned, giving Liam his back, and angrily yanked his clothes back on.

Liam didn't argue with him. Didn't try to reason with him, didn't tell him to *sit down, kid, and listen to me.* None of it. He was just . . . letting Austin go.

Well, fine. If he was going to give up that easy, then maybe he didn't deserve the kind of loyalty Austin had to give in the first place.

Before the whole Bobby . . . thing, Austin and Rob had often pulled all-nighters playing video games. Two guys who couldn't be any more different, finding common ground. Maybe now that they were over the worst of those differences—or rather, Austin was over them—they could find that place again. He hoped so. Since things had so spectacularly gone to shit with Liam, he was feeling fiercely determined to salvage *something* out of this whole mess of experimentation, and hadn't his inability to play nice with Bobby been the very thing that had started him on this path in the first place?

If he couldn't have the punishment and absolution he craved, and he couldn't stop himself from getting turned on by locker room trash talk, maybe he could at least get back on Bobby's—and therefore the rest of his roommates'—good side. Maybe once he was there, *they* could help with the mess he'd gotten himself in. Because really, what was the use of two gay roommates and one bisexual one if he couldn't go to them for advice on how to manage matters of not-straightness?

And so, a few days after things had imploded between him and Liam, Austin set out on Operation Win Back Bobby. First plan of attack? Woo him with a video game.

Austin wasn't any kind of connoisseur gamer or anything, he just liked to shoot big guns at Nazis, zombies, or whatever combination of the two game developers were generous enough to throw at him. Give him a good first person shooter with urban warfare levels, a good selection of weaponry, and lovingly rendered hyperviolence, and he was there. Bobby was a good opponent on multiplayer: no spawn-camping bullshit, only plain old-fashioned skill. Throw in some energy drinks, and they had themselves a great night. Sometimes Max would pop in, dragging Christian along, and they'd have a four-way.

But Bobby wasn't really into war games, so much. He preferred creepy Japanese import games with complex puzzles and freaky monsters and gruellingly realistic running mechanics that had your character tripping and gasping for breath every time you so much as nudged the joystick. Three hours of shoot-'em-up and Austin would agree to at least an hour of postmidnight survival horror. Bobby did most of the game play; Austin found the puzzles impossible and the scarcity of ammo or weaponry to be insufferable. They'd sit up together playing, Austin complaining about nearly everything, and both of them getting more and more jumpy as the night wore on, and it was good. It was like being friends. It *was* friendship.

Austin wanted it back.

Wanted it back enough to solve fiendishly difficult puzzles for it. To that end, he took a detour on his way home from class that afternoon, stopping at one of those cramped little video game stores that perpetually smelled like BO. Strode right up to the counter. "I need the most obscure and difficult Japanese survival horror game you've got."

The nerd behind the counter, still hung up on the nerds versus jocks bullshit from high school, gave him the evil eye. "Are you sure you don't mean *Call of Duty 4*?"

Austin didn't respond, just stared at the guy until he started to squirm, then hit his headset. "Hey, Richard, customer thinks he's man enough for *Lobotomy Hospital*."

A few minutes later, Richard arrived with the disc, the nerd behind the counter was a condescending shit some more, and then Austin was on his way home, *Lobotomy Hospital* in hand.

When he got there, he found Bobby in the kitchen making himself a mug of tea.

Austin cleared his throat awkwardly. Held out the bag at arm's length. "So, uh, I got you this. Thought maybe you'd wanna play it with me this weekend. Or something."

Bobby's neatly groomed eyebrows lifted. "Oh?" he said, gingerly plucking the bag from Austin's hands. He gave Austin a kind of bewildered, confused look, like he was half-afraid the bag was full of dog shit, and then he opened it and his eyes bugged out. "Is this—" he squeaked. "Oh my God, *Lobotomy Hospital*!"

"You don't have it already, do you?" Austin asked, nervous.

"I don't! I mean, I've been thinking of buying it since it came out, but I've been too chickenshit, to be honest. Guess fate has made the choice for me."

"I, uh, I guess it did," Austin said. "So it's good? I did good?"

Bobby smiled at him. "You did good. So is this supposed to be a peace offering, Austin? Buying me nice things?"

Wasn't that technically a bribe? Buying Bobby gifts to get back into his good graces? Austin supposed it kind of was.

And yet it wasn't like that at all. He thought of Puck/Liam's little differences, the way he was so careful to make sure Austin really thought about them. Nuances, that was the word.

"Kinda," Austin replied. "But mostly I miss you and thought maybe we could play it together."

Bobby cupped his own cheek in one hand. "Awww," he said. "I'd love to, Austin. Love to."

"R-really?" Would it really be that easy? That simple?

"Really. I miss you too, even if I'm sick of killing Nazi zombies with machine guns."

"You'll be happy, then. The dude at the store said in this game you're armed with nothing but rusty old wheelchair parts."

Bobby wiggled with delight. "Ohh, I'm getting goose bumps already! I guess I better go on an energy drink run if we're gonna do this thing tonight. No way *Lobotomy Hospital* isn't gonna be an overnighter."

Austin was about to agree when his cell phone buzzed in his pocket.

One new text message.

From Liam.

My house. Tonight. 8pm sharp. I know you know where I live.

Austin stared at the screen, his mouth going dry. Another text message arrived.

& wear a jockstrap.

"Jesus fucking Christ," he said.

Bobby's face lit up with concern. He leaned in, anxiously rising to his tiptoes. "What? What is it?"

"Uh, I, uh, nothing serious. I mean, nothing, nothing to worry about. But I'm gonna have to take a rain cheque on *Lobotomy Hospital*. This weekend, maybe?"

"Oh, come on!" Bobby griped, falling back to the flat of his feet again in obvious disappointment. "You can't tease me like that. Whoever it is, tell them it'll have to wait because you have a date with a sentient straitjacket."

"I really can't," Austin said. He tugged at his shirt collar, still trying to get some spit into his mouth.

"Really? Who's more important than me, huh?" Bobby was teasing, putting on a big ridiculous pout, but even Austin could pick up on the fact that he was only exaggerating in order to hide the fact that he really was hurt.

Jeez, Austin couldn't leave him like this.

Well, hadn't he seriously considered talking to him about the whole Liam thing anyway?

"It's Liam," he admitted. "Williams. From the porn store."

Bobby's eyes widened. "The porn star?"

Austin's face went hot. "Jeez, do you gotta put it like that?" he complained, but oh God, it was totally true. Liam was a porn star. A porn star was propositioning him, texting him, ordering him to wear a jockstrap and making his dick harder than survival horror games. "B-but yeah. Liam the porn star. He and I uh—"

"You *what*?" Bobby took him by the shoulders, fingers digging in. "Don't hold back on me, Austin."

Austin squirmed in his grip. "I don't know, okay? I just, I don't know. I kind of asked him to, you know, teach me some things."

"You two are fucking!" Bobby was practically shouting. "I knew it!"

"Keep it down!" Austin groaned. "But yes. I mean, no. I mean, it's complicated. We haven't had sex, exactly, but I'm not going to his place to shoot the shit and watch hockey, either. Fuck."

"Oh my Gooooooood," Bobby said. "Forget video games. You want to get back in my good graces, you tell me *everything*."

"Can it wait? I kinda gotta have a shower. And catch a bus. Apparently." He stared down at the text in disbelief, half-expecting it to disappear the next time he blinked.

Wait, wasn't he angry at Liam? Oh, fuck it, maybe this text message was Liam's Dom way of admitting he'd fucked up and wanted to try again. Whatever it was, Austin wasn't about to say no to a proposition like that, even if it kinda made him want to puke.

"Go, then!" Bobby was bouncing up and down, practically squealing, hands flailing like the wings of some kind of bird. "Go, go, go! *Lobotomy Hospital* can wait. Oh, this is too good, this is too, *too* good."

Austin nodded robotically and headed for the stairs and the shower.

Well, as embarrassing and fucking weird as this whole thing had gotten, there was no doubt he and Bobby were back on the path to being friends.

Even if it had ended up taking the most awkward and humiliating route humanly possible.

Maybe he deserved that.

CHAPTER 16

The woman across from him on the bus kept glaring at him. Probably because he was jiggling his leg so much.

Well, she'd have to glare some more, or move to another damn seat, because there was no way he could summon the self-control to stop now. Not with all this anxious energy coursing through him.

Not with this itchy ass, bare against the insides of his jeans where the jockstrap didn't cover.

Austin was wearing a jockstrap.

He'd showered, taking care to clean his ass extra well, and now he was wearing a jockstrap. For fetish purposes, not to keep his cup in place. Wasn't wearing a cup at all, actually, which may have been a bad decision seeing as his dick was trying its damnedest to bust right through his fly.

He was really doing this. He was really, really doing this. He wasn't going to Liam's place tonight to rehash their argument. He was going there, potentially, to fuck. Or rather, be fucked. Or whatever version of fucking Liam would do without taking out his dick, since that was apparently how it went with straight guys like Austin.

And Austin told himself that was almost certainly for the best, despite the way the disappointment of it twisted inside him, getting all mixed up with his arousal and turning into some kind of volatile Mentos-and-Diet-Coke mixture. By the time he rang the bell for his stop, he was ready to explode . . . in more ways than one.

Hopefully Puck wasn't the type of Dom to toy with denial.

Oh, who was Austin kidding: if he was, Austin would fucking love every second of it, then ask for more.

That was the kind of person Puck made him.

No, that was the kind of person Austin *was*.

Nothing wrong with me, he recited to himself as he made his way up the sidewalk, and knowing where he was going, what lay ahead, made it easy to believe. He could deal with the crippling self-hatred later, if it came. Now it was all anticipation and adrenaline and buzz, and he wanted to distill and drink it.

He rang up to Liam's apartment. "It's me," he said. "Uh, Aus—"

The buzzer went off and the lock clicked. Apparently they weren't doing small talk. Well, that was totally fine by Austin. Completely one hundred percent fine.

A short but somehow simultaneously *looong* elevator trip later, and he was standing outside of Liam's door.

Puck's door?

They were getting all tangled in Austin's head. He didn't need to knock; the door opened right in front of his face.

Liam didn't say hello, just stepped back and let Austin shuffle through the doorway.

"So, uh, your roommate isn't here?" he asked, because he was nervous about *something* here and God, please let it be that, please let Liam think it was that.

"You think I would invite you over if she was? Tell me your safeword."

"Luongo," Austin recited. And as for the other question? "And I . . . don't know? I don't actually know what's going on with you and her, to be honest. You're roommates and you do porn together and you call her *baby* but you're still doing this thing with me . . .?" That wasn't a question, but somehow his voice rose up at the end there.

"Would it bother you, if I told you I was sleeping with her?"

Austin recoiled a little. He hadn't really thought about that. He supposed he didn't have a right to be jealous, but on the other hand, he kind of was anyway. "Well, it would mean you're getting more pussy than me," he joked.

Puck grabbed him by the hair, yanking him close. "Don't talk about her that way, understand me? She told me you came here. You scared the shit out of her. She thought she was gonna have to call the cops."

"So . . ." Austin grunted in pain, lifting onto his tiptoes as Puck kept on tugging. "I take it that you *are* sleeping with her, then?"

His back hit the wall. Puck's free hand closed around his throat. They were up close and personal, now: Austin could feel the gust of Puck's breath on his face, could practically hear the grit as he bared his teeth. "Not anymore, I'm not, but I still respect her, which is why I don't let little bitches like you talk about her that way."

"Sor-ry!" Austin rolled his eyes.

Wait, not *anymore*?

"Not yet, you're not," Puck said. "You're just lucky she thinks your cluelessness is kind of cute in hindsight, because otherwise your complete lack of boundaries would be a deal-breaker. That's why you're going to spend tonight proving how sorry you are." He leaned in, and Austin thought he was about to kiss him, but then he turned his head a couple degrees and bit Austin right on the cheek. As Austin shouted and twisted in pain, Puck leaned forward, his body hard and heavy, and whispered, "But here's the fun bit: we're going to do it without me *punishing* you."

Shit. Fuck. He had no idea what that meant. No idea what Puck planned to do to him—make him do?—and no idea whether that statement meant that this meeting wasn't the Dom-apology Austin had thought it was going to be.

He should ask for clarification. He should demand an apology from Liam for his point-blank refusal to accept what Austin needed from him. He should . . . he should . . .

Puck's hand was cupping Austin's cock through his jeans, the heel of his palm rubbing firmly down the hard length of it, and suddenly Austin didn't give a shit about punishment anymore. He bucked and moaned, then flushed in shame.

"Ready to prove yourself to me, kiddo?" Puck asked, pressing their foreheads together.

Austin shut his eyes, and God help him, he nodded.

"Very good. You can start by stripping down and showing me the jock you're wearing for me."

No question there, no *Did you remember to wear a jock like I asked?*

Because Puck didn't ask for favours, he made demands. And he expected to have them followed.

Austin was no exception. Still crushed to the wall by Puck's broad chest, Austin's shaking hands moved to his fly, which he unzipped. He shimmied until his jeans were pooled around his ankles. Puck's big hands closed around his hips, holding him there like guys held cute, tiny girls, and then he pulled Austin's shirt up over his head.

And then he walked away.

Speechless, panting, Austin stepped out of his sneakers and jeans, left his shirt on the floor, and followed.

The condo's huge windows were all open, and a cool night breeze was blowing through the living room. Austin was covered in goose bumps by the time he found Puck: sitting on his couch, legs spread with the windows at his back, like the king in his castle, and here was Austin come in from the cold begging.

Austin wrapped his arms around himself.

"You know, you're revealing more than you're hiding by doing that," Puck said casually. "Maybe I can't see those hard little nipples, but I can see how *vulnerable* you feel." He licked his lips—slowly, obscenely. "I like it. C'mere."

Austin forced himself to drop his arms to his sides as he walked forward. Puck, meanwhile, openly fucked him with his eyes, mouth curved in a wicked smirk.

"You have a real nice body, kiddo. You wax your chest?"

Fighting the urge to cover himself again, Austin shook his head.

"Missed out on a few parts of puberty, huh? That explains your balls." Puck's leg shot out, the bare sole of his foot rubbing against Austin's dick. He pushed it from side to side with his toes.

He wasn't wearing boots. Wasn't wearing any of his bondage wear, actually, only a low-slung pair of grey sweats and a sleeveless workout top. Like one of those guys at the gym who stared too long and made everybody around them feel uncomfortable, like meat on display, assessed and measured.

It was different from his usual look but just as threatening and intriguing.

Austin's shoulders slumped when Puck finally put his foot on the ground again.

"That's enough play for your dick tonight, I think."

What?

"Oh, don't give me that puppy dog look, kid. You're supposed to be proving how sorry you are, remember? Me letting you shoot your load is hardly any kind of penance. Now get on your knees. Ass in the air."

Austin did as he was told, feeling more exposed than he had before. Somehow the jock made him feel *more* naked than actually being naked, and those full-length windows weren't curtained. The room was full of hazy moonlight. He didn't think anybody in nearby buildings could see, but that thought didn't do much to comfort him.

There was something plastic on the floor. Sturdier than a garbage bag. One of those painter's sheets? An outdoor tablecloth? He wasn't sure, but whatever it was, it reminded Austin of movies about mob murders, ones where the victim would walk into a room lined with plastic, knowing that soon the whole thing would be splattered with his blood.

Austin shuddered when Puck's hand touched his lower back. He hadn't seen the guy come over. He'd had his eyes closed. Hadn't even realized it.

"You look sexy in that jockstrap, buddy. Nothing nicer than a bitch with his worthless dick hidden and his slutty ass on display." His dry hand slid down the crack of Austin's ass, not really lingering. The touch was almost clinical, which made Austin shudder harder. "Now, I seem to recall that me and your hungry little boypussy have some unfinished business, isn't that right?"

Austin whimpered.

"Answer me, Austin."

"Yes," Austin gritted out.

"Yes, what? Answer with a full sentence."

"Fuck you," Austin spat. He knew what Puck wanted from him, but he wasn't going to say it. Puck was lucky Austin was letting *him* call Austin's ass that.

Puck didn't strike him. "Wrong answer, Austin. You have one more try, and after that, you can leave. Your call."

Austin's heart sped up at the thought of being sent away. He had zero doubts Puck would follow through on the threat.

Why couldn't the guy just spank him and get on with it?

Because there's nothing wrong with you.

Puck was sticking by his resolution not to punish Austin with the pain he'd asked for. Other punishments, sure. Send him away? Sure.

But cause him pain and, regardless of intentions, he'd be playing right into Austin's craving.

"What's it gonna be?" Puck asked.

Austin blew out a breath, muscles absolutely *twitching* with tension. He wanted to explode outward, rage and flail and scream and punch shit, but at the same time, he didn't want to do any of those things. All that energy returned to his body until he was a quaking, shaking mess. Every word was a battle. "Yes, you and my h—my hungry boypussy have unfinished business."

Puck's voice softened, turning sweet and soothing on a dime. "That's it, buddy. That's good." His hand massaged Austin's hole, not too hard but not lightly either—there was definite intention there.

Austin moaned in abject pleasure, but not at Puck's *touch*. No, it was the sound of his voice; it was the way he was praising Austin.

Austin was a team player. He was obedient. He *craved* this.

Approval.

"We're going to try something new now," Puck said. His hand began to rub circles on Austin's ass cheek, just firm enough that as he moved outward, Austin felt himself being spread open for a second before Puck's hand shifted the pressure and hid him again. And then the circles slowed and that spread moment stretched out, longer and longer on each round. It was almost hypnotizing. The pace, the motion, the cycling of emotions from baseline anxiety to acute humiliation and back again. Around and around and around. "That's it," Puck praised. The tension drained from Austin's body as the strange massage continued, as Puck murmured to him. "Getting nice and loose for me, aren't you, buddy?"

"Yesss," Austin hissed, letting his cheek rest on the plastic material covering the floor. His eyes rolled back in his head. He barely registered the clicking sound of a squeeze bottle being opened, not until Puck's other hand was between his spread ass cheeks smearing him with warm lube.

"Feels nice, doesn't it? Nice and wet and ready, just the way you're meant to be. One day I'll be able to do this to you and sink my cock right inside you without the slightest bit of resistance. We'll train your ass, won't we?"

"Yes."

"Flying pretty high for me now, aren't you, kiddo?"

"Yes," Austin said, mostly because right now he wanted to agree with Puck about *everything*.

"Hold on to that," Puck said, and then there was a sharp, unyielding feeling, a pressure, an intrusion, and his curved index finger was right inside of Austin's ass.

Austin's hands balled into fists. He tossed his head back and forth on the plastic, growling through clenched teeth. Pushed *back*, wanting that finger *out out out*, but somehow in the process only opened himself more. Puck was down to the second knuckle inside him now, the pad of Puck's finger massaging him from the inside, crooking and rubbing. Firm. Searching.

"How's that feel?" Puck asked softly.

"Nngh." Which, garbled as it was, was pretty accurate to how Austin felt right now.

He didn't know.

Scared? Full? Good? Flying?

Not pain, anyway.

As the finger inside him continued to stroke, Puck's other hand reached between Austin's trembling thighs, right inside his jock to roll and tug on his balls. "That's it, kiddo. Nice and relaxed. Don't clench, don't flex, just relax. Nice and loose and open for me."

Puck's finger withdrew, but only for a second or so, and then the pressure was back, and two fingers stretched past Austin's resistance. Another tug on his balls, another slippery rub up and down his inner walls, and Austin was moaning, broken and needy.

The whole time, Puck didn't once touch his dick, and Austin didn't ask him to, either. He liked this open, receptive place, this place where he didn't have to fight or think or struggle or worry about how he looked to anyone. To preserve it, he'd go along with whatever Puck wanted from him. He wouldn't argue, and he wouldn't make any demands.

And anyway, whatever Puck was doing in his ass was starting to feel damn good.

Because you're a fag. He'd seen Puck saying that in his videos, saying fags didn't need their dicks because the only place they got pleasure from was their hole. Well Austin still loved having his dick sucked, but maybe the truth wasn't that his ass—boypussy, that's what Puck wanted him to call it—was the only place he *could* feel pleasure, but that it was the only place he *deserved* to feel pleasure. He arched and twisted, crying out as Puck's fingers dragged across a particularly sensitive spot.

"Don't clench," Puck reminded, and pulled his fingers free. Austin found himself whining, wanting that feeling back. Puck didn't give him it though, just crouched behind him and rubbed his ass and thighs, gentling him. "Nice and loose. Loose and relaxed. Don't want you shooting your load, now, do we?"

"Wh—" The mind-fog haze of lazy pleasure lifted, leaving Austin blinking and shaking his head in shock.

"You're doing this to apologize, remember? You're doing it to prove yourself. It's not supposed to *get you off*." Puck sounded almost disgusted at the mere suggestion of such a thing. "But it'll make me happy with you, and isn't that even better?"

Part of Austin screamed *Fuck no, asshole, I'm not your toy!* but it was drowned out by the whispering fuckdoll fag part of him that kept repeating *Yes yes yes yes.*

"Yes," Austin moaned.

Puck's fingers slid inside him again. Homed in, this time, on that spot that made him shiver with pleasure and fucking *stayed* there, rubbing it over and over again, up and down, then in sweeping little circles. Fuckdoll Austin started to make little yelping crying noises, intense pleasure ratcheting up inside him.

All the while, Puck rubbed those soft circles on his lower back, chanting softly, "Nice and loose. Nice and relaxed."

And the more he said it, the more his voice blurred in Austin's head, until the words weren't words anymore, just waves of sound washing over him, following the currents of Puck's touch inside and outside of his body.

The yelping turned to one long, low moan. Austin's whole body turned to liquid, and speaking of which—

His eyes popped open. "I need to piss," he said. Bad. Like, right now. Like, the pressure had suddenly built and was already releasing.

Puck didn't leap away from him in disgust. He kept up his assault of hypnotizing pleasure. "No you don't, buddy. It just feels like that. Come on, now, let go. Nice and loose for me. Let go."

Austin didn't want to refuse him. Couldn't, even if he did want to, even if he tried. Something inside him *broke*, and suddenly his cock was fucking leaking, not piss like he thought, but a steady stream of cum. Dripping out of him pleasurelessly, not shooting like it should. Soaking the fabric of his jock. Puck kept rubbing that spot inside him, but now his other hand moved to Austin's cock, pulling downward on it, his tight fist bringing more dribbles of Austin's cum with it.

Milking me. He's milking me.

No other description of the motion. No other word for how it felt.

Humiliating. Horrible. A defeat, instead of the triumph coming usually felt like.

And all the while, Puck murmured to him "That's it, buddy, that's my boy, let it all go, let it all go."

Let it all go.

Let it all go.

Body slumping forward, Austin did. Let go of everything, as surely as he'd let go of the tension in every single one of his muscles.

It didn't even bother him when the tears started.

CHAPTER 17

At some point, Liam cleaned his ass, but not his dick in the cold, sticky jockstrap, a decision Austin didn't argue with. Then he wrapped Austin up like a burrito in a fuzzy fleece blanket printed with the Canucks logo, helped him to his feet, and got him to the couch, where he immediately collapsed in a pile of shivering and sniffling tears. He thought that now there'd be more of that awkward cuddling and pillow talk like the first time, but instead Liam tossed himself onto the other end of the couch, pulled Austin's blanket-wrapped legs over his lap, and turned on the TV.

Really? That was it? He'd teased and tortured Austin to the point of coming in his pants and *crying*, and now they were gonna watch TV?

Okay, so yeah, Austin had been the one to draw the line on cuddling with the whole *I'm not gay!* flip out, but still. Couldn't Liam see he was a fucking wreck right now? His hands were actually vibrating, and his body was running hot and cold at the same time. He was pretty sure his eyes were still leaking tears, even though he wasn't really crying anymore.

Liam fiddled with the remote for a minute or two while Austin shook himself to pieces, and right when Austin was about to curl up into a ball on the couch and start wailing in distress, Liam patted and rubbed his legs through the blanket and turned toward him. "You watch Olympic hockey, kiddo?"

The question surprised him so much that he almost forgot how shitty his body felt coming down from its high. "Uh, yeah, who doesn't?" he replied. His eyes flicked down to where Liam was still rubbing slow, easy circles on his legs, the touch no more sexual than the massages he got from the sports therapist. It felt good. Relaxing.

Safe. Austin slumped back into the corner of the couch and sank deeper into the warm hug of the blanket. The trembling slowed.

"How about a classic, then?" Liam smiled, his eyes twinkling in the reflection of the television. A DVD booted up. "Twenty-ten winter Olympics? Gold medal game?" He looked so eager, like an excited kid.

"Is it really classic if it's only been a couple years?" Austin asked with a sceptical raise of his eyebrow.

"Maybe not, but I didn't want to date myself by showing something from the twentieth century."

"How old are you, anyway?" Austin asked with half an eye on the familiar game. He'd watched it on TV live, with his dad and stepbrother. The game had been heart-pounding, epic, an overtime win—everything that was good about hockey, but that wasn't even the best part. The best part was after Canada had won, when the whole city had *roared*. Tens of thousands of cheering voices. In the streets, in their condos, in their cars listening to their radios, in malls watching on electronics store TVs, on stopped buses watching on smartphones.

"Thirty-five," Liam replied. "Does that bother you?"

Austin shook his head. "Nah. Where were you, when Canada won gold?" He reached out of his cocoon of blankets to gesture at the TV in illustration.

"Davie Street with my buds, pissed fucking drunk."

"You have a lot of friends on Davie Street who like hockey?" Austin asked, mostly joking. "You'd think on Davie Street the only hockey fans would be more into *women's* hockey, if you get my drift."

"I'd slap you upside the head for stereotyping, but I was down there in 2002 for the Salt Lake City games, and I tell you, it was a good damn day to be a woman who loves hockey as much as she loves pussy."

Austin laughed, life and strength returning to his body, and sat up enough to list in the other direction, nudging Liam's shoulder with his own playfully. "What about you? Hockey ever get you laid?"

When Austin didn't retreat to his own end of the couch, choosing to lean against Liam's warmth instead, Liam dropped an arm around his shoulders. "Maybe," he teased. He rubbed Austin's upper arm briskly.

"You think I could make that a definite yes?" Austin asked, before he even realized what he was saying, let alone in time to stop himself.

Liam shot him a look that was as shocked as Austin felt.

Well, no going back now, not that Austin wanted to, if he was honest. He wanted to get this over with, break this tension, quiet this sick anticipation humming inside him. He also wanted to pleasure Liam even half as much as Liam had pleasured him tonight. After all, hadn't Liam withheld Austin's orgasm as a form of punishment? Did that punishment mean anything if Liam, as the Dom, didn't orgasm either?

Austin let the blanket fall from his shoulders and leaned in closer, one hand reaching out and making contact with Liam's hard chest. He licked his lips, out of nervous habit, at first, and then slower out of some hope of turning Liam on. Liam looked back at him with his dark, unreadable eyes. He didn't move. Austin could see in the shifting TV's light that his jaw was tense. Holding back?

"Please?" Austin asked, because it seemed right, because it made this craving make sense somehow. "May I?"

Puck's head fell back against the couch, his hand around Austin's shoulder digging in. "Yeah," he said, and spread his legs.

Oh. He wants . . .

Austin looked to him—for reprieve? for encouragement? for strength?—then reached with both hands for the elasticized waistband of his sweats.

The grey fabric was soft and plush and warm, and under it, Puck's massive cock stirred and started to lift, shifting the fabric. Austin stared at it in a heady, horrible mix of admiration and fucking terror.

The thing was huge. Imposing. Austin had no idea what to do with it, had no idea what it made him that he wanted to do anything with it in the first place, only knew that he was going to. Had to. Needed to.

He should say that aloud. Keeping it a secret felt akin to lying. "I need this," he said, mouth carefully shaping each word, wanting to make it perfect.

The hand on his shoulder lifted to cup the back of his head, fingers tightening in his hair. "I know you do, buddy."

"Why didn't you . . ." Austin's hands moved almost on their own, finally pulling the waistband of Puck's sweatpants so that massive pierced erection of his sprung free.

"Why didn't I just make you?" Puck's mouth quirked. "Because you needed to ask for it, Austin. You needed to get to the point where you wanted it enough to ask for it yourself. No deniability now, kiddo. Nobody forcing you, nobody coercing you, nobody to blame. This is all you."

That should have scared the shit out of him or made him angry, but it didn't, not right then.

Because Puck was *proud*. Of him.

"How should I—" Austin stared at that big curved dick, almost afraid to lean toward it. Which was dumb as shit, because it wasn't like it was gonna jump out and bite him on the face.

"Do what comes naturally to you, buddy. Give it a lick, give it a taste, hell, if you're feeling romantic you can give it a kiss with those cocksucking lips of yours."

Austin touched his mouth self-consciously.

"Oh yeah, you heard me. Cocksucking lips. Soft, pretty pink lips like yours are *made* for sucking dick. Kissing dick, worshipping dick. Lips like that, you're gonna be a natural at this, so get in there and give it a go."

The hand on the back of his head pushed a little.

Austin leaned in the rest of the way on his own. Parted his cocksucking lips and pressed an open-mouthed kiss to the very tip of Puck's substantial dick, taking the heavy piercing between his teeth.

"Mmm," Puck murmured, encouraging, and gently tugged his hair.

Austin moaned, wet and breathy, around Puck's girth. Stretched out his tongue and gave the firm, salty skin a lick. The taste made him shudder, the weight of it made him gag, but he wasn't gonna quit now.

"Don't be shy. Give it a little suck, huh?"

So he did. Gently at first, little tentative suckles, not sure if he was doing right, and then, when he heard Puck groan, a little harder. Bobbed up and down over the head of Puck's dick, the way Austin liked girls to do to him.

He supposed that made *him* the girl. His wrung-out cock tingled and twitched just thinking of it.

Couldn't get hard, though. Maybe Puck's training was already sinking in. Maybe his body knew instinctively that he wasn't going to be fucking anything anytime soon.

The bobbing motion seemed to be what Puck liked, because he grunted and pushed back against the couch, fingers scraping the upholstery. Like he was *struggling*. Maybe he was. After all, he never fucked Austin's face. Never took Austin by the hair and shoved him down onto his dick. Never acted the remotest bit impatient with how timid and likely lousy Austin was at sucking dick.

Didn't do any of the things he did to the guys in his videos.

And far from being disappointed that Puck wasn't being forceful enough with him, it almost turned Austin on more, knowing that Puck expected him to figure it out on his own, make it happen on his own, prove his enthusiasm. Prove himself.

Or maybe Puck was trying to be a considerate lover.

Nah.

He reached out, taking the base of Puck's dick in hand, and jerked him off as he licked and sucked on the head.

"Now you're getting it," Puck praised. "Yeah. Getting into this whole cocksucking thing, aren't you?"

Austin's jaw was getting tired. His lips were numb to the point of hurting. He pulled off, stomach twisting at the sight of his own drool all over that engorged dick, then slapped the head against his outstretched tongue. Did Puck like that? He'd certainly seen it enough times in STRAIGHT SUB SETUP.

Puck hadn't needed to set Austin up. Austin had come to him.

A natural cocksucker. That was all Austin was. He should be on his knees on the floor. Yeah, that was where he belonged, wasn't it?

Never letting go of Puck's shaft, he slid to the floor, legs spread wide where he knelt, and looked up into Puck's face. Puck stared down at him, corner of his mouth twitching.

Laugh at me, Austin thought, and suddenly it was the thing he wanted above everything else. To be on his knees for a man, to have that man laugh at how desperate and pathetic and cock hungry he was.

But Puck didn't laugh. He swept his fingers through Austin's floppy, half-curled bangs, and that little twitch at the corner of his mouth turned into a soft smile. "Aren't you so pretty," he said, and there was nothing about his tone that suggested he was trying to be humiliating about it this time.

Austin knelt there perfectly still, letting Puck get his fill of looking. Nobody'd looked at him like this before.

He didn't know, exactly, what he was supposed to do.

A hot little blush hit the highest point of his cheeks. His eyes twitched momentarily to the left, and that seemed to break Puck's concentration, because he shook his head a little, expression hardening, and dug a hand into Austin's hair hard. "All right, cocksucker, not that I don't enjoy the view, but I think it's high time for me to get off, so I'll give you a choice."

Austin nodded and swallowed, forcing himself to look up at Puck and not away.

"You can either let me fuck your face and take my cum down your throat, or you can kneel there nice and pretty while I jerk off on your face and give your cute little nose a few new freckles. What'll it be?"

"You're giving me a ch-choice?" Austin's hands, resting on his knees, curled into fists.

"That's right. Boy's choice. So?"

It was almost too much to wrap his head around. Choosing? What was the goal, here? To get what he wanted? To give Puck what *he* wanted? God, he didn't know what Puck wanted! How could he possibly? Hell, he didn't even know what *he* wanted!

And then he thought of *STRAIGHT SUB SETUP 4* and Puck fucking Danny Domino's face, and the horrible guttural noises Danny had made, the way the tendons in his neck had popped out, the way his face had turned almost purple. And then there had been the drool and the mucus, running down Danny's face, gushing out of his mouth in sticky clumps. Would Austin be able to withstand that? Puck obviously thought he could, or else he wouldn't have offered.

On the other hand, it would probably hurt, that big, pierced dick battering his throat. Getting painted with Puck's cum, though, that was so disgusting and demeaning that it made his nipples pebble.

"Come on my face." Austin licked his lips. "Please. Sir."

Puck's eyebrows went up. "*Sir*, is it? Hmm. No, I don't think so. Try *Coach*."

Austin's throat went dry. That word was sacred. Puck must have some suspicion of how sacred it was to Austin.

Yeah, that's why he's getting you to pervert it this way. He wants under your skin.

And Austin was fucking letting him.

"Please...Coach," Austin said, nearly choking on the word. It was like his mouth was full of sand and dust.

"Please what?"

"Please come on my face, Coach."

Puck grinned cruelly. He was already jerking his dick slowly, his foreskin sliding up and down the taut shaft. "Can do, sport. Chin up, tongue out."

Tongue out?

Of course. Puck wanted him to taste his cum.

Didn't want him to take it on the face or swallow it, he wanted him to really *taste* it.

Austin stuck his tongue out. Shut his eyes.

"Ah, ah. Keep 'em open. Keep 'em on me."

He opened them again, turned them up so they were locked on Puck's face.

Puck was looking at him too. His hand on his dick squelched with Austin's drool, but turned to that familiar slapping sound as the spit dried. Austin couldn't see how fast he was going, how he was holding himself, whether his cock was pulsing and ready to blow. He was looking at Puck's face, Puck's fierce eyes. The line of tension in Puck's jaw, like he was either angry or concentrating really, really hard.

And then Puck's eyelids half closed, and his lips pulled back over his teeth, and Austin knew he was about to come.

It surprised the hell out of him when the first hot, white rope of it striped across the bridge of his nose. He recoiled, but didn't pull his tongue in, so the change in position meant the next shot hit his tongue and mouth. He didn't think about what to do next: he spat. Puck's cum was nasty, salty and bitter. It bubbled out of Austin's sealed lips and coated his chin as Puck got him one last time, on his cheek.

Puck grunted in satisfaction and leaned back. "Not bad for your first time, kiddo. We'll have to keep practicing. Teach you to keep your eyes on me and your mouth open. Hold position. *Mmmm.*" He pulled his sweatpants back over his dick and closed his eyes. Austin knelt there, panting and unsure of what to do next. Puck's cum was already going cold on his face, and he was pretty sure he'd gotten a bit of it on his eyelashes. After a couple of long, awkward minutes, Puck sat up again. *Now* he laughed. "You look like a cat somebody threw in a bathtub."

Austin narrowed his eyes. "Yeah, a bathtub full of cum."

They shuddered simultaneously as the mental image of that hit them both at the same time.

"All right, all right," Liam said, still laughing a little, and stood. Walked away, leaving Austin still kneeling like an asshole on the living room floor.

It seemed to be the right thing to do, though, because when Liam returned, hot washcloth in hand, and saw Austin still kneeling there, glazed with cooling cum, he got that soft-around-the-edges look again.

Austin blushed furiously. Yeah, maybe he could get used to a guy touching his asshole, but no way was he ever gonna get used to a guy looking at him like *that*.

Maybe noting Austin's distaste, Liam coughed, cleared his throat, and knelt, gently wiping the mess from Austin's nose and cheeks and chin.

"You have something to drink?" Austin asked, a little hesitantly, not sure if it would offend the guy.

"Sure, kiddo. Orange juice okay?"

"Beer?" Austin tried.

Liam laughed. "Yeah, there's some Granville Island Pale Ale in the fridge. What say you get dressed, and I'll open us up a couple bottles?"

Austin struggled to his feet, refusing Liam's hand up and was about to pull the crusty jockstrap off when Liam caught him by the wrist.

He wagged a finger. "You're wearing *that* home."

"You can't be fucking serious."

"Dead serious." Liam reached for the red-and-blue-striped elastic around Austin's hips and snapped it against his skin. "You wanna test me?"

Austin shook his head. As gross as it was, being forced to sit around in his own cum like the bitch he was kind of turned him on, anyway. But there was no way he was going to give in to that urge without at least a little bit of *token* resistance. If Liam ever figured out what an eager, depraved little fag he was, it would be game over. He'd be crawling around on all fours with a dog tail plugged into his ass or something. Or—God forbid—wearing lipstick.

By the time Austin had dressed, Liam had returned with their beers. They sat together on the couch and drank, like two normal dudes, except for the whole time, their respective inside knees stayed pressed together.

And once or twice, when Liam dropped his hand by his side, it landed on Austin's thigh, or—once, only—on top of Austin's hand.

After Canada's game-winning overtime goal, after Austin relived that electrifying stadium roar, it was finally time to go.

Liam walked him to the door. Waited while he put on his sneakers. And then, just before he was about to open the door, pushed him back against it. Austin thought—with stomach-dropping dread—that Liam was about to kiss him, but then he pushed their foreheads together instead, held Austin by the nape, and drew away again. "That was fun," he said, and then his soft smile turned into a stern line. "And you're officially forgiven for showing up here and scaring the shit out of my roommate. But from now on, you wait for *my* call."

Next time, Austin thought, bewildered, and practically fell out the door.

CHAPTER 18

Liam texted him nine days later. Austin knew that because he counted. He drew the line at marking off the days on the calendar, though.

Barely.

Nine days of watching more porn than ever. Nine days of finger-fucking himself, trying to re-create that moment on the floor of Liam's condo. Nine days of trying his hardest not to jerk off. Nine days of failing. Nine days of spilling his dirty secrets to Bobby, who he realized probably had enough collected dirt on his roommates by now to destroy each and every one of them. Nine days of Bobby not destroying anybody, except for the lobotomized reanimated dead on *Lobotomy Hospital* while Austin watched the game play with his hands over his eyes.

Nine days of practice and workouts with his teammates, who were finally adjusting to his alternate captain position and finally forgetting all about Drew, especially now that their game was shaping up to be ten times stronger. Nine days of almost no inappropriate boners when the trash-talking got personal.

And then the ninth day, and Austin was at Liam's place in his jockstrap again, ready for anything.

Which was good, because on the ninth day, Puck plugged him for the first time, his ass training begun in earnest.

Afterward, they had three beers each and watched a Canucks game from last year's Stanley Cup play-offs, but spent less time watching than they did shooting the shit about prospects for the upcoming season and arguing over the best and worst trades of the summer.

It was nice, Austin realized, to be able to talk about hockey with Liam. Not because he didn't have anybody else to talk about it with—because in Canada you were never far from someone willing to talk hockey, whether it was a bus driver or your TA or the server at any given restaurant, not to mention Austin's actual hockey *team*, who of course lived and breathed hockey. But it was nice to talk hockey with someone who also *knew* Austin, all of him, and in that aspect, Liam was one of a kind. His teammates could talk NHL until their faces turned blue, but the secret Austin was keeping made it sort of . . . hollow, in a way. Like in the back of his mind Austin knew that if they *really* knew him, knew what Liam knew, they wouldn't be willing to argue over who was this season's team to beat anymore. And Bobby, who *did* know him and still liked him, didn't know jack shit about hockey, other than the fact that when the Canucks lost the cup on home soil, Vancouverites had a bad habit of going completely apeshit.

And who wanted to talk about that?

So in a way, Liam became the fixed point in Austin's life: the tiny place where the disparate sides of him overlapped. And that place was warm, and safe, and good, and Austin looked forward to being there. Looked forward to every text, every dirty phone call, every time Liam showed up at Rear Entrance Video and he was on shift. Started looking forward to the aftercare in their evenings together as much as he looked forward to the play.

Which was saying quite a lot, actually, because he really, really, *really* looked forward to the play.

He licked Puck's black leather boots. Wore progressively bigger plugs. Had his balls bound off or stretched by thick silicone rings. Learned to deep-throat. Assumed the position. Got tied up and even suspended in the rigging at the Mischievous Pictures studio after hours. He begged, and sometimes he fought, but no matter what, Puck always won. And when Puck won, Austin did too. And though it still made him shudder, he learned to love being called fag and pussy and slut and bitch, which Puck used interchangeably with the kinder pet names: buddy and kiddo and little guy, affectionate but still deliciously humiliating in their own way. Through it all, Liam's steady voice cooed to him, praised him, helped him fly.

And afterward, he could always count on Liam for a warm blanket and a cold beer and a good old hockey game on the "telly."

June moved to July, and July to August. Austin's life was busy as hell, but he still found time to sit around waiting for Liam's next text or booty call. In between, Rear Entrance Video was Rear Entrance Video, now with the added stress and drama of an upcoming wedding. Living with his roommates was living with his roommates, now with the added happiness and security of calling those roommates friends. Austin's classes got harder, and his homework got more overwhelming, and his practices got more intense. His team evolved into a well-oiled machine, everybody working harder and harder as they came to realize they actually had a chance this year of making the University Cup play-offs. And while none of them were ass-kissy enough to say it aloud, Austin couldn't help but think that maybe his teammates had accepted that Austin had at least *something* to do with that.

Hard to believe Austin had started the summer lonely and demoralized on a fragmented, middling hockey team, no real friends to speak of, disliked by his roommates and a month away from being kicked out of his place and fired from his job.

Hard to believe, though, what could still be undone in a single day.

August 16th

On the last day of summer semester, Austin walked out of his last, three-hour kinesiology exam nauseated but relieved. For better or for worse, whether he got Bs or Cs or Ds on his transcript, he was glad to be done with his summer schoolwork so he could focus on hockey and the upcoming season. Maybe one day, he'd be in the NHL and his university grades wouldn't fucking matter. Maybe this was the season he'd get scouted and he wouldn't even have to *finish* university.

In the grand scheme of things, the academic side of his schooling was nothing but a distraction from what mattered: the game.

Luckily, not all distractions were as tedious and time-consuming as academic credit hours.

Case in point, the text from Liam burning a hole through his pocket, promising him a reward for finishing the semester.

Austin liked rewards. Bonuses at Rear Entrance Video, nights out for pizza after a good practice or exhibition match, achievements unlocked on Xbox. But he liked rewards from Liam most of all. Last time had been after he'd taken his biggest plug yet without whining or complaining, and Liam had tied him down to a bench and sucked him until he'd shot right down Liam's throat. Liam had swallowed and it had been the most mind-blowingly hot thing Austin had ever witnessed. Sure, people had swallowed his cum before, but never with such enthusiasm, and never within the confines of a relationship where, by rule, only Austin did the swallowing.

So yeah, he was looking forward to tonight. Looking forward to his reward, looking forward to forgetting about the stresses of the week and of the months to come, looking forward to curling up on Liam's couch and watching some classic hockey from Liam's massive collection of vintage games.

Austin hadn't known reruns of sports could be so enjoyable. Sure, he'd watched games multiple times, but that had been to study them, to analyze them, to figure out what went wrong and what went right and how to apply it to his own game and to his team's strategy. He'd never watched them for fun, because once you knew how it ended, where was the excitement?

The excitement, it turned out, wasn't as important when you had the comfort and familiarity and memories of a good game. And it especially wasn't as important when you were sharing all those things with Liam.

It was nearing five by the time Austin reached Davie Street, so he stopped by Liam's favourite sushi place to pick him up some dinner on his way. By the time he arrived at Liam's door, styrofoam containers in hand, buzzing with pleasure at being able to do this small thing for Liam, he'd completely stopped worrying about his test scores.

Liam opened the door with a smile that turned to a full-on grin when he saw what Austin was carrying.

"Is that food?" he asked, letting Austin in. "Did you *buy me dinner*?"

Austin hunched into his shoulders like a dog about to get a newspaper to the nose, uncomfortable with how big a deal Liam was making. "Uh, well, you know, it was getting on five, so I figured why not?"

Liam took the containers, giving his cheek a hard pinch. "That is adorable! So domestic!"

"Jeez, it's just takeout," Austin mumbled.

"I should make you scrub my floors naked next . . ." Liam continued, ignoring Austin's expressions of discomfort.

Which was okay, actually, because that last bit didn't make him uncomfortable at all. Perking up considerably, he followed Liam into his kitchen.

"Oh! Or maybe not," Liam said.

"Huh? Why?" Austin couldn't keep the puppy disappointment out of his voice.

Liam grinned, not at Austin, but at the opened styrofoam container on the kitchen counter in front of him. "Because I just got a better idea. Hope all that hockey means you've got a high tolerance for cold."

Liam refused to explain what he meant by that. He shoved Austin into his small bathroom, watched him strip, then ordered him immediately into the shower.

"Do I stink that bad?" Austin complained, stumbling into the tub nonetheless.

"Shhh. No talking unless it's to safeword, got me? Get nice and clean, then towel off and meet me back in the dining room. *Don't* dawdle."

Whatever Liam had planned, he had Austin's attention now. But then, he usually did when he specifically brought up Austin's safeword, because it meant whatever he was about to do was going to test Austin's limits somehow.

Austin liked that.

Feeling twin prickles of nervousness and eagerness, he moved to turn on the shower taps.

"Oh," Liam said. "Let me handle that."

He reached in through the shower curtain and yanked the cold tap to full blast.

Only the cold tap.

Austin yelped and scrambled for the far shower wall, trying to avoid the ice-cold shower stream.

"None of that," Liam snapped in a tone that left no room for argument. "Come on, you can take it. Can't you?"

Austin hugged himself, covered in goose bumps and dripping frigid water. He could take it, damn it. It suddenly became crystal-clear why Liam had brought up the hockey/cold-tolerance connection. There was no way Austin could allow himself not to meet this challenge.

With a shudder, he stepped under the stream again.

Liam peeked around the edge of the curtain and gave Austin a mean-but-nonetheless-pleased smile. "That's my boy. I'm gonna get things ready outside for you now. You make sure to give yourself a good scrub. Don't be shy of the cold water. I'm sure it sucks, but you're not gonna get hypothermia or anything either. And the longer you can take being in there, the happier you'll make me, huh?" He reached into the shower and gave one of Austin's hard nipples a possessive little pinch.

Touching Austin like Austin was *his*. Yes, Austin would definitely pass this particular test. To make Liam happy? To solidify Liam's claim on him? He would.

He did.

After Liam left the room, Austin forced himself to stand directly under the frigid spray, ignoring the way it shrunk his dick and made his whole body shudder and ache. He just had to do it. Just do it. Teeth chattering, he soaped himself off, washed every inch of himself. Paid particular attention to his pits and his dick and balls and his ass, like he always did for Liam.

Motivated by thoughts of pleasing Liam, he was able to stand the cold water a lot longer than he'd have thought. And then, when he thought he couldn't take anymore, he forced himself to endure a minute more.

Shivering, skin simultaneously stinging on the surface and aching deep down, he finally got out of the shower. Towelled off briskly. Didn't bother wrapping the towel around his waist, because he knew Liam wouldn't want him hiding how shrunken his dick was. This was what Liam wanted. Austin accepted it. That was all he had to do, accept it all.

He was still shivering and covered in goose bumps, hair half-dry, when he met Liam in the dining room.

"Gorgeous," Liam said, when he looked up from the table and saw Austin standing there. "C'mere."

Austin went.

Liam's hands cupped his shoulders, then immediately flinched back. "Damn, you are freezing. Good. That's good. Very good, buddy."

His words almost warmed Austin, until he realized Liam obviously wanted him cold.

"Arms up," Liam directed. Austin didn't think, didn't question, just raised his arms above his head. His icy-cold skin ached.

Liam turned around and picked up something off the table. A roll of see-through cling wrap?

Austin must have made a questioning look, because Liam smiled that smug fucking smile of his, the smile he got when he was impressed by his own cleverness. The guy sure did have a fucking ego on him. He was lucky he mostly earned it. "Gotta be food safe, right?" he asked Austin, and began to wrap the cling wrap around his torso. Around and around and around, tighter and tighter, layer after layer, from his nipples right down to his pathetic dick. Austin stood completely still, allowing himself to be captured, to have all that plastic slowly tighten around his body.

At last, Liam reached the end of the roll. He tossed the paper tube over his shoulder. "Up on the table now, kiddo. Need help?"

"Fuck no," Austin snapped, although he did. The cold shower had made his body sluggish and stiff, and the cling wrap—even wrapped as it was just around his torso—made movement difficult.

Together, though, they got him up onto the table on his back. Liam pushed Austin's arms and legs spread eagle. Tied off his wrists and ankles to the four legs of the table with lengths of smooth rope.

Normally after he tied Austin up, he liked to stand back with his hand on his chin, admiring his own work like you always saw artists do in cartoons, but today he moved economically, single-mindedly. "Time is of the essence," he explained as he bustled around the room. "Take this." He pressed a cloth napkin from his cupboard into Austin's hand. "I think I'm gonna be keeping your mouth busy, so you drop that if you need to safeword, okay?"

Austin mutely nodded, mentally preparing himself for the sensation of being gagged. It was the one thing he hadn't quite gotten used to, having his mouth taken over and used and silenced. It was almost *more* intimate than anything Liam had ever done to his dick or ass. And Austin didn't think he was that big of a talker.

Liam didn't gag him, though. Not with the ring gag or the ball gag, not with his own socks or underwear—which Austin loved best of all—not with tape or a handkerchief. Instead, he took a small round dish and had Austin balance it on his puckered lips.

"I've always wanted to do this," he said, and that was when Austin felt the first cool, soft piece of sashimi come to rest on his plastic-wrapped abdomen. "Ever since I saw it in some shitty old yakuza movie, and you bringing me sushi tonight reminded me of it. Human furniture Japanese-style, except I think more people in Vegas do it now than anyone *ever* did in Japan. I could never ethically justify going to a restaurant that serves sushi this way, though. But with a sub, knowing he's consenting? Knowing I'll take care of him after?" He cast Austin a reassuring smile as he continued to lay out the pieces of sashimi in orderly lines on either side of Austin's torso "Not to mention knowing he's clean and well wrapped with a month's worth of cling wrap?"

At last, he poured a splash of soy sauce into the dish Austin still had on his lips.

Now he stepped back.

"Gorgeous," he breathed, again. "Can I take a picture? I won't share it anywhere—" He flashed Austin a rakish smile. "Unless you want me to, that is. Blink once for yes and twice for no."

Austin, drunk on Liam's loving expression and unabashedly eager voice, gave him one solemn blink. He kinda wanted to see this for himself, too. He could always ask Liam to delete the picture after, once he came down from this frigid-cold high.

He closed his eyes, breathing slow and deep through his nose. He heard the artificial camera shutter sound from Liam's phone, then the sound of a scraping chair.

The cling wrap made it a little hard for Austin to really breathe. The stuff was thin in one layer, but in the multiple layers Liam had used, it slightly limited the movement of his ribcage. It felt like a tight, firm hug. Consistent. Safe.

Liam rubbed his bare upper thigh with a warm palm as he ate, delicately picking up one piece of sashimi in his chopsticks at a time. He dipped them in the soy sauce. Continued touching Austin absently as he ate.

Most of all, he took his time. He didn't talk to Austin, didn't look him in the eye, just treated him as the human plate he was.

Gradually—very, very gradually—Austin began to warm. With it, his dick tried its damnedest to get hard. The cling wrap kept it pinned down in position. Liam had laid his serving of pickled pink ginger right over the head.

When he'd finished everything else—absolutely every slice of fish from Austin's prone body—he finally went for the ginger. The tips of his chopsticks pinched Austin's swollen dick through the plastic. Liam didn't react to any of it. He ate his ginger with slow, lizard-like satisfaction, then leaned back in his chair with a sigh.

Austin didn't move. Couldn't move, but didn't want to. Liam wasn't acknowledging him now. He wasn't important. His purpose wasn't to demand attention or affection, it was to be still and quiet and wait.

It felt like hours, although it was probably more like the ten minutes it typically took Liam for his stomach to settle after a meal. At least he wasn't a stickler for the half-hour rule, because then the wait might have felt like days.

Somehow in the process of warming up from the cold shower and cold fish laid out all over him, his body actually felt the remaining cold more keenly. He couldn't help it—he moaned miserably around the heavy porcelain dish that weighed on his lips and twisted in his bonds.

Liam didn't jump up to free him; he still had the handkerchief safely clutched in his hand.

But he did run a slow, absent hand up Austin's inner thigh, slipping into the triangle made by the cling wrap and Austin's legs. "Shh," he said softly. "Shh. It's okay, buddy. You're doing good."

That praise, so genuine, so freely given, so completely fucking commonplace and subtly stated, rocked Austin back into a safe, patient lull. He stayed there, silent and still and accepting, until Liam got up and finally took the dish of soy sauce from his mouth.

It was a little hard to move his lips, thanks to the combination of the cold and having held that position so long. He flexed them wordlessly, trying to soften them.

And Liam . . . Liam stared. Stared at Austin gaping like a fish, his expression soft, but other than that unreadable.

Then he gave his head a shake and moved to untie Austin's wrists and ankles.

Didn't do Austin much good, though. He was way too stiff to *consider* closing his legs or lowering his arms. Liam gave him a cautious look, eyes on his mouth, eyes on the handkerchief, waiting for a signal that wasn't coming. At last, he got a pair of scissors and cut Austin free.

Of the cling wrap, at least.

In all other respects, he'd cut Austin free already.

CHAPTER 19

ustin was way too big for even a guy the size of Liam to carry, but Liam sure did try his hardest. He got Austin off the table, got him mostly upright, threw one of Austin's arms around his big shoulders, wrapped his own arm around Austin's naked, chilly waist, and together they hobbled down the hall.

Not to the living room. Not to the couch, with the fuzzy Canucks blanket. Not to the TV with its vintage games.

To Liam's bedroom.

Austin was too woozy to really grasp how big a deal this was, to finally see the inside of Liam's personal space for the first time.

It wasn't all that interesting of a room, anyway. It was dark without the full-length windows, and small, most of its square footage taken up by a massive unmade bed, which Liam helped Austin into.

"There you go, kiddo," he murmured in that gentle voice he always used when the games were through. Austin curled up on his side and hugged himself, gritting his teeth to keep them from chattering. Strange how the further away in time he got from that ice-cold shower, the more frigid he felt. He drew his knees up to his chest and tucked his head. It didn't help that he always felt cold and shaky after coming down from the soaring highs Liam brought him to.

Think warm. Think warm. Think warm.

Which turned out to be easier than might be expected, because the mattress creaked and then Liam was curled up naked behind him, spooning his body.

They must have looked ridiculous, two buff, manly guys snuggled up like a needy couple.

And Austin playing the girl, of course.

Fuck it, he didn't care, not when Liam's body was radiating waves of musky heat, not when Liam was pulling his heavy duvet over them both. Austin pressed back, seeking that heat, and ignored the way their bodies fit together.

Liam gathered him in close.

Wrapped a big arm around Austin's shoulders. Toyed with the hair at Austin's nape with his other hand.

Austin didn't fight any of it. He'd given up fighting. He didn't see the point anymore, not when not fighting felt so damn good. If that was taking the pussy's way out, then fine, Austin was a pussy. He and Bobby could become a two-man army of pussies.

Liam made him feel good. Made him feel safe and wanted. Wanted him for him, all of him, flaws and all. Hockey player and cocksucker together.

The longer he lay there, though, and the warmer he got, he realized he must have taken this session hard for Liam to have brought him back here instead of their usual routine on the couch. Liam had been rough with Austin so many times in this apartment, had pushed Austin to the brink over and over, but it had never been anything that couldn't be salved by some time on the couch together. To be brought to the bed . . . It was abnormal. It was too much.

Austin squirmed in Liam's arms. "I'm okay now," he said, keeping his voice light to prove he really, really was.

"Mmm," Liam replied.

Was that a *yes*? A *no*? A *yeah right, kid*?

Of course Austin's brain went to the most offensive option. He twisted in Liam's arms to face him. "Seriously, I mean it!"

Liam looked like he was in pain. His jaw was tense, and his eyes were narrowed in a flinch. "That's the thing," he said, voice strained. "I know you are. It's me who's not."

Liam? All-knowing, all-powerful Liam? Always prepared, always in control Liam? *Liam* wasn't okay?

But though Austin couldn't logically believe it, his heart still squeezed. Looking at Liam, seeing that expression, hurt. He wanted to make it better, but not in that urge-to-serve way that might have him ducking under the covers to suck the guy's dick. This was something else, something not sexual at all, a purely emotional feeling. He didn't want Liam to hurt. He cared too much to see him like this. And that thought was fucking terrifying. He couldn't bring himself to tear out of Liam's arms, though, not when Liam seemed so vulnerable. "I don't understand," he said instead.

"I know you don't, buddy. You can't. That's okay."

Except it wasn't fucking okay. Austin didn't really want it to be okay. Not as much as he wanted to understand Liam. Wanted to *know* Liam.

Liam heaved a sigh. "It was just . . . You looked so beautiful tonight. You've changed so much in the last couple months. Just— God, the way you *give* yourself to me now." With Liam staring into his eyes like that, Austin couldn't possibly summon up those old feelings of shame and disgust at being called a girl word like beautiful. Liam could call him whatever he liked, if he was gonna look at him like that. "But the problem is, I want to *take* more. More, and more, and more."

Austin furrowed his brow in confusion. "So . . . take it? Aren't you the Dom here? Aren't you in charge?" The thought that Liam might answer *no* to any of those questions filled Austin with a quick, powerful surge of panic, which quickly transformed itself into anger. "If you want something, take it!" he shouted, and gave both of Liam's shoulders a hard shove.

Liam's hands shot up to clamp Austin's wrists. Austin couldn't help it; he yelped. "What kind of man do you think I am, Austin? An animal? A rapist, taking things from you that you don't want to give?" Finally he must have noticed his vice grip on Austin, because he made a disgusted face and threw Austin's arms down. "I *am* the Dom here. I *am* in charge," he insisted, but then all the anger left his voice. "And being in charge means controlling myself—my own urges—too. Maybe more so than I ever try to control you." He petted Austin's hair. Leaned in to press their foreheads together briefly, the way he always did when he was overcome with one of those emotions he refused to tell Austin about.

But Austin wasn't accepting that self-sacrificing bullshit speech, not now, not even if it kind of made him feel all squishy inside to know Liam cared about him and respected him that much. "And what if I want to give them to you, huh? Did you ever think to ask? You just assume I'm gonna say no?"

"You said you were straight," Liam said softly, regretfully. "That usually comes with certain limits, and I respect that."

"Yeah, yeah, yeah. You never take your dick out with straight guys, right? I thought we kinda crossed the bridge when I got on my knees and sucked you off."

Liam didn't reply to Austin right away, and that was when it dawned on him.

Yes, Austin had given Liam a blowjob. Plenty of times, now. And he liked it. Liked the way it made him shudder with equal parts pleasure and revulsion. Liked how submissive it made him feel, how owned and controlled and converted. Liked that when the tears fell, he could blame it on all the choking and gagging he was doing.

So yeah, they'd definitely crossed that bridge . . . but Austin had been the one to take the first step, hadn't he? That night on the couch, that was all Austin. Liam had straight-up said it: *You needed to ask for it.* And Austin had.

They'd crossed *that* bridge, but there was still another one, wasn't there? Something Austin *hadn't* given to Liam yet. Something Austin *hadn't* asked for.

Liam had brought him here to his bed. Naked. Spooned around him from behind.

All of that, and Austin hadn't thought to ask. Not until now.

"Fuck me. Please." Austin's face burned. "That's what you want to take from me, right? You want to claim my ass?"

That was when he felt it: Liam's erection lengthening against his hip. Liam's silent reply.

Yes. I want that.

Austin puffed up his chest, bolstered. "You can do me raw, if you want. I get tested as a part of the team health exams. And you get tested to do your videos, right?"

Liam nodded mutely.

"So go ahead and take what you want from me, Coach. Come inside me. B-breed me." Austin licked his lips, then rolled to one side, onto his back. His legs fell open. "Please. I need it. Please."

Those were the magic words. Not *please*—please was easy if you didn't think too hard, anybody could say please—but *I need it.* Liam loved giving Austin what he needed. Loved hearing Austin admit to what he needed. After fighting so hard and so long, to just come right out and say it—but only for Liam—must have driven him crazy with power.

"*What* do you need?" Liam growled, and suddenly he was on top of Austin, pinning his hands to the bed, straddling Austin's hips with his big monster of a dick trailing streaks of pre-cum over Austin's abs.

"I need you to fuck me," Austin replied, and it was so easy to say, so, so easy. To give this thing he'd been holding back, to let go of the final line he'd drawn around himself, the final fence he'd built between gay and straight.

With Liam.

For Liam.

Liam put extra weight on Austin's pinned wrists. "And what else?"

"Come inside me."

"Nngh. No. The other one."

Austin's stomach dropped, his fingers flexing in abortive fight-or-flight, but he said it again. "Breed me."

"That's right, buddy. And *where* do I breed you?"

No question where this was leading. Liam lowered himself, nipping a trail down Austin's neck to his shoulder. The pleasure of that was enough to distract Austin from the humiliating words his mouth was forming: "Breed me in my boypussy."

"Mmmm." Liam lapped at Austin's skin with the flat of his tongue, wetting him from collarbone to jaw. The sensation—the wetness of it—made him shudder. "Love making you say dirty things like that, kiddo. Love the way you blush and look so ashamed, but you do it anyway. Love that it gives you a little boner." His hand closed—hard—around Austin's dick.

Austin bucked into Liam's palm, gritting his teeth. "Come on, man. I know you like cutting me down, but there's nothing little about *this*." It was true. Austin had done his fair share of covert comparing in locker rooms, and he knew he wasn't remotely bad off in that department.

"I could make it little, if I wanted," Liam threatened with a show of teeth.

As far as threats went, it didn't make much sense, but Austin still shivered with want. He wanted to be reduced to nothing, brought down, made to beg and scrape and crawl. He'd wear a leash. He'd let Liam write SLUT on his skin in permanent marker. Whatever. He didn't care. "Please," he begged, again, not sure what he was begging *for*.

"You really want it, huh?" Liam teased, slowly jerking Austin's dick. "Really want my big cock inside you raw?"

Austin shut his eyes. "Yes, fuck. Yes." He squirmed beneath Liam's weight, trying to fuck into his hand.

"Prove it." Liam lifted himself off Austin completely, let go of his dick, let the cold air in the room hit him. He sat up on his knees, and when Austin opened his eyes again, Liam was looming over him in the darkness, watching him pant and twist in confusion for a minute before leaning forward to pick up something off the shelf built into his headboard. He put the bottle into Austin's hand, closed Austin's fingers around it. Austin recognized it by feel: lube. "Go on, fuck that boypussy with your fingers for me, show me how much you want my dick in there instead. Do it well enough and maybe I might be good to you, all right?"

Austin nodded feverishly, popping the cap on the lube and letting it drizzle over his fingers. He'd seen Liam do this enough times by now, he knew what to do.

Didn't stop his hands from shaking, though.

At least Liam liked that, seeing his fear and shame and desperate need to please. It was all there for him, laid bare in the way Austin trembled, the way he so slowly reached between his legs and petted his hole, afraid to penetrate himself.

But wanting it.

So, so badly.

So he fingered himself. Pushed past the pain, past the tightness, past all the defences of his uncooperative muscles. Fucked his own ass with two fingers like he'd been told to. He stretched himself the same way Liam sometimes did to prepare him for a plug, or to tease him into begging to be milked. Tried to look in Liam's eyes the whole time he did it, tried to make it good for him even if his face burned and his heart and lungs felt like somebody had dropped a fridge on his chest.

The whole time, Liam seemed . . . different. He didn't have that same patient hunger in his expression. Didn't seem to get that same lazy satisfaction out of just watching Austin. In fact, he looked almost *im*patient. Or was that desperation? Because now he was grabbing Austin roughly by the wrist and yanking Austin's fingers out of his hole. "All right, buddy, I think that's enough of that. Points for slutty enthusiasm, but we don't want you getting *too* loose for me now, do we?" The words themselves were the usual disaffected smugness, but Liam's tone was anything but. He sounded breathy. A little shaken.

Austin reached up and cupped his cheek, solemnly shaking his head and never breaking eye contact the entire time.

Liam winced. "God," he rasped, and fell forward on top of Austin's body. Pressed his face to Austin's neck, hot steamy breath damp on Austin's skin. "Austin— Buddy—"

Austin didn't know what was happening now, didn't know what was going through Liam's mind, but fuck, he liked it, was driven to go along with it even if it scared him on one level, too. And fuck, Liam was thrusting against him, their cocks nudging together then glancing off each other clumsily. Liam was out of control. Out. Of. Control. That was what this was—what it meant. Liam was always in control, was always strict and authoritative and distant, and now he wasn't anymore. He was losing it. Shuddering himself to pieces. Baring himself to Austin in a way he'd never done before.

Because of Austin.

Because of *Austin*.

Austin moaned and arched, lifting both legs and wrapping them around Liam's hips like the whore he was.

Liam didn't make him beg. Not this time.

As soon as Austin's ankles hooked together in the small of Liam's back, he felt the bump and nudge of Liam's cockhead as it notched against his slippery hole. "Gonna take you nice and slow, buddy," he said, and it was simultaneously a promise and a threat; yes, Liam would be gentle and careful, but he was still claiming what was his. Thinking of it that way did something to Austin, something he couldn't name or explain. He felt emotionally touched and physically *consumed*, and it was powerful, so powerful, so close to something beyond any of this, maybe even on the edge of love.

Ownership. That was what it was. Not love, of course not love. But he knew the minute he felt the unbearable pressure, knew the minute

Liam shushed his pained cry and kept on pushing, tearing into him and claiming him with every joined inch.

Liam owned him.

The thought of it made him fly, made him open up, made him so pliable and receptive, and every inch he gave of himself, Liam took, until Austin was bathed in sweat at the pure exertion of it all.

He felt so full. Felt like there wasn't a single part of him, now, that Liam hadn't claimed. Filled and surrounded at the same time. Liam was all around him. Felt like he was in the air Austin *breathed*. Felt like without him, he couldn't breathe again.

He clung to Liam's back. Rolled his hips up, taking another inch.

This time, Liam was the one who cried out. A broken, masculine sound that felt like a fist to Austin's heart.

A fist that *squeezed*, wringing a single word out of Austin's deepest, darkest, most secret places: "Master."

Liam froze. Lifted himself up on his arms, their sticky chests breaking free from one another. He stared down into Austin's face, demanded, "What did you just say?"

Austin flinched back against the mattress, face flushing. "I—"

That was when it happened. Liam's lips parted, and his eyes went all heavy-lidded, and he leaned down, and despite his pinned wrists Austin still arched up and—

Turned his head.

The kiss died before it had a chance to live. Austin had killed it, and he'd never felt so relieved and gutted at the same time. No time to consider the feeling, though, because suddenly Liam's rough hand had caught him by the hinge of his jaw, turning and posing his head so that he faced Liam again, mouth pinched cruelly open.

He was too stunned to close his eyes, which meant he saw the ugly, raw fury in Liam's—no, *Puck's* eyes when he drew his head back and spat down into Austin's mouth.

Austin spluttered and gagged, his whole body flexing and clenching in sheer revulsion. This wasn't good humiliation, wasn't the kind of casual cruelty that made him fly.

It made him feel like shit.

"Luongo," he begged, trying to push Liam off him, *needing* Liam off of him *right the fuck now*, and at least, for as angry and animalistic as Liam seemed, that word still held power.

A horrified expression overtook Liam's features, and he wrenched back, cock ripping free of Austin's convulsing body. Pulled away from Austin all together. Tripped out of bed and stumbled backward to his bedroom door. "I'm so sorry," he choked out, turned the knob behind himself, and fell into the hallway.

The door slammed closed behind him, and Austin was alone.

CHAPTER 20

When Austin finally managed to stop shaking long enough to get out of bed, Liam still hadn't returned. The bedroom door was still closed, the condo quiet. Austin couldn't stay in here forever, though. Didn't want to, really. The bed reeked of sex, and Austin didn't see himself staying the night, not after how fucking disastrously things had gone.

If this had been Austin and a girl, if a girl had told him no, effectively kicking him out of his own bed? He'd expect her to get the fuck out and make her own way home.

Well, Austin wasn't about to act like he had less balls than a fucking puck bunny. He squared his shoulders and strode for Liam's bedroom door. Yanked it open like he fucking owned it.

And found a neat, folded pile of his clothes on the hallway floor at his feet.

He nearly fell over in relief. He hadn't realized, before now, how humiliating in a bad way it would have been to slink nude into Liam's front hall to retrieve his clothes, then silently and shamefully get dressed before slipping out the door.

At least this way, he didn't have to do the walk of shame *naked*.

He wasn't about to fucking thank Liam for that, though, he decided as he yanked his clothes back on. Felt absurd to be getting dressed at all, honestly, like a different person had taken the clothes off in the first place, so why should Austin be putting them back on now?

Well, like it or not, he fucking was. This was all him. Nobody else to blame. Not possession, not sleepwalking, not Liam.

Time to get this over with. He stormed out of Liam's room, down the hallway, and into the living room, where he found . . .

Lalita, sitting on the couch in a modest sweater dress and knee-high boots. She looked up from her smartphone and gave Austin a tight, apologetic smile. "Liam said you needed a ride home," she said. She didn't ask him why. Nothing in her tone suggested she knew, but then, maybe she was being discreet.

Probably a good skill for a dominatrix to have.

"No, thanks," Austin said, and jabbed a thumb over his shoulder. "I can grab a bus."

"Don't be ridiculous," she snapped without venom. "I know I can't force you to do anything, but come on, now. It's a free ride. Hell, I'll throw in a cup of coffee from Starbucks to sweeten the deal."

Austin's shoulders slumped in defeat. He really didn't feel like standing out in the cold night air waiting for a bus, not after everything that had gone down. What if it was raining? He already felt like shit. He wanted to get home and crawl into bed.

"If it helps, you can think of it as a favour from his jilted ex instead of one from the man himself?" Now she had a mischievous smile, and Austin couldn't help smiling back.

Even if the expression combined with his mindset made him feel a little unhinged. "Fuck it, fine. Not like this night isn't crazy enough."

"Good boy," she said, and rose gracefully from her seat on the couch.

Liam didn't come out to say good-bye, not that Austin expected him to. He and Lalita left the apartment, locked up, and headed for the elevator. They spent the ride down to the parking garage in silence.

They were silent when they got into Lalita's older model BMW.

They were silent when they drove out into the rainy, glistening Vancouver night.

Silent as they stood in Starbucks lineup.

"Want anything?" Lalita asked after she'd ordered her black Americano.

Austin shook his head.

He thought they'd pass the rest of the drive like that, with Lalita sipping her coffee and Austin staring sullenly at his reflection in the passenger-side window, but a few minutes later, their bubble of silence burst.

"I'm going to come right out and say it," Lalita said, her voice clipped. And when Austin looked over, she didn't look harried at all. She kept her eyes on the road, executing a smooth turn. "Liam asked me to drive you home tonight. He wanted to make sure you got taken care of. Can't say I'm too fond of taking over someone else's aftercare duties, but I'm not about to leave you out on the line, either. The bastard probably knows that, too." She clucked in disapproval. "He told me to tell you he's sorry for losing his temper with you, too, and that he's sorry for not driving you home himself, but he thought you'd like a little space."

Space, was it? Did Liam think Austin was some kind of moody teenager? Or the kind of guy who couldn't handle the humiliation of sex going sideways?

Lalita made eye contact with him in the window's reflection. They were stopped at a red light. She had a ruthless look about her, pitying and half-angry like Austin imagined a big sister would look. "Between you and me," she said, "I think he's a fucking coward."

Austin let out a single, bitter "Ha." Not exactly a laugh; he hoped Lalita wasn't expecting one.

"I suppose I don't need to tell you he doesn't want to—how do I put this delicately—see you in this capacity anymore?"

Now Austin *did* laugh, a raw sound that felt in his chest like it was a coin's toss away from crying. "He got one of his girlfriends to break up with me for him? Shit, is this junior high?" And Austin had been worried that Liam thought of *him* as an immature teenager? "What the fuck? I mean—" Okay, that choked feeling in his throat was definitely the beginning of tears. "I mean what the fuck, right? What the fuck? So he lives with you—his ex—but he can't break it off with his—his—his regular fucking booty call—" Austin was too upset to feel humiliated to name it that way, to acknowledge that's what he was to Liam. "—can't break it off with *me* like a fucking man?"

Lalita pursed her lips. "It's different, with me and him. We were one another's first loves, I think, but as intensely as we felt for one another, we were only ever meant to be friends. Sometimes you mistake the nature of a relationship. What's between the two of you is as strong as you think, but in a different way from what you believe."

Austin had no idea what any of that meant, other than that Lalita and Liam had to be some pretty fucking good friends to be doing porn with each other. "Shit," he said, and laughed raggedly. He dropped his head into his hands. "Shit. So what does all that mean for *me*? What the fuck do I *do*?"

Lalita didn't answer—just continued to focus on her driving. She flicked her turn signal on, made a sharp right, and before Austin knew it, they were outside of his house. Liam must have given her the address—not that Liam had ever been here either.

No point thinking about it, really.

At least the lights were off. He didn't want to face Bobby now.

Sure, he'd have to talk to the guy eventually, but . . . not now.

He didn't think Lalita had anything more to say to him, but right as he was about to open his door, she spoke up one last time. "You want my advice, little one?" She flashed him a smile that was at once motherly and intensely sexual. Austin's whole body prickled looking at her. It was like a static shock. Friction between two incompatible forces, sending off sparks. He wasn't sure if it was a good feeling, or a bad one. "You and Liam had an intense connection, just like he and I do. And just like he and I, it didn't take the form you initially thought it took. You want someone to dominate you? Find someone to dominate you." She shrugged. He had the absurd thought that if he propositioned her now, asked her to take on that role, then she would say yes.

Not absurd at all, really, not with the way she was looking at him, her eyes wide and dark and full of possibilities, a whole universe waiting to be explored.

Her dark eyes daring him: *"Find someone to dominate you."*

He licked his lips and opened his mouth.

But that was who Liam was supposed to be.

And now I don't want anybody else.

He closed it again without saying a word.

At least Liam had picked the ideal time of year to dump Austin's ass. If ever he needed a distraction or something to keep his body busy or to make himself hurt, there was always hockey.

Workouts. Drills. Practices. Training camp with his team. Preseason exhibition matches. Analyzing and planning strategy. Watching footage of rival teams' games. More drills.

Hell, as August became September, even if he and Liam had still been seeing each other, Austin wouldn't have had time for the guy anyway.

Okay, that was a lie. For Liam, Austin would have *made* time. Somehow. Now, summoning up the energy to *use* that time together would have been an entire other issue . . .

What did it matter, though? It was all a daydream, because Liam hadn't called, and wasn't going to call, and the sooner Austin got his mind off the asshole, the better.

So Austin played hockey.

Week of September 1ˢᵗ
(Five weeks to the start of the regular season)

Their crop of first years arrived with the usual small town egos. Not much talent to go around, but plenty of attitude. Ronny Hanson from Prince fucking George up north thought he was God's gift to hockey. Maybe he was in Prince George, but here he wasn't exactly hot shit. More like lukewarm shit. And he didn't like hearing it, either. Like it or not, though, he wasn't good enough to be their team's star anything. He'd likely spend this season on the bench. Maybe after a hard summer spent training next year, he'd be ready for minimal ice time. For now, though, he was just some asshole eighteen-year-old kid calling Austin a faggot for supporting Warren's decision to put him on the bench.

It wasn't until after practice that day that Austin realized it: Ronny Hanson calling him a faggot hadn't given him a boner. It had made him fucking mad that the kid could be so fucking disrespectful, and determined to straighten his ass out before he took his bullshit onto the ice.

Week of September 8th
(Four weeks to the start of the regular season)

Austin wasn't sure how long he'd been cured. Thinking back, he couldn't remember the last time trash-talking had gotten him horny. Now that he was paying attention, though, he made it a whole week without a single incident. That was eleven *pussy*s and four *fag*s and even a couple *you skate like a girl*s. Not to mention Ronny Hanson telling him to go suck off Johnny Weir when they did some figure skating–inspired exercises on the ice.

He'd never been so happy to return a DVD in his life as he was to take back his pilfered collection of Rear Entrance Video discs. Good-bye emaciated Eastern European twinks. Good-bye buff muscle studs grunting and fucking in a tastefully decorated fake living room. Good-bye glory hole videos. Good-bye black guys still wearing their sneakers. Good-bye "artsy" compilation of tattooed guys sucking each other off in abandoned buildings. Good-bye football team gang bang. Good-bye STRAIGHT SUB SETUP.

He deleted the stash on his computer, too. Cleared his browser history, so he wouldn't be tempted to revisit any of the gay porn sites lurking there. That Friday, he went to a party up on campus and found a cute girl with wavy brown hair and very short shorts.

He leaned over the back of her chair, resting his elbow on her small shoulder. "I'm on the hockey team," he said.

"I know," she replied, not looking at him. "We slept together, remember?"

Well, no, but . . . "Cool. That means we can skip the bullshit, then. Wanna go for seconds?"

She cast a bored look around the party. "No, but this party fucking sucks, so you can eat me out. Take it or leave it."

Her disaffected tone kind of turned Austin on, so he took her by the hand, she led him back to her dorm room, and he ate her pussy until she fell asleep. It was as good as it had ever been, and in the middle of the night she rolled over and gave him a half-awake handjob.

Cured.

Week of September 15th
(Three weeks to the start of the regular season)

Austin got home from practice still keyed up, wanting to get the excess energy out. He thought of killing some pedestrians on *Grand Theft Auto*, briefly considered lifting weights in his room alone, but in the end, he saw Max in the hall with his running shoes on and his earbud cord hanging over the back of his neck.

"Hey," he called. "Going for a run?"

Max stared down at his getup, giving Austin an incredulous look. "Uh, yeah? I mean, I'm not going to the Commodore Ballroom like this." He laughed.

"Good, good. Can I come? Can you wait for me to throw on a hoodie and my sneakers?"

That surprised Max, but when he shook off the shock, he smiled. "Sure, man. Don't make me wait too long though."

Austin didn't. He trotted to his room, quickly changed into a pair of shorts and a sweatshirt, and threw on his running shoes.

He and Max didn't talk, but they did jog side by side, matching one another's pace on Max's usual route through their neighbourhood.

When they got back, Austin was sweating and panting and in desperate need of a shower, but he hadn't puked.

"That was fun," Max said when they parted, and it was only then that Austin realized Max's hand was on the knob to the bathroom door. First dibs on the shower, damn. "We should do it again."

Austin didn't take his eyes off that doorknob. "Yeah, sure, but next time I get first shower."

"I got a guy to fuck right after this. Can you say the same?"

Austin grunted. Didn't reply.

"That's what I thought. *I* get first shower."

It didn't hurt as much as he'd thought, though. Thinking about it. Having it pointed out. In fact, it hurt so little, he called out, "Hey, Bobby, you wanna fuck?"

He and Max both laughed.

Max still got the shower first, though.

Week of September 22ⁿᵈ
(Two weeks to the start of the regular season)

Practice. Class. Work. Tuxedo fitting. Practice. Running with Max. Video games with Bobby.

Austin was alone so rarely, and *bored* so rarely, that when it finally happened, it completely threw him off.

He had to assume that was why he randomly found himself on the Mischievous Pictures website, looking at the teaser clips for their latest STRAIGHT SUB SETUP DVD, coming out next month.

There was Liam in his Puck getup, jacking off a blindfolded sub who was tied to a table and *blubbering* as Liam casually (borderline bored, really) edged him over and over again. Austin wondered if this sub was the guy who'd failed to show up that day. Had he rescheduled? Or was this a different guy, someone who'd been waiting in the wings for his chance?

It didn't feel good, watching this. Not the way it used to feel, and that goodness had been a very complicated thing.

This was straight-up bad.

Austin couldn't blame it on jealousy. He'd never had—or wanted, honestly—any kind of claim on Liam. He didn't mind seeing Liam with other guys. Kind of thought it was right, in a way, that monogamy was a rule pathetic slavering little fags like Austin would have to follow while masters like Liam did as they pleased. That was Liam's right.

In fact, it kind of got Austin hot to think about being forced to watch as Liam used other men, telling him he wasn't as good the entire time. That he wasn't worth being faithful to. That he could never hope to satisfy a guy like Liam and he'd just have to put up with the fact that Liam sought satisfaction elsewhere.

Austin had a boner, now, so he *definitely* wasn't jealous.

But fuck, he was sad.

No wonder he was sad. He was sitting here getting hard to his ex-Dom's porn, thinking about his ex-Dom forcing him to watch while he fucked other—better looking, smarter, less sexually confused—guys. Or hell, Lalita. Maybe they still fucked sometimes. It seemed like the kind of friendship where they could.

Even if they didn't, shit, he was still below Lalita on the ladder, wasn't he? At least Liam had broken it off with her mutually, not fucking kicked her out of his place and never talked to her again. He'd stayed friends with her. She was obviously worth the effort.

And Austin? He wasn't worth any-fucking-thing.

How could he be worth anything, sitting here watching minute-long clips of Liam fucking other men? Men he'd chosen over Austin in every conceivable way?

And he was jerking off to it now, too. Pumping his shaft dry, making it hurt a little, and feeling all the better for it.

Oh, and crying too. Pathetic.

He'd cry and jerk off, and then he'd come, and maybe he'd force himself to lick it off his hand, gagging the whole time, or maybe he'd wipe it off on his chest or his boxers, and then when the endorphins fled him, he'd be left with nothing but a compulsion to run and run and run and run. Get nowhere, but hurt himself, like he deserved. Like, deep down, he wanted.

No.

He didn't want this.

He'd *never* wanted this.

And he'd never deserved it, either.

He wiped his eyes with a sniff. Stabbed his computer off—hit the power button and didn't bother with the shutdown command. Put his dick back into his boxers.

And still in his underwear, still with a shameful erection, he got up and went to Bobby's room.

Bobby didn't question. Just welcomed him in with open arms and a gentle, accepting smile.

Austin was still sad, and he was still hurting, but at least he was trying to make the hurting stop.

And at least he wasn't alone.

Week of September 29th
(One week to the start of the regular season)

Bobby and Dylan had a project due and had commandeered the kitchen table as a workspace for laptops and massive books of art and scraps of notebook paper. Whatever they were talking about, Austin didn't understand a word of it, and they didn't seem to want him around, anyway. Max and Noah were working—Max the night shift at Rear Entrance Video and Noah at the restaurant. Christian was locked up in his room doing lesson planning for the upcoming week of classes. All the sports channels were showing baseball. All the other channels were showing shitty reality TV. It was pissing down rain. He wasn't feeling macho or motivated enough to play the latest *Call of Duty*. Also, *Call of Duty* was way more fun when he was using it to torture Bobby.

After a half hour of channel surfing Austin finally gave up on the TV and headed upstairs, intending on doing some biceps curls. Instead, he opened up his computer and surfed to YouTube. His suggested videos playlist were all hockey clips, of course.

And at the top of the list?

CANADA WINS GOLD! 2010 OLYMPICS MEN'S HOCKEY FULL GAME

Settling back in his seat, he selected it, and was lulled immediately by the familiarity of it all. The familiar stadium, the familiar team roster, the familiar rendition of the Canadian anthem. Now came the first face-off . . .

He'd memorized every play, every call, every comment by the announcers, every snippet of music, every sign held up in the audience. There was no suspense. No tension. He already knew who won, and when, and how.

But God, it felt good. Relaxing, safe, familiar. Like Liam. Like Liam's couch, curled up in the Canucks blanket while Liam rubbed his shoulders and murmured the play-by-play in his ear.

And then the older memory, sitting with his dad and stepbrother, cheering and hugging and practically fucking crying with joy. The only time it would have ever been okay, growing up, for Austin to cry.

Liam had given him so much. Permission to be weak, to give in, to cry.

And now, he'd given him *this*. This quiet, steady contentment, where everything went right, and there were no upsets or surprises. A calm, safe place. Austin rested his chin on his folded arms, the screen of his computer filling up his entire vision, and let the 2010 Olympic hockey team skate him to sleep.

CHAPTER 21

Their first game of the regular season, and they lost.

No, lost was too generous. They were annihilated. Massacred. Humiliated.

They made the fucking Toronto Maple Leafs look good.

Ben choked in net first period, and by the time Coach finally benched him and brought Yves in, they were four goals down and *pissed*. But not the good kind of angry where you regrouped and turned your fury into an amazing comeback, the likes of which Liam would include in his collection of classic games. No, it was the kind of angry where you got *sloppy*.

First, they got done in for icing after Calabresi let the frustration get to him and took a wild shot that went nowhere useful, and then some obnoxious dickhead playing pest for the opposing team goaded Riley into a two-minute penalty for roughing. Of which he served roughly forty seconds, because that was how long it took the other team to score their fifth goal of the game. They skated around aimlessly after that, playing only marginally better than they might have done blindfolded or drunk or both, making stupid mistakes and fumbling passes and failing on every conceivable level to get their shit together and play as a fucking team.

The third period started with Austin finally scoring their team's first and only goal of the game thanks to an assist from Warren, but it didn't mean shit, because there was no hope of tying up the game by that point and even if there was, nobody was in the mood to give Austin any credit for anything after the way Calabresi had played. Because Calabresi's fuckups were Austin's fuckups now, and Calabresi had been fucking up all night. Worse than Ben, maybe. Which probably came as a relief to Ben, but didn't do much to improve the spirits of anybody else. Even Warren couldn't summon up his reliable staidness for the team to rally around. Oh sure, he tried, and the words were all right, but the feeling was all wrong.

By the time they shook hands with the opposing team and limped off the ice, they were demoralized, cagey, and set to eat their own.

Austin, focusing too hard on unlacing his skates in an attempt to avoid the angry glares aimed his way, thought things couldn't get any worse—and then they did.

Because that was when Coach barged in for his postgame scolding-slash-pep-talk that he liked to give after they sucked bad on the ice, but this time he wasn't alone.

Liam was with him.

Looking completely sorry to be there, like he wanted to fall through the floor, which was pretty much exactly how Austin and his entire team felt when they saw the look on Coach's face.

Guy was *pissed*. Red-faced, meaty hands in fists. "Just in case you weren't feeling sorry enough about playing like crap tonight, I thought you'd like to know you embarrassed yourselves in front of one of our star alumni."

What? Liam was *what?* Austin gaped as Liam bashfully stepped forward.

Coach clapped him on the back, not sensing Liam's awkwardness. "Yep, this here is Liam Williams, not that I expect any of you sorry bastards to know that. Don't expect you to know your sticks from your dicks, after what I just saw. Williams here was my star centre back in the day, weren't you, Williams?"

Liam didn't reply. Was staring at Austin, eyes all big and watery, giving himself away.

Austin turned his head, finding some speck on the wall to focus on instead.

Coach continued. "Won us our last university cup in—what was it, again?"

"Two thousand one," Liam replied, his voice scratchy.

Brimming with so much emotion, Austin's skin prickled.

No.

"So, how's that, huh? You gonna apologize to Williams for taking a piss all over his legacy tonight, or are you gonna sit there staring at the walls like a bunch of sissies?"

"Why should we have to apologize?" Ortega shouted. Because of *course* it was Ortega. Austin flinched in advance. "Make Austin apologize. He's the one who screwed us tonight. We never played this bad when Drew was on the team." A rumble of agreement went through Austin's teammates.

And all he could think was *not in front of Liam, please not in front of Liam.*

"Fucking narc pussy ruined our game," Ortega rambled, jumping to his feet when he realized no one was standing up to him this time. "Him and his butt buddy Calabresi."

Oh for fuck's—

Before Austin knew what he was doing, he was on his feet, too. "Can you fuck off with the fucking homophobic bullshit, Ortega? Look, fine, Calabresi's green and he didn't play as well tonight as I'd hoped. I'm fucking *sorry.*" *Sorry Liam has to see me like this, had to see me play so fucking bad and now has to see my team turn on me, calling me out as a fag, ruining every last shred of credibility I had.* "But I didn't give him Drew's spot because we're fucking, all right? So cut it the fuck out. I gave him Drew's spot because I thought he was the best man for the job. Maybe he's not. And maybe I'm not the best man for *this* job." He reached down, fingers scrabbling at the edge of the A badge sewn to his jersey. Gave it a tug, but it didn't tear. His hands were shaking too bad.

"Sit down, Austin," Liam commanded.

That steady, calm, powerful voice. Austin dropped down to the bench instantly.

"And you," Liam said, turning. "What was your name, again? Ortega? Maybe in your little gay panic you didn't notice Austin was the only one on this sorry fucking team to score a goal tonight. Maybe instead of worrying he might want to fuck your ass, you could try wrapping your head around the fact that the way he played tonight makes him one of the best players on your fucking team."

Ortega returned to his seat, sulking, arms crossed over his chest, and muttered under his breath: "What, did that fag suck your dick, too?"

Oh, that was fucking *it.* The fag that broke the camel's back. "What," Austin barked, the rage inside him boiling over as he shot to his feet again, "is your fucking problem, Ortega? So what if I *was* sucking his dick, huh? I still scored more fucking goals than you. I still got this team into shape over the summer after Drew nearly fucking sank us. As far as I'm concerned, as long as I play good hockey I can suck as many dicks as I want. I can suck *fifty* fucking dicks, and as long as I'm the team's strongest scorer, then there's nothing you can say or do about it." He made a circle with one hand, jerking off an invisible dick while he poked the inside of his cheek with his tongue. Ortega snarled, but still shrank into the wall like the coward he was. Austin dropped his hand. "And if you don't like it, you can get the fuck out of this locker room right fucking now and go see how many NHL scouts Drew has on speed dial."

Warren stepped in between them with his arms spread, but he really didn't need to, because no way was Austin risking a suspension fighting a scumbag like Ortega. "Okay!" he shouted. "Okay, okay, that's *enough*. Both of you. I think we already embarrassed ourselves enough tonight on the ice." He gave Austin an earnest, wide-eyed stare. "Let's not embarrass ourselves in the changeroom, too."

"Who's embarrassed?" Austin scoffed, turning away and returning to his seat to finish unlacing his skates.

"I'm hitting the fucking showers," Ortega announced. He rounded on Austin, jabbing the air with one finger. "Puett better fuckin' stay here, or else I won't be held responsible for what I do the first time I catch him checking out my dick."

Liam shoulder-checked him on his way past. "Hey, kid, speaking as a real live fag? I promise you, nobody's checking out your two-inch micropenis for anything but a laugh, so rest easy."

Ortega snarled wordlessly at him and stormed out.

A minute or so later, Austin's teammates kicked out of their skates and followed after him.

Not one of them made eye contact with Austin before they did, not even Warren.

Coach just stood there and gawked.

"Great start to the season," Austin joked, voice quaking.

Coach gave his head a bewildered shake, then nodded. "Nice goal tonight, Puett," he managed to say, still looking stunned. "Keep it up."

And then he wandered out, leaving Austin and Liam alone.

Adrenaline gone, Austin slumped forward, head between his knees, as his body shook and his heart pounded and his poor brain tried to figure out what the fuck he'd just done.

Oh God oh God oh God oh God.

He'd fucking ruined himself. He'd *ruined* himself.

And for what?

His fucking dignity, that was what. Because he was tired of his teammates treating him this way. Treating *anyone* this way, really, even people he didn't like anymore, like Liam.

He was sick of the talk. Sick of the way they used words like *fag* and *pussy* to put people down, put them in their place.

When the truth was, Liam, who really was a *real live fag* in their eyes, was more of a fucking man than they could ever hope to be. And a hockey star, too. Shit. Not that Austin hadn't suspected, but still. Holy shit.

And now here he was, crouched in front of Austin, draped over him, arms wrapped around him in a gentle, comforting hug, as warm and safe as the Canucks blanket on his couch.

"It's okay, kiddo," he said into Austin's shoulder. "It's okay. I'm here. I'm not going anywhere."

Wait, wait, wait. Liam and Austin weren't fucking together anymore. What the hell did Liam think he was talking about, saying shit like that? And why the fuck was he *here*?

Austin pushed him off. He sat up straight, putting his shoulders back. "Yeah," he said, giving Liam a hard glare. "It is okay. It's fine, actually. I'm fine. I don't know why you're here right now, because I don't . . ." His mouth firmed into a hard line. "It's fine, because I realized something. I don't *need* you anymore."

Liam didn't move, didn't flinch. He gave Austin that calm, in control look he was so good at. "Oh?"

I don't have to fucking explain myself to you, Austin thought, but then his mouth opened and the words came out anyway. "Yeah. That's right. I *don't* need you anymore. Because I realized something tonight. Originally I came to you because my life was out of control. I was getting turned on when my teammates trash-talked me, and I was scared of being gay, and it was making me treat my friends bad because I thought it was their fault. I was hoping you could cure me. Maybe you did, because I'm cured. Trash talk doesn't turn me on anymore. It just fucking makes me angry, you know?" His chest heaved. He was breathing hard, as hard as he'd been at the end of the third period, after fighting to the very last buzzer. He pressed on. "Because it turns out there's a difference between when they call me fag and when you do it. You do it to make me feel good and give me something I need and let me feel something I need to feel, and that turns me on, and that's okay. B-but they do it to put me down and make feel like I'm less than them when I'm not. I wouldn't be less than them if they were wrong about me being a fag, but you know what? I'm still not less than them even though they're right."

Liam didn't argue. Didn't try to talk him out of what he was saying. Didn't put him down or tell him to slow down or take it easy. He crouched there, listening. Respectful.

"So . . . so I'm cured. Shit, before tonight my life was actually back on track. I don't need you any more, Liam. I don't."

Now Liam winced, but then he nodded and smiled, laying a gentle hand on Austin's knee. He was about to pull it away when Austin reached down, covering Liam's hand with his own.

"But maybe . . ." He grunted in frustration. "I don't need you, Liam. Hear me? But maybe . . . maybe I want you," he admitted. *Because I might be cured, but I really do like the things you do to me, and if there's nothing wrong with that—and there isn't—why should I deny myself? What makes want less valid than need, anyway?*

Liam didn't smile. Didn't kiss him.

Instead he flinched and pulled away. "I'm glad to hear that, Austin. Really, I am. But you should go take a shower. Fix things with your team before it's too late. Don't let Ortega get them on his side."

Oh, hell no. Liam wasn't avoiding a confrontation with Austin this time. He cupped Liam's cheeks in both hands, forcing his head straight. "Don't even try it, man. Fuck Ortega. Fuck my team. It's over. Didn't you hear me? I *want* you." He swallowed hard, heart thrashing, waiting for Liam to respond, to say something, *Oh God, please say something*, and then, when Liam didn't, it hit him. "Don't you . . . oh God. You don't want me."

He pulled back. This time Liam caught *his* hands. "Oh, buddy. Oh buddy. Oh buddy, buddy, buddy. You couldn't be more wrong."

"You kicked me out of your place. You stopped talking to me. I threw away my hockey career, and you don't even want me. But then— Why are you here if you don't want me? I don't get it. I don't get it."

"Shh, shh, shh." Liam leaned forward, pressing their foreheads together.

Austin couldn't resist that, couldn't resist that familiar touch, couldn't fight the calming effect of it.

"I'm here because I couldn't stay away. I wanted to see you play, buddy. Wanted to cheer you on, even if you didn't know I was there—until your coach spotted me in the bleachers, anyway." His smile wobbled. "I'm here because I *do* want you. That's the problem, Austin. I want you way too much. Like I said. I want what you can't give me."

Austin narrowed his eyes in confusion. "But I did give you—"

"Yeah, you let me fuck you that night. I know. Thanks for that, but that's not what I meant. Don't get me wrong, I did want that from you, still do, but that's not the thing I'm talking about when I say I want something you can't give." He laughed, briefly, the sound as sad as a cough. "Honestly, after the blowjobs, I figured sex would only be a matter of time. And I thought—I thought that was okay. I mean, I thought we could *just* have sex. After all, I'm in porn. It's not like I don't have ample experience with no-strings-attached sex."

Austin laughed weakly.

"But at the risk of being completely cliché, you were different from the start. You were a project, and you *needed* me, and fuck, I loved that. But then you turned out to be this sweet kid with a good heart and you were so trusting and so giving and— *Shit*, you were a Canucks fan too!"

And you were good from the start, too. You made me feel good. You helped me trust. You taught me it was okay to give all the things I had to give. You taught me how great it was to watch a years-old hockey game. "So why did you send me away?"

"Because—" He sighed, pulling Austin into another hug, but this time he didn't draw back. He crouched there with Austin in his arms, holding him. "Because of that word you used. You probably don't remember it, and that's half the problem. You called me *Master*,

Austin. Nobody's ever done that. The subs I have on set, that's one of the things I tell them they *can't* do in a scene. It's not a word you throw around. Not to me. It's not like Coach or Sir or Daddy, not for me. It's a word that means commitment. Means that we're bound to each other. Beyond sex."

Austin relaxed against Liam's body, closing his eyes. He should have been afraid to say what he said next, but in Liam's arms, eyes closed, feeling that familiar sense of safety—*he can help me fly, and he'll never let me fall*—he couldn't feel anything but calm and sure. "What if I want that?"

Liam stiffened. Let Austin go. "I don't think you understand what you're saying, buddy. I'm not talking about us regularly hooking up like we were. That was great while it lasted, but this is so much more. I'd want to be 24/7 with you, Austin. Not boyfriends, exactly, but committed just the same. Master and boy, that's a commitment, and I don't think you're really capable of that. I don't think that's what you want." He put a hand to Austin's lips before he could argue. "What we've been doing, it's a thrill and a kink for you, and that's okay. Nothing wrong with a bit of thrill. It doesn't need to be more to be real and valid. But I . . . I *want* more. I tried to deny it, I tried to ignore it, I tried to dial it back, but then that night you submitted so beautifully and called me Master, I realized that it wasn't enough anymore. Not with you. It could *never* be enough, and you could never give me what I needed from you. Which is why it had to stop. So I sent you away."

"There you go treating me like a kid again," Austin snapped, but he wasn't angry, not even about that night Liam had sent him home. Not anymore. He felt like he was about to laugh, actually. Because it was all so simple and so straightforward and in hindsight, he didn't understand how it had taken so fucking long. "Pretending like you know best, not giving me a say. Did it ever occur to you to fucking *ask* me what I was willing to give you, huh? I mean, isn't that what you've been doing for me this whole time? Teaching me it's okay to ask for what I need? And then giving me it? So how come you won't ask *me* for what *you* need? How come you won't let me have the chance to give that to you?"

"You're straight," Liam sputtered. Austin had never seen the guy look so pathetically outmaneuvered.

He rolled his eyes. "This from the guy who spent weeks convincing me things weren't so black and white, that the world couldn't be divided into *straight* and *gay* no matter how much I tried. Look, you were right. Things *aren't* just gay and straight. Sometimes you're something in between. Sometimes there's exceptions. Sometimes people don't follow the rules. Well, newsflash, *I* don't follow the rules." And to prove it, Austin lunged forward and kissed Liam square on the mouth. Hard and fearless and real. By Austin's old rules, it was possibly the gayest thing he'd ever done. Gayer than sucking dick. Gayer than getting it up the ass. Because fuck, it was *romantic*. It wasn't humiliation, and it wasn't animal need.

It was sweet and perfect and giving, everything Austin wanted to be for Liam, and give to Liam, all those emotions he'd been so afraid to feel—so afraid to be emasculated by—before Liam had come and changed everything.

It was love.

Even if Austin couldn't name it aloud quite yet.

Liam pulled back, mouth swollen, eyes wide and startled and a little sad. "Kiddo, I'm touched, I really am, but do you understand the ramifications of this? Yes, I said straight and gay weren't black and white. And I meant it. I still mean it. I believe it. I'm glad you believe it too. But the rest of the world—your team especially—isn't going to see it that way. And before you suggest it, if we took it to the next level . . . If it stopped being just sex . . ." He looked briefly hopeful, but then his expression hardened, determined. "I have too much self-respect to be any bi-curious jock's dirty little secret, you get me?"

Austin laughed and shook his head. "Who said anything about keeping you a secret? In fact, I, uh—I have a thing. Tomorrow. A public, kinda formal thing. I'd like you to come with me." He wet his lips. No going back, now. He didn't want to. "As my date."

Because it's not just sex for me either.

I'm not sure it ever was.

Liam's hand curled around the back of Austin's neck, drawing him close. Their foreheads touched.

But this time Liam followed through on the familiar gesture; he gathered Austin in the rest of the way and finally kissed him, like Austin realized he'd meant to all along.

CHAPTER 22

"With this ring, I promise to respect our differences of opinion. I promise not to get too mad when you leave your nail polish all over the house." Sandra gave Beverly's orange nails a meaningful look as she clasped Beverly's hands and gave them a squeeze. "I promise to kiss you every single day, regardless of whether or not you've brushed your teeth. I promise to never talk over you. I promise to listen. I promise to never let money get in the way of loving you. I promise to be there for you, no matter what happens: if this remission ends, if your store fails or if it becomes a wild success, if Vancouver falls into the sea . . . if your nephew can't find a teaching job and winds up moving in with us."

Christian barked out a laugh, which had the rest of the wedding party and the guests all laughing too. At Austin's side, Bobby sniffed, dabbing at his eyes, then returned the wadded up tissue to the neckline of his puffy orange dress.

Beverly took a deep, tremulous breath as Christian handed her the second wedding band. She slipped it onto Sandra's hand, staring into her face like there was nothing in the world she'd rather look at. "With this ring, I promise to let you cook. I promise not to *complain* about your cooking. I promise to go with you to all your favourite stores, even if they don't sell my size. I promise not to spend the whole time complaining that they don't have my size. I promise to braid your hair when you're sick. I promise to ask your opinion. I promise to fight for you and for what we have together, whether it means fighting the world or fighting my own body. I promise not to take you for granted."

Now it was Sandra's turn to break down, and she paused to fan her eyes a moment before taking over the vows again, concluding, "I promise to love and respect you, and give you as much of myself as I can for as long as I can."

Austin couldn't help it; his gaze wandered from Sandra and Beverly in their white dresses to Liam sitting in the third row, looking strange but handsome in his neat grey suit. *As much of myself as I can, for as long as I can.* It wasn't a promise of forever, but maybe forever wasn't the true measure of partnership or love. It had only been a day since that kiss in the locker room, and they hadn't gotten to spend any of it together, but Austin felt like whatever was between him and Liam was already on that scale. Their eyes met, and Liam grinned, giving him the thumbs-up. Austin flushed and quickly looked away.

Beverly nodded rapidly, like she couldn't agree more, then repeated back, giddy and tearful, "I promise to love you and respect you, and give you as much of myself as I can for as long as I can."

"Couldn't have said it better myself," the man officiating said with a shrug, the first thing he seemed to have said in the entire ceremony, and everybody laughed. "Sandra Bowie, Beverly Blake, I am absolutely overjoyed to say that by the power vested in me by the province of British Columbia and the Unitarian Universalist Church, I now pronounce you wife and wife! Make with the kissing!" He raised his arms, Sandra and Beverly fell into one another's arms like they'd lost their respective abilities to stand upright, and when they kissed, everyone cheered and applauded, including Austin. Next thing he knew, Bobby's arms were thrown around his shoulders and Bobby's lip-gloss-sticky lips were pressing a happy kiss on his cheek.

He'd never been happier to return an embrace in his life.

"Can I just say you make an adorable bridesmaid?" Liam said, sidling up and giving Austin's orange tie a tug.

"Brides*man*," Austin corrected with a crooked grin, folding his arms over his chest as he watched Bobby twirling around on the makeshift dance floor in his dress and black high-top Chucks like he was a little girl in her first tutu.

Man, Austin couldn't judge, because it wasn't like he would have done anything different if he was wearing one of the puffy orange bridesmaid dresses instead of a suit and tie like Christian, Max, and Noah were all wearing.

There'd been no point in renting a hall when they had a whole store already paid for, so they'd pushed the racks of videos and toys to the walls, opening up the centre space of the store as a dance floor. There was a table set up for a potluck dinner, and for decoration, they'd filled the room with flickering jack-o'-lanterns. Max had provided better speakers for the store computer and made up a dance playlist. Which was currently cycling through a selection of shamelessly fun seventies and eighties music while they waited for the brides to arrive.

When they finally walked through the door, everyone applauded again. Lacking a glass to clink, Christian cupped his mouth and shouted at the top of his lungs, "Kiss!"

"Kiss, kiss, kiss!" they all chanted, until Sandra finally grabbed Beverly by the waist and dipped her like a pro, planting a dramatic smooch on her lips . . . and then her chin, and cheeks, and forehead, and nose, until the two of them fell back against the door giggling.

"Ladies and gentlemen and everyone in between!" Max announced, Bobby giving an excited shout at the last bit, "May I present to you Mrs. and Mrs. Bowie-Blake!"

There was no spotlight, but Sandra and Beverly still walked into the centre of the dance floor like there was one trained on them. They took each other by the hand and shoulder or waist, falling so easily into their roles that Austin had no doubt they fit together perfectly. The song they played for their first dance was sultry and heartfelt at the same time, a love song and a sex song all at once. As it went on, Max hopped the counter, grabbed Christian by the hand, and yanked him onto the dance floor. Bobby and Dylan were next—Bobby eager to resume twirling in his skirt—and after them, Noah and his girlfriend, Amber, and the store's old manager Vicks, with her chubby Mohawked baby in her arms. One of Sandra's bridesmaids and her date joined in soon after, and the other . . .

The other made a beeline for Austin. "You wanna?" she asked, gesturing to the dance floor with her thumb. She was gorgeous, tall and slim and redheaded, with eyes as sharp as Sandra's but a soft, sexy mouth.

Austin automatically turned to Liam. Didn't consider how it would look. How it would be interpreted. Didn't really care.

Liam, leaning against the wall next to him, raised his eyebrows but gave Austin a nod of permission.

Permission, it turned out, that Austin didn't want. He shook his head at the bridesmaid. "Sorry. Spoken for," he said, and flashed her an apologetic smile as he took Liam by the hand and led him out onto the dance floor.

His roommates and his coworkers and Sandra and Beverly and their guests and the sexy bridesmaid could all see him. They could even be staring, gaping, *whispering*, but Austin didn't care if they were.

He pressed against Liam's body, let Liam's arms enfold him. Wrapped his arms around Liam's neck and rested his head on Liam's shoulder and let himself . . . dance.

Liam had given him that.

The party was still in full swing when Liam looped an arm around Austin's waist and drew him close, whispering, "Wanna come home with me?"

Every muscle in Austin's body seemed to twinge in anticipation. "*Please*," he replied, not the slightest bit embarrassed that it came out in a breathy moan.

Liam gave him a squeeze, and the look in his eyes said he was feeling the same powerful desire that was currently overrunning Austin. And then, because Austin was too stupid with want at that point to really move, Liam took him by the hand and led him across the room to where Sandra and Beverly were nestled together on the floor in their dresses, a bottle of wine between them. "Congratulations," Liam said, and Austin nodded dumbly.

"Going so soon?" Beverly asked, eyes twinkling mischievously.

Liam elbowed Austin in the ribs. "Tell Beverly where you're going," he ordered.

Austin's spine straightened, and his cheeks went hot. But he didn't try to resist. "I'm going home with Liam."

"Oh, isn't that nice," Beverly said. She looked downright evil, now. "Well, have fun, both of you. Liam, you take care of him. Don't play too rough."

"Wouldn't dream of it," Liam replied smoothly, but what Austin heard was, *I love him too much to ever hurt him.*

And that, more than anything Liam had ever said or done, made Austin fly.

After making the rounds of the reception, they finally ducked out the front door, out into the cool Vancouver night. The walk to Liam's place was brisk and beautiful, and though Austin hadn't had so much as a mouthful of wine, he felt deliriously drunk, neon lights dancing in his vision. He swore he could feel Liam's heartbeat in his hand.

They walked down Davie Street like any other gay couple, hand in hand and fingers interlaced, Austin's head on Liam's shoulder.

When they finally arrived at Liam's condo and the door was shut behind them, Liam didn't need to say anything; Austin automatically fell to his knees. Felt like he'd been waiting to do this for months. Maybe he had been.

Liam laughed softly. Not cruel, but affectionate. His hand landed in Austin's hair, fisting it tightly. "Eager, huh?"

"Yes," Austin hissed, eyes falling shut as Liam jerked his head back.

"Good. I am too." Liam's other hand came to rest on the side of Austin's face, his thumb pressing against Austin's lips. *Cocksucking lips.* Austin remembered, now. How they fit together. He opened his mouth, staring up into Liam's eyes as he sucked his thumb in. "That's my boy," Liam murmured, and Austin didn't miss the way his tailored slacks shifted.

Austin rested his palms on his knees. Arched his spine. Kept on looking up at Liam like he was a god on earth. To Austin, he was, and he planned on worshipping accordingly. With his eyes, with his mouth, with every inch of his body. *I promise to give as much of myself as I can.*

Right now, that meant everything.

He only wished he was naked.

"I still remember the first time I met you, kiddo. You were so nervous. Your palms were sweaty. You obviously felt threatened by me, but in a good way. God, *such* a good way. Even thinking about it got me all . . . predatory. Yeah. Made me want to see how much more I could get under your skin. I thought, I could really get off on toying with this kid." His smirk softened into a wistful smile. "And then you practically begged me to believe you were straight, and it nearly broke my heart. After that, all I could think about was how I could help heal *yours*."

He dragged his spit-wet thumb over Austin's lower lip, drawing a line down Austin's chin and holding Austin delicately by the jaw. "I was so scared," Austin admitted, barely above a whisper. He stared up into Liam's eyes, seeing nothing there but patient acceptance. No judgment at all, but why would there be? There never had been. "Terrified. Felt like my whole life was spinning out of control." He balled his hands—still resting on his knees—into fists. "And then you were there and you made things make sense again. Even—" He swallowed. "Even when it was only Puck, in your videos. Or even . . . even after you sent me away and we weren't seeing each other anymore. You made me feel like there was still order in the world. Like even if it felt like everything was falling apart, I knew it never would completely, because you would always be there. In the centre."

Like the sun. Hell, maybe that spinning Austin felt was actually *orbiting*. Hurtling through the universe, but anchored, always following a safe, set path. He'd never go flying off into nothingness, so long as Liam was there.

Liam's expression turned fierce and determined. "I will *always* be there for you, Austin. Just like that, whatever you need. So long as you want me."

Austin's eyes slid shut. "I want you." His voice shook. His shoulders trembled. His eyelashes felt wet. "I want you."

Liam laid a sweet, gentle kiss on his open mouth. "Then you have me, kiddo. Get undressed, hang up your suit, and I'll meet you in my bedroom."

CHAPTER 23

Liam was waiting for him in the bedroom, seated on the edge of his bed with his jacket off and his tie loosened, his sleeves rolled up to bare his muscular forearms. Austin fought the urge to cover himself as he walked in, suddenly shy of his nakedness. Liam hadn't seen him naked since the night he'd sent him home, and that night, they'd both been naked. This was different, Austin could feel it.

"Having a tough time, huh, buddy?"

Austin nodded, flushed hot from his chest to his ears.

"Put your arms behind your back, then. Hands on opposite elbows. Hold nice and tight."

It felt good to follow specific instructions. Made his nakedness a more active thing, something he participated in rather than something he ... was. His dick was hard, and Liam was looking at it, half-smiling, pleased. Austin tightened his grip on his elbows and took a deep breath that caused the slightest strain to run through his chest and shoulders.

"Damn you're pretty." Liam slipped from the bed and walked to Austin's side, taking a handful of his hair as he continued around Austin's body to stand at his back. "But I'm the only one allowed to call you that, aren't I?"

Austin licked his lips. Remembered he was supposed to answer direct questions. "Yeah."

"What else is there that only I'm allowed to do?" He pulled Austin's head back a couple of degrees and ran a finger up the underside of his dick.

"Touch me like that," Austin replied. "F ... fuck me."

"Oh, hmm. Is that only in your ass—" Liam's hand moved from Austin's dick to the crack of his ass, tickling teasingly at his hole. "—or in your mouth, too?" Now the finger touched

Austin's lips. Austin should have been disgusted at where Liam's finger had been, but oh, he wasn't. Or, he was, but he was helplessly turned on at the same time. He shuddered. "If I invited a friend over, would you suck his dick too?"

Austin wished he could say yes, give Liam everything he desired, but he shook his head.

"Good boy. I appreciate the honesty. Frankly, I think I'd like to keep you all to myself anyway. But the thought of it—the fear—gets you a little hot, huh?"

That was true. Austin pictured himself on his knees, hands tied behind his back, blindfolded, sucking dick, and then Liam would pull the blindfold off and it would be another man. Another man's scent in his nostrils, another man's cum filling the back of his mouth and his throat, sticking to him no matter how many times he swallowed or spit. A little moan escaped him.

"Yeah, it does. That's okay, buddy. It's okay to want things and be afraid of them, or to only want to think about them but not make them real. It's even okay to pretend, a little."

The words were out of Austin's mouth before he could stop them. Before he could think of where they were going. "Before we started all this, I'd finger myself and pretend it was you. When I watched you—" He shook his head. "When I watched *Puck*."

Liam groaned, pressing up against Austin's back, letting Austin feel the long curve of his thick cock. "I knew you were perfect for me. But you do know Puck is me, right? It's not like I have some alternate personality who does my scenes."

"No, but Puck—Puck I have to share. Liam is all mine." *God*, Austin said that now, but was it true? He had no idea. Liam had made no promises of fidelity. Hadn't mentioned quitting his job, or even being exclusive with each other outside of it.

Liam's arms slid up Austin's chest, drawing them closer together. Austin's strained arms twinged in pain. Liam pressed his face into Austin's hair and breathed deep. "Yes, Austin. Yes, I am. And God, I'm so fucking relieved to hear you put it that way. I knew we'd have to talk about my job eventually, and to be honest with you, I was kind of dreading that conversation, because I'm not ready to give up my work. Maybe one day, I can move to doing most of my work behind the scenes—well, I'll probably pretty much have to unless I want to do old dude fetish stuff, I guess—but not yet. But working the job I do doesn't make what's between us any less important or any less meaningful." He kissed the back of Austin's head. "And you're right. Liam is all yours."

Relief hit Austin like a tidal wave, and he would have fallen, except for Liam standing behind him with his arms wrapped around his chest, holding him upright. Holding him steady. "I love you, Master," he blurted out.

Liam grabbed him hard by the shoulders, turned him, and gave him a shove so he fell backward onto the bed. He loomed over Austin, face unreadable, and Austin's heart pounded. He ached to take it back, to make it out like he was joking, but he couldn't. He couldn't tell a lie, not to Liam . . . not to his master. So he lay there, awaiting Liam's response, even if it was a punishment.

But Liam didn't respond. Didn't say a word as he stripped out of his clothes and tossed his shirt and tie and trousers to the floor. His jaw was tight, his eyes dark. Austin couldn't tell if he was angry or possessed. He climbed onto the bed, straddling Austin's body, and the pressure of his weight brought Austin instantly to a safer place. "I love you too, buddy. I love you, and I want to make you mine."

I already am, Austin thought dreamily, but didn't get to say it aloud because Liam had climbed up to straddle his head, was dipping the head of his cock into Austin's waiting open mouth. Salty. So big. Austin let out a half-smothered moan as Liam fucked his face twice more, then went to work tying his wrists to either bedpost. The rope was soft and slick, but the knots were secure. Secure. Austin liked that.

Liked it better when Liam grabbed his calf next and bent his leg up over his body, folding Austin in half in order to tie his ankle to the same post as his wrist. And then the other leg, leaving his back curved and half-rolled off the mattress, his ass exposed, his legs spread to the point of aching.

Completely at Liam—his *master's*—mercy.

And secure.

Austin floated in that painful but safe place as Liam slicked his ass, then slipped two fingers in to milk him. He knew he was being milked right from the start, because Liam used his free hand to gentle him, kept murmuring and whispering "Easy, easy," and "Nice and loose for me, buddy."

Took him by the cock and gave it slow, rhythmic tugs as his cum poured out and drenched his own belly and chest, finally releasing him from his horrible pleasure.

And then, taking advantage of his loose hole and upraised, offered body, Liam finally claimed him. Nine inches of thick, bare cock. Stretched him to the point that he gritted his teeth and wailed, but Liam didn't stop, and Austin didn't want him to stop. He wanted to be fucked and pounded and used and *owned*, until there wasn't a single part of him Liam hadn't claimed.

He didn't want to be his own person, not anymore, not when it was so much better, so much safer, so much more *right* with Liam.

And he knew he could have gone on without this. He did. Their weeks apart had taught him he could manage himself, could enjoy his life, could find a peaceful place even when the rest of his world was completely out of control, but oh, it was so much better with Liam, he knew. Having Liam to lean on, to support him, to help him continue to grow into the man he'd begun to become.

Yes, this was exactly where he wanted to be.

Nope, correction. Right here, but with an ass full of Liam's hot cum.

This was where he wanted to be.

Austin didn't remember being untied. Didn't remember Liam coming inside him, either, not really.

But both of those things must have happened, because he was lying curled on his side in Liam's bed, cooling cum dripping out of his aching ass.

The sensation snapped him out of the happy, floaty place. Felt sloppy and horrible and humiliating, but also right. Yeah, right—at the same time. He relaxed again, eyes drifting closed.

But wait, where the fuck was Liam?

He sat up.

"Liam?" he called, although it was more of a croak. He hadn't realized Liam had gotten so deep into his throat, but damn, he could sure feel it now. He coughed and tried again. "Liam?"

Liam appeared at the bedroom door, still naked with his cock hanging huge but limp between his legs.

It still made Austin's mouth water. That was, until he realized Liam had Austin's phone in his hand.

"What is it?" Austin asked carefully, heart thrashing, like he had something to be afraid of or feel guilty for. He didn't, of course.

"It kept buzzing. You got like eighteen texts from some bloke . . ." He lifted the phone and squinted at the screen. "Warren?" He tossed the phone at the bed, and even in his dopey state, Austin's reflexes were quick enough to catch it. "I didn't read them."

"He's my—the SFU hockey team captain." Austin didn't want to look at the texts, but Liam was waiting, so he did it anyway.

9:04 p.m. I prayed about what happened

9:04 p.m. And talked to my pastor

Oh, great. Austin looked to Liam for strength, and Liam—obviously sensing his need—sat beside him and wrapped an arm around Austin's shoulders, tilting his head so he could read along.

9:07 p.m. He said I already knew what to do

9:08 p.m. And I do

9:08 p.m. You were out of line talking like that, but Ortega goaded you into it

9:09 p.m. You had your back to the wall so of course you fought

9:09 p.m. I would have too

9:10 p.m. I don't know if ur actually gay or if you were just saying that

9:10 p.m. But it doesn't matter. Coach says the school has antidiscrimination policies and we all have to follow them

9:11 p.m. So I expect u at practice monday morning ready to help us win our next game

9:12 p.m. Leave the guys to me

"Well, that's good, isn't it?" Liam asked, tentatively chipper.

Austin groaned, tossing the phone down to the end of the bed and putting his head in his hands. "Are you kidding me? My life is over. You think school *antidiscrimination policies* mean jack shit on the ice?" He couldn't help but say *antidiscrimination policies* in a mocking, whiny tone, like they were a pathetic joke, because that was exactly what they were. "You think because there's *antidiscrimination policies*, my team is gonna march in a gay pride parade now? C'mon, man, you played hockey. You know how it is. It's over."

"No, I know how it *was*. You know, before school-wide antidiscrimination policies?" He gave Austin's shoulder a brisk rub. Kissed his temple. "And it's true. I stayed in the closet the entire time I was on the SFU hockey team, and I never considered going into the NHL, because I had to choose between my sexuality or a hockey career, and the choice was easy. I don't regret it. But you don't *have* to choose, Austin. You have to take advantage of that."

"What, and spend the rest of my fucking life getting bullied? Seriously. It's hockey. There's no room for guys like us. Especially not a guy like me, with my history of popping a boner every time someone calls me a sissy." He turned, grabbing both of Liam's hands. Looked him in the eye, as sincere as Beverly and Sandra had been during their wedding vows. "So maybe I don't have to make a choice, but I'm gonna anyway. I choose you, Liam. I choose being yours."

"God, buddy, you don't know how flattered I am, and how much that means to me, but you're still wrong. You're wrong about having to choose, and you're wrong about there being no room for us, and I'm gonna prove it to you. But first . . ." He swept his hand through Austin's bangs. "First, I want to give you something. I thought it might help you with at least part of your hockey problem, and to show that I still most definitely want you to be *mine*. And as for the rest, well, I'll help you through it. That's what I'm here for." He ruffled Austin's hair affectionately. "Now, wait here a minute."

Austin didn't understand how a guy who had quit hockey out of fear of homophobia could stand here and tell Austin that he had go through the exact thing *he'd* opted out of. And damn if Austin wasn't going to call him out on that. As soon as he got back.

When Liam returned, though, he didn't sit on the bed; he knelt on the floor between Austin's knees, which startled Austin into forgetting what he was about to accuse Liam of.

Seemed like it was unnecessary, anyway, because Liam beat him to the punch. "I know what you're thinking, Austin. You're mad at me, right? Think I'm a hypocrite? Maybe I am. Or maybe I believe in you. Look, if I'm going to be your master, that means more than just fucking you until you beg for mercy. It means guiding you. It means giving you everything you need. You *need* to play hockey, buddy. I can't promise you the NHL or the Stanley Cup or the Canadian Olympic team, but I can promise to help you give it your best shot. If you don't succeed, then you don't, but we'll both know you've tried. And we'll both know I did everything in my power to help. Which is where this comes in." He reached down, picking up a black cardboard box about the size a watch might come in.

He must have had it in his hand when he'd walked into the room and Austin had been too angry to notice. Well, he noticed it now.

Liam pulled the lid off the box. Inside it, nestled in white tissue paper, was something made of a clear, plastic-looking material, or maybe silicone. And a tiny gold padlock. Austin's brow furrowed.

"Here," Liam said with a paternal smile, and gently took Austin's soft cock and balls in one hand. In the other, he picked up the clear silicone . . . whatever it was. "I honestly think you've cured yourself of the whole getting-boners-you-don't-want thing, so maybe this isn't necessary, per se, but maybe it will help with your confidence. Whether or not you need it, it'll be there." And then he slipped the silicone thing over Austin's cock. It was a sheath, sort of, with a little hole in the end over the head of his dick and a ring that went back around his balls. Now Austin realized. A cock cage. It was a cock cage. To keep him from getting hard. And now Liam was locking it. The key was nowhere to be seen. He settled back, looking at his handiwork, and said, "Okay? You need to safeword?"

Austin stared down at it, at the stiff material covering his cock, keeping it small and soft and . . . yes, secure. Safe and secure. He shook his head. "It's okay."

Liam grinned in relief. "Oh, good. I've always wanted to put one of these on a boy, but never really been in the position to ask for it. But you, you're all mine, aren't you, buddy? You like control. You like giving *me* control."

God, it was true. And the teasing way Liam said the words . . . Austin squirmed, his dick trying to rise in its unrelenting cage. He bit his lip, cheeks going hot. He didn't safeword.

"Don't worry. I won't abuse my power. Much." Liam's grin turned to a smirk as he reached up, grabbing Austin by the hair at the back of his head, and yanked him down into a hard, demanding kiss.

Austin moaned into his mouth . . . and once again felt his dick pinch inside the cage.

"Beautiful," Liam said, watching it, watching Austin's dick filling the tight space and squishing up against the barrier of the clear silicone.

"I'm happy, Master," he said, because he thought he should. "Thank you. But I still don't believe you about the hockey thing."

Liam cupped and rolled Austin's balls, weighing them thoughtfully. "That's okay. You will."

CHAPTER 24

Austin didn't believe Liam one bit, but he did agree to give it a chance. For his master's sake. To help his master take care of him the way he needed, Austin had to cooperate. So he did. He went to practice that Monday, which was awkward as fuck, but not unbearable. The insults were few and far between, though, and the word "fag" didn't get dropped once. Ortega glowered at him nearly constantly, but Austin really didn't give a fuck, because Austin was alternate captain and Ortega wasn't shit. And despite Ortega's attempts to turn them against him, Austin's team did seem to acknowledge— however grudgingly—that he really was their best scorer. No matter what had gone down with Drew *or* with Austin's sexuality, his skill as a hockey player wasn't in doubt.

They didn't ask. He didn't tell. And on the days he didn't have to shower with his team, his cock was nestled safely in its cage, Liam's wordless promise to give Austin whatever he needed so he could have the best shot possible at realizing his dreams.

Then that Saturday, Liam asked him to meet at their usual sushi place after his day shift at Rear Entrance Video, but when Austin arrived there, Liam wasn't alone. Eleven guys, including Austin.

Liam beamed at him. "Have a seat, buddy. Guys, this is Austin."

"Hi, Austin," the men around the table all greeted. Mostly big, burly dudes with moustaches and beards, a couple muscular, a couple kinda fat, but there were two skinny little fuckers as well.

"So, Austin," Liam said. "This is Dave, our goalie." A man with a goatee and a shaved head raised his hand. "And next to him on the left, that's our centre, Mike." He went around the table like that. "John, left defence. Andy, right defence. Loren, our star right-winger—"

"That's on the ice, not politically," Loren butted in, which got a laugh.

"Ken, our left-winger . . ."

He went on, introducing all the players and alternates. A hockey team. Austin was sitting with a hockey team. Amateur, definitely, like a house league team, but a hockey team just the same.

"I don't understand," he said, when the introductions were through.

Dave, the goalie, flashed Austin a cocky smile. "What, Liam here didn't tell you? We're the Davie Street Gay Men's hockey team."

"Excuse you," John hissed. "Gay? I thought we voted to change it to queer, seeing as we're *not* all gay?"

"You're not gay?" Austin asked in disbelief.

John laughed. "Oh, I'm gay, all right. But Liam's bi and Mike goes by queer, and you're not gay either, right? Just not quite straight?" He said it so simply, condensing all of Austin's confusion into such a gentle phrase. And it didn't bother Austin at all. Made him feel like he was among friends, more than anything. Because it was true. He wasn't gay, for sure. Hadn't decided if bisexual was the right word, either. But whatever he was, he loved Liam and wanted him as a master, and he was still the same meathead hockey-playing Austin otherwise. In the end, that was all that mattered.

Dave cleared his throat. "Gay, bi, queer, transgender, straight-with-exceptions . . . whatever, it's all good. And we're always looking for new players, if you've got time in between your big-league college games, eh?"

It's hockey. There's no room for guys like us.

So they made room.

Suddenly, it all became clear.

"Puck here says you're good," Loren added. "Are you? Because we're headed to the rink after we're done eating here."

"I don't . . ." God, Austin didn't even want to say it. He wanted to say *yes* to them, to everything they were offering him, with every fibre of his being. "I don't have any skates with me."

Liam's hand closed around his shoulder. "Don't worry," he said smoothly, "I took care of your skates and pads. I've got your back, don't I?"

Austin's stomach twisted. His dick twitched in its cage. "Yes, you do."

Always. Liam would always be there for him, no matter what he needed, whether it was a pair of skates, or a guiding hand in life, keeping him safe and steady.

Wait . . . Puck.

Puck.

Liam's porn name.

Puck. Not as in the Shakespeare character, like Mistress Titania, or maybe that too, but Puck, as in hockey puck.

Austin turned against Liam's chest, right there in public, and laughed until it hurt.

Find more love and laughs at *Rear Entrance Video*:
riptidepublishing.com/titles/universe/rear-entrance-video

Dear Reader,

Thank you for reading Heidi Belleau's *Straight Shooter*!

We know your time is precious and you have many, many entertainment options, so it means a lot that you've chosen to spend your time reading. We really hope you enjoyed it.

We'd be honored if you'd consider posting a review—good or bad—on sites like **Amazon, Barnes & Noble, Goodreads, Twitter, Facebook, Tumblr,** and your blog or website. We'd also be honored if you told your friends and family about this book. Word of mouth is a book's lifeblood!

For more information on upcoming releases, author interviews, blog tours, contests, giveaways, and more, please sign up for our weekly, spam-free newsletter and visit us around the web:

Newsletter: tinyurl.com/RiptideSignup
Twitter: twitter.com/RiptideBooks
Facebook: facebook.com/RiptidePublishing
Goodreads: tinyurl.com/RiptideOnGoodreads
Tumblr: riptidepublishing.tumblr.com

Thank you so much for Reading the Rainbow!

RiptidePublishing.com

acknowledgments

Special thanks to Julio-Alexi Genao, who helped me with the hockey details. As it turns out, being Canadian only takes you so far. Any remaining mistakes, though, you can pretty much guarantee are mine.

also by
heidi belleau

Rear Entrance Video series
Apple Polisher
Wallflower

The Professor's Rule series, with Amelia C. Gormley
Giving an Inch
An Inch at a Time
Inch by Inch
Every Inch of the Way
To the Very Last Inch

The Burnt Toast B&B (A *Bluewater Bay* novel), with
Rachel Haimowitz
The Harder They Fall, with Lisa Henry (in the
Rules to Live By anthology)
The Flesh Cartel serial, with Rachel Haimowitz
King of Dublin, with Lisa Henry
First Impressions. Second Chances
Blasphemer, Sinner, Saint, with Sam Schooler (in the *Bump in the
Night* anthology)
Bliss, with Lisa Henry

With Violetta Vane
Mark of the Gladiator
Cruce de Caminos

about the
author

Heidi Belleau was born and raised in small town New Brunswick, Canada. She now lives in the rugged oil-patch frontier of Northern BC with her husband, an Irish ex-pat whose long work hours in the trades leave her plenty of quiet time to write. She has a degree in history from Simon Fraser University with a concentration in British and Irish studies; much of her work centered on popular culture, oral folklore, and sexuality, but she was known to perplex her professors with unironic papers on the historical roots of modern romance novel tropes. (Ask her about Highlanders!) When not writing, you might catch her trying to explain British television to her newborn daughter or standing in line at the local coffee shop, waiting on her caramel macchiato.

You can visit her blog: heidi-below-zero.blogspot.com, find her tweeting as @HeidiBelleau, email her at heidi.below.zero@gmail.com.

Enjoy more stories like *Straight Shooter* at RiptidePublishing.com!

Capture & Surrender
ISBN: 978-1-62649-030-7

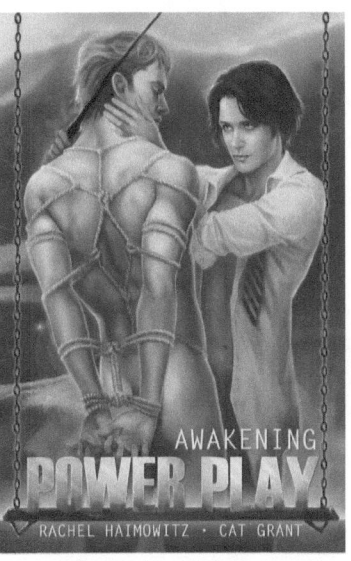

Power Play: Awakening
ISBN: 978-1-937551-44-5

Earn Bonus Bucks!

Earn 1 Bonus Buck for each dollar you spend. Find out how at RiptidePublishing.com/news/bonus-bucks.

Win Free Ebooks for a Year!

Pre-order coming soon titles directly through our site and you'll receive one entry into a drawing to win free books for a year! Get the details at RiptidePublishing.com/contests.